Everybody Got A Secret

A Drama-Filled Romance

By

Princess Diamond

Twitter & Instagram: @authorprincess
Facebook: @authorprincessdiamond
Pinterest: princess diamond

Everybody's Got A Secret: A Drama Filled Romance

Text COLEHART to 22828 to sign up for the mailing list & for updates on New Releases. Also, Check out Cole Hart Releases at www.colehartsignature.com

Acknowledgements

I give all praises to God who anointed me with this wonderful gift of writing. Through Christ I can do all things.

To my father in heaven, you passed away too soon. You have never seen any of my work, but I write in your memory. Love always.

To my mother in heaven, I still can't believe you're gone so soon. I miss you every day. I wish you were here with me. My biggest supporter. Love Always.

To my family and friends, I couldn't have done this without your endless days of listening to me talk about my stories, offering ideas, and giving me advice. You all are my rock. Thanks for everything.

To all the authors that have helped me. From giving me advice to supporting my work to the positive interactions. Much love.

To my readers, without your support, there is no me. I appreciate you all.

A special thanks to my sisters. Your input is priceless.

XOXOX

Princess Diamond

Princess Diamond's Books

Element of Surprise

Element of Surprise 2: Lust Unleashed

Put My Name On It

Hott Girlz Series (1-3)

Dream & Drake Series (books 1-4)

Chapter 1

Vanity

Buzz. Buzz. Buzz. Buzz.

"Man, if you don't roll your ass over and get that damn alarm," my husband Ivan said, turning his back to me and putting the pillow over his head.

Half asleep, I reached over feeling for my phone, trying to cut it on snooze again.

"And don't hit the damn snooze again. Either get your ass up or stay in bed. Shit don't make no damn sense."

"Ugh! You're such a grouch in the morning." I opened my eyes, cutting the alarm off. "I couldn't snooze again if I wanted to. You keep talking to me."

"But look who's talking now?"

"Cause you talking to me."

"Whatever."

"Whatever then."

If I wasn't going back to sleep, neither was he. I walked around to the other side of the bed, snatching the pillow off his face. "Get up."

Ivan stayed in the same spot with his eyes closed.

"Fuck outta here. For what? I'm not on vacation. I got to go to work." He rolled back over on his side with his back to me again. "Always on bullshit."

"You can't avoid me," I said, jumping in the bed, playfully landing on top of him.

He tried to push me off with one hand. "You play too damn much. Get off me."

I didn't budge. "Make me."

Ivan groaned. "Now, if I did this to you, it would be an argument."

I began to ride him like a pony. "Giddy up. Giddy up. Giddy up, now."

Ivan quickly rose from the bed, grabbing me by the wrists, pinning me under him. "Is this what you want? Huh? The reason why you won't let me sleep?" He used his knees to open my legs up.

I started to tease him, telling him no. That was until I felt his gigantic hardness pressing between my legs.

"All you had to do was ask instead of getting on my damn nerves."

My eyes scanned his handsome chocolate face. He was so sexy when he got angry. All frowned up, looking like a stripper. My baby had it going on. He had a football build with muscles, a nice ass, and a humongous dick. Smooth skin, a baldhead, pretty teeth, and he was super smart too. I had to fight hoes off of him night and day.

"You love this big dick, don't you?"

When I didn't answer him, he pulled at my panties, ripping them.

"Don't rip my shir—" Before, I could finish my sentence Ivan ripped my tank shirt from my body, totally exposing me. "And you gonna buy me a new one," I exclaimed with my pinky finger in his face.

"Shut up," he said, entering me with ten inches. "Take this dick that you woke me up for and shut the fuck up." Letting go of my wrists, he jerked my hips upward, pounding me hard and fast.

I couldn't say another word even if I wanted to. The feel of him stroking me so deep, shut me down completely.

Ivan knew he was hitting it right when I started bucking in the air like a bull, grabbing the sheets, cursing and clowning. He had my pelvis tilted upward, which caused this euphoric sensation to travel throughout my whole body. Within seconds, I was having an intense orgasm.

"That should calm your ass down."

Ivan rested on top of me, slowing it down, cradling me in his arms. I locked my legs around him, gripping his firm backside. His lips found my left breast, sucking and lightly biting it, driving me insane.

"You love me?" Ivan whispered.

"Yes!"

His tongue traced my harden nipple. "No, you don't."

"Yes, I do," I mumbled as his dick connected with my spot again. "Oh, Ivan!"

"You just love the way I freak you." He stopped sucking my boob, staring me in the face. "Do you really love me?"

"Yes, I promise, I do." Ivan had me so hot. I would have told him that I walked on water just to keep him inside of me.

"And what about this?' Ivan asked, thrusting deeper inside of me, hitting my g-spot repeatedly. "This is the only time we're not arguing. Why do I have to be deep in your pussy to get you to cooperate?"

He was right, but I didn't want to talk about our marital problems in the middle of being fucked.

"Babe, I love you," he moaned. "I'll go crazy without you in my life."

I buried my face in the crook of his arm, enjoying every stroke. I was on the verge of cumming again. Holding back, I tried to savor the feeling a little longer.

Stopping, mid-stroke, Ivan's lips desperately found mine.

"Why'd you stop?" I whined.

Ivan silenced me by slipping his tongue into my mouth. I put my arms around his neck, closing my eyes, savoring our kiss.

"Nice, huh?"

"Stop talking." I pulled his head back towards me so we could continue.

Cupping my ass, Ivan slid his big rock-hard dick back into me to the hilt. I clenched my vaginal muscles around his shaft, loving every inch of it.

"Ah, your dick feels so good."

"I want to stay in this pussy forever," Ivan groaned, pounding me with force.

I cursed loudly wiggling under him moaning nonstop. I held onto him with all my might as the orgasmic spasms claimed me.

"Now, it's my turn," Ivan said, breaking out of my grip, flipping me over with my ass in the air.

He gently slid back into me, stretching my wet walls. Once he was in deep, he began to thrust so hard that his balls smacked against my clit.

"Open your legs wider."

Lying flat against me, Ivan reached under me, rubbing my clit with one hand. He knew how much I liked dual stimulation.

"You ready for me to bust?" he asked me.

"Yesssss," I said feeling horny all over again.

The tingle of my sensitive clit being rubbed, and the feeling of his hard dick sliding in and out of my peach, sent me over the edge. I squeezed my coochie muscles real tight, contracting my third orgasm.

"Ahhhhh. Fuck!" Ivan yelled about to cum.

"Don't pull out," I begged him. I was about to ovulate. "I want you to cum in me." Ivan was always careful. He never deposited sperm inside of me or he wore condoms. That would be cool if I wasn't trying to get pregnant. He knew how much I wanted a baby.

He pulled out, shooting a hot load all over my ass. "Damn, that was fire. I wish I could bottle your pussy up and sell it," he said, rolling onto my side of the bed. "I'd be a billionaire."

Beyond frustrated, I retreated to the shower, crying. I was trying so desperately to get pregnant. And Ivan wasn't cooperating at all. He hadn't cum in me in years.

By the time I got out, Ivan was snoring. I couldn't help but smile at him. He was sprawled out on the bed like he'd been in a fight.

I bent down, kissing his sexy lips. "Bye."

I couldn't resist pulling back the bed sheet to take another look at that big fat dick. It still had girth even when it was soft.

"See you when I get back," I said, kissing it bye too.

Looking at the time, I realized that my ride would be here shortly. I didn't have time to cook breakfast like I usually did. Ivan was going to be pissed. He loved my cooking.

Dressing in my mini skirt, halter shirt, gym shoes, and hoodie, I wheeled my suitcase to the front door. Just in time to see my cousin pull up.

Chapter 2

Pebbles

I should have known that leaving the club with Chip was a bad idea.

"Get off me," I said, pushing him away.

Chip was on top of me, kissing my neck. "Peb, c'mon, let me get some, damn."

"Nooooo." I used the palm of my hand to push his face away from mine.

"I don't know why you acting like you don't want me anymore." He kissed my lips softly. "We were so good together."

I stared deep into his eyes, getting lost for a moment. His sculpted body and his charming personality were addictive. "Yes, we were until your lying ass cheated."

"Aw, that was in the past. Stop bringing up old shit."

"Bullshit. It's not in my past. I see it right now, replaying in my head. Do you really think I forgot about you fucking my roommate?"

"That was a year ago. I've changed."

I sighed. "See this is why I never agree to see you. Cause you always trying to freak me. Move!"

"Well, let me lick you then. I know you want that."

A grin spread across my face. I couldn't stand Chip. He knew me too well. Getting my pussy licked was the shit. I liked getting licked almost more than getting dick. I said, almost. Cuz I loved me some dick too.

"See, look at you, cheesing." His lips found mine as his hands roamed under my skirt. "You gonna let me do it?"

Chip wasn't fooling anybody. I felt his swollen dick inside his pants. I smacked my lips. "I don't know."

"You know I lick you the best."

I didn't want to give him his props, but his lying cheating ass had the best tongue action. Actually, he was skilled in the bedroom, period. That's why every chick back in college wanted to fuck him. He was a sexy brown-skin brother with a presence that begged women to be all on his dick and stay in his face, like he had fuck me pretty please written on his forehead.

"Get off me."

His fingers traced my inner thigh, making tiny hearts. "Puh-lease," Chip begged, giving me the sweet little boy face. His long eyelashes always sealed the deal, helping him get his way.

My vagina throbbed, messing up my judgment. "Let me think about it, damn."

I bit my lip thinking about how much he enjoyed sucking on me. He sucked on my coochie like it was a T-bone steak. "Ok. But we not together. I hope you heard me."

"Yeah. I heard you. We not together. I got it." Chip looked my body over as if he was taking it in for the first time. "You gotta come out your clothes."

"Why?"

"Cause I want to touch you all over while I do it. I need to feel your skin."

"You better not be on no bullshit," I said, undoing my shirt.

Chip climbed off me, undressing as well.

"Uh-uh, what the hell you doing?"

"I want to please myself while I please you."

I eyed him strangely. "That sounds like bullshit."

"Don't act like you haven't seen me do it before."

I guess he had a point. "Whatever. You better lick me better than ever."

"Oh, I am."

Chip stood over me naked. His manhood was erect, pointing ten inches from his body. Thoughts of how we used to have sex flooded my mind, making me real hot.

"You ready?" Chip asked, kneeling down.

"I guess." For some reason, I felt like this was a mistake. Chip was too eager. I know he had something up his sleeve.

My body quivered as soon as I felt his tongue between my legs. He started slowly licking from my vagina all the way to my clit. His licks were similar to the way a kid licked an ice cream cone.

"Oh, this pussy tastes good," Chip said, spreading my legs wider, opening my lower lips. "I just love putting my face all in it."

"Ssssssssssss."

"I miss licking you," he mumbled sucking on my pearl.

"Mmmmmm."

"Feels good, baby?"

"Yeeeeesssss," I purred, feeling his finger inside me.

My hands landed in his curly hair, guiding his tongue where I wanted it to go. I rotated my hips on his finger while his tongue did magic.

"You miss me, baby?"

"Mmmmm. Yeeesss," I said, not hearing a word he said. My concentration was on the wonderful feeling between my thighs.

"You ready to cum?" Chip asked, making slurping sounds.

"Hell yeah," I said, wishing he would shut the hell up so I could cum.

Simultaneously, Chip sucked hard on my clit and pressed his finger deep inside me, connecting with my gooey center.

Pleasure jolted through me. "Ah, Chiiiiiipppp!"

"You cumming, baby? You want to feel me inside of you?"

Opening my legs wide, I screamed out in orgasmic bliss. "Yesssssssssssssss! Fuck me with that big ass dick."

Out of my mind with pleasure, Chip took full advantage of my lustful rant. While I was in the middle of my climax, Chip slid his super thick girth inside of me, holding my legs steady in a Chinese split.

I wanted to cuss this muthafucka out. He knew I was in the heat of the moment. But I couldn't because his dick felt amazing. Always had. Always will.

I touched Chip's ripped stomach as he rolled his body, fucking me like a true professional. He was positioned on his knees, working in and out of me effortlessly. I couldn't help but surrender to his stroke. It was like I was in a sexual trance when Chip fucked me. Each stroke had me open for more.

Before I could catch myself, I said, "I miss you inside of me."

"I miss being inside of you," he said with his hands all over my body. Starting with my tender breasts, squeezing, rubbing, and pinching. Then, he cupped my ass, tracing the opening with his finger.

Panting like a dog in heat, I begged and screamed for him to fuck me harder. Chip was the only man who could truly handle me in bed. It was like he had the blueprint to my body, touching me in all the right spots, at the right time. Making me cum like no man could.

Chip slowed his movements down, teasing me. He pulled all the way out with just the tip left in, and then slowly worked his way back in.

Why is he playing with me? "Would you just give me the dick? I'm ready to cum."

Smiling, he continued teasing me.

The slow controlled motions had me on the brink of insanity.

Chip lifted my butt in the air, my feet dangling. He twisted with circular pelvic thrusts, digging deeper and deeper each time. By the time he sped up, I was gushing like a fountain. My eyes rolled into the back of my head as my body quivered. I'm sure I looked like I was being electrocuted.

"That's what I like to see," Chip said in a cocky manner. "Thick white cum all over on my dick."

He has always given me unbelievable orgasms.

I was still feeling the effects of my orgasm when Chip laid on top of me, holding me tight. My legs were pinned in the crook of his forearms. His soft lips connected with mine. Our kiss intensified in the midst of our passion. His low moans and husky breathing indicated that he was near the finish line. Clawing my ass, he lifted me up and down, meeting his rough thrusts. The powerful jerks sent my body into another orgasmic fit, making me cum harder than the last time.

"Ahhhhh! Shiiiiit!" His body twitched. "Fuck Yeah!" His body twitched again. Then he shut his eyes tight, depositing deep inside of me. "Can't nobody do me like that but you."

He was right because I felt the same way.

"I need you in my life."

"No."

"I want to get back together."

"No."

"Why not?"

"Didn't we have this conversation already? I told you just cuz I break you off sometimes don't mean we're getting back together. We're done."

"Think about it," Chip said, kissing my face, my shoulders, and finally my breasts. "Don't you miss me? Don't you miss us? Don't you miss fucking?"

Truth is, I did miss him. A lot. And not just his incredible out of this world sex either. We were more than a couple. We were best friends. Not only did we have a lot in common, we enjoyed each other's company as well as companionship. We had history. He was my first and only love to this day.

I wasn't ready to give us another chance. Our break up was hard. I still haven't been able to replace the void that Chip left in my life.

"I better go." I tried to slide from underneath him.

"No," he said, holding on to me tighter. "We can do this."

"No! I can't do this."

Being intimate with Chip brought back so many emotions. So much hurt. A lot of pain. Before I knew it, I was tearing up, thinking about the past. "Let me up."

Chip noticed immediately. "What's wrong?"

"See, this is why I didn't want to be intimate with you."

He kissed away my tears. "That's because you still love me."

I looked away from him. "Stop making things complicated."

"I still love you too." He turned my face back towards him. "Admit it. You still love me."

"I don't," I lied. "I'm over you."

"No, you're not."

"Yes, I am," I replied with a fresh stream of tears.

"Then why are you crying?" he whispered.

I rolled my eyes at him and then looked away. I couldn't stand how much he knew me. Reading me like a book.

"I didn't mean to upset you." He kissed my wet face again. "Let's go to breakfast and talk about it."

"Is that a trick too?"

He grinned. "Nah, I'm starving."

I giggled, knowing he was dead serious. Real talk, I was starving too.

"I think I drank too much. My stomach is on E."

"That was all those stripper moves that got you on E."

We both laughed.

"I don't want no damn White Castles."

"Me either. Let's do IHop."

"I don't care where we go. I just want to sit down and eat."

Chip was a true gentleman. Not only did he drive, he opened all the doors for me, pulled out my chair in the restaurant, and he offered to pay. He might have done one or the other back in the day, but he never did all this. For as long as I've known him, he could be quite selfish. Things were always about him.

His behavior had me so stunned that I got up from the table, nearly leaving the restaurant. I was almost out the door when Chip ushered me back inside, seating us at the nearest booth.

I eyed him suspiciously while the waitress placed our food on the table. “I guess you have changed.”

“I told you I did.”

“I’m sure the old Chip is in there somewhere. The selfish, egotistical bastard that I once knew.”

Chip chuckled. “Nah, I’m all grown up,” he said in between bites of pancakes. “I’m not on that foolishness no more. I want to settle down. I got one more semester to go before I finally graduate. I already have a decent job, a new ride and a crib.” He stopped chewing, looking dead at me. “Now, I just need a good woman to make it complete. I want to marry you, like we always talked about.”

I rolled my eyes. “I don’t know why you looking at me.”

Chip dropped his fork in the plate, stood to his feet, and slid into the empty space by me. He moved real close, pinning me in the corner of the booth with his right arm around my waist, and his left hand resting on my thigh. “Look, our parents are best friends. My brother and your sister are married. And we—”

“So, that’s them. Not us.”

“Stop fighting what is meant to be. We go way back. You’ve known me your whole life. I was at the hospital when you were born.”

“Hold up,” I interjected. “You were at the hospital because we have the same birthday, dumbass.”

That’s how our parents became friends. Because of us. And the reason why my sister Vanity married his brother Ivan.

“So what, though. I was still there, lying in a crib right next to you. We were always destined to be together.”

I shook my head, taking a sip of my juice. “This conversation is stupid.”

“No, it’s not. Check it. We experienced the first of everything together. Kindergarten dance. Eighth grade dance. Kissing. Making out. Sex. Skipping. Detention. Prom. Graduation. We even went away to school together. That has to count for something.”

I faked a yawn. “You boring me. Get to the point.”

“You know I’m your past, present, and future.”

"What?" I asked, nearly choking on my juice. I laughed.

"You heard me. Get your head out your ass and let's do this."

"No, you get your head out your ass. That shit you just tried to kick to me, was the same exact thing I said to you when I found out you were cheating. I begged you to work it out for us. And you gave me some lame ass excuse about how we out grew each other. You turned your back on me. Not the other way around. Get it straight."

"You're just in your feelings right now."

"The only thing I'm not feeling right now is your tired ass. I'm not going to stop my life and accommodate you because you tired of dealing with those hoes. I was good to you. And you did me real dirty."

"You'll change your mind. I'll be here when you do."

"I'm not changing a damn thing." This whole ordeal with Chip was giving me a fuckin headache. I felt myself getting pissed, real quick. He's the only one that could push all the right buttons, making me want to fuck him up. "It's time for me to bounce. Back the hell up."

"You want to get out, move me then." Chip's six feet frame stayed posted up so I couldn't get out.

"If you don't get the fuck out my way, I'm going to step right on your dick."

I was about to slap the piss out of him and cuss his stupid ass out when my phone rang. It was my cousin Juicy. She was back at Chip's house with his roommate Dino. Juicy fucked Dino hours before me and Chip so they were fast asleep when we rolled out.

"Talk to me."

Juicy laughed. "Is that really how you answer the phone?"

"Yep, pretty much."

"Where you at?"

"IHop."

Chip leaned in, kissing my neck and rubbing my inner thigh. "Give me some more before you go."

"Stop it," I demanded. Chip stayed horny. I used to like it when we were together. He was always in the mood. His dick never took a break. That's one of the reasons why I didn't think he could remain faithful.

"Who is that?"

"Chip."

"It figures. He's probably trying to get some more booty. I heard y'all fucking a little while ago. The shit was loud as hell too."

"Take notes. That's what good dick sounds like." I was still fighting Chip off me. If he didn't piss me off, I might have given him some more.

"Humph. The way you was calling out Chip's name, I thought he was your boo again."

"Naw. Never that."

"Y'all getting back together. I already know it. Watch and see."

"I don't think so."

"Yes, we are," Chip said into the mouthpiece. He must've overheard Juicy's loud ass mouth.

Juicy smacked her lips. "Damn, is that nicca on the phone too? Tell him to get out of our business and get a damn life."

"You heard her," I told Chip.

He paid me no mind, still trying to seduce me. "Let me get some, sexy." I gave him the stank face.

"Girl, you see the time?"

I looked at my phone. It was almost five. "Oh, shit. I completely lost track of time. I'll see you in a few."

"Hey, wait a minute, pick up some L. I wanna get wasted on the way."

"Girl, we don't have time for all that shit. We are going to miss the damn bus."

"But you had time to fuck and go eat, though. You—"

I hung up while Juicy was still running her mouth. I'm not trying to hear that garbage. She got me fucked up.

I shoved Chip. "Look, we gotta go. Go ahead and pay the bill and pack this shit up or leave it. I don't give a fuck. Either way, I'm out." Chip finally slid out of the booth so that I could get out.

"I can take you to the airport," he offered.

"Boy, please. Vanity ain't having that. She already said anyone who don't make the bus, won't make the trip. I'll be damn if I forfeit my free vacation messing around with your cheating ass."

I stood from my seat with my hand out. "Give me the keys." Chip willingly handed them over. "I'll be waiting in the car. You got five minutes to handle this before I pull off." I strutted away in my five-inch heels.

Chip ran up behind me, smacking me on my ass. "You are so sexy when you take control like that. That shit makes my dick hard."

I wiggled out of Chip's embrace, walking towards the door again. "Now, you only got four minutes."

Chapter 3

Vanity

My cousin Shay made a sharp right, leaving me holding my expensive cup of coffee with two hands so it wouldn't spill. I bought a gourmet coffee every morning, but I wasn't thinking about Shay's insane driving when I ordered it. She peeled out of the drive-thru like a maniac.

"Just so you know, I'ma get my freak on while we're there. I can't let all this goodness go to waste," she said emphasizing on her voluptuous curves.

"I already know," I chimed in so she wouldn't keep repeating herself. She made the same remark three times already.

I don't know why in the world, out of all the people who offered to pick me up, I allowed my big mouth cousin Shay to do it. She is too damn much at five something in the morning. I love my cousin, but I've only been in the car with her for ten minutes and she hasn't stopped talking yet. Not to mention, I already had a headache cause I couldn't drink my coffee due to her zigzag ass driving.

"Cuz a bitch got needs, you feel me? And I'm not coming all the way out there to be playing around with Moneaco's ass. He better recognize that he is replaceable."

Moneaco was her Bahamian boyfriend that she met during our visit to the Bahamas last year. Up until this point, I thought things between them were great. If I knew they weren't, surely, I wouldn't have let her pick me up. I could have gotten this story later on in the day, like when we arrived.

"Last time, he was too busy to give me some action. I wonder what the excuse is going to be this time."

"I thought you said you had a good time with him when he came to visit last month?" Here I go getting sucked into her nonsense. I should have just nodded my head or gave an uh-huh or something.

"I did. We had a great time when he came to visit me. The problem is when I visit him. Let me find out he got a wife and some kids in this muthafucka. I'ma set that tiny ass island on fire. Watch."

I laughed hard, knowing her loud mouth, crazy ass would do just that. "You don't want to go to jail over there. It's not the United States. Ain't no three hots and a cot. They'll have your looney ass behind bars and chained up on concrete floors with no windows."

Shay laughed hysterically while driving at top speed through the yellow light that just turned red.

"Will you slow down? You rushing like we about to be late. The bus doesn't leave for another hour or so."

"Girl bye. This is how I drive. I don't slow down for nobody. Not even the Smurfs."

Giggling and shaking my head, I knew there was no reasoning with her. If she wasn't afraid of the police, aka the Smurfs, then I know I wasn't going to talk no sense into her.

"I know one thing, if you make me miss my trip cuz we get pulled over, I'm going to beat your ass."

"Fuck the police," she said whipping around the corner down a side street, avoiding morning traffic.

I don't see how my cousin Jerome, Shay's brother, managed to stay sleep the whole trip, stretched out in the backseat. He would have to be dog ass tired. I'm sure if he didn't have to drive her car back home, he'd still be in the bed.

I couldn't wait for Shay to park. As soon as the car was still, I leaped out with my suitcase and hauled ass to the waiting bus. On my way, I tossed my cold coffee in a nearby trash. It pained me to know that I spent nearly six dollars on it and I couldn't even drink it. A waste of time and money.

"Good Morning," I said, greeting everyone as I made my way on the bus. Shay was in tow, squeezing her big booty past me, taking her seat.

Not everyone was present, but the three I was most concerned about were the ones that were late to everything. My cousins Piper and Juicy and my sister Pebbles.

"You can stop staring at my empty seat, dammit. I'm here," I heard Piper say behind me, boarding the bus. She was huffing and puffing, breathing hard, like she just ran a mile.

"Why you so out of breath?"

With no tact, she raised her shirt showing her tiny baby bump. "Cause a bitch is pregnant again and those steps nearly took my ass out."

Piper was the realest white girl I knew. She wasn't fake or phony, keeping it one hundred all the time. Even though she was adopted into our family at birth, she couldn't be any closer than my blood cousins. The family loved her. Well, almost everyone, except for Shay. I think Shay was jealous of Piper because she was so beautiful. Easily, she could have passed for mixed Black or Hispanic with her long wavy hair, full breasts, big booty, and tiny waist. Men threw themselves at her constantly.

"So, where am I sitting?" Piper locked eyes with Shay for the first time since she stepped on the bus. "Put me with anybody except for that big mouth heffa. You know I can't stand her fat ass."

"Who you calling a heffa?" Shay stood up three seats away. "I got your big mouth, bitch."

"Oh no! Oh no!" I jumped in front of Piper who already kicked off her shoes and was taking off her earrings. Pregnant and all, I don't think Shay was ready for the heat Piper was about to bring.

"I got your, bitch, bitch. You think because I'm knocked up, I can't kick the shit out of your trifling ass. You besta believe, hoe, I can still beat the fat off your funny looking ass. I did it before. I'll do it again."

"This is not going down. Have a seat," I said to Shay while still blocking Piper's path.

"You always taking up for that ghetto bitch," Shay complained. "Just like when we were kids. Some shit never change. Have your favorites, Vee. I see how you are."

"I don't have any favorites."

"I'm not a bitch, bitch!" Piper yelled behind me as she tried to push her way pass. "Straight up, Vee, let me handle her ass. I promise, she will never pop her gums again."

"Would you chill?" I said to Piper. "I'm not letting you handle nothing. Besides, you're pregnant. You've been through a lot recently so relax. Put your damn shoes back on." I cut my eyes at Piper's unacceptable behavior. "Now, back to you," I said addressing Shay again. "I'm not taking up for her. She's pregnant. And she's right, you do have a big mouth. You wouldn't be in this mess if you hadn't told Piper's business and fucked her man."

"And I apologized for it. I'm not going to keep being attacked for some shit I said sorry for."

"I'll attack your fat ass if I want—"

I covered Piper's mouth with my hand. "I don't give a damn what's going on with you two, we are taking this trip together and you two are going to act like you got some sense. I don't care if you have to fake it all the way there and back."

"I'm not faking shit," Piper exclaimed. "I just won't speak to the ugly bitch."

Shay was very pretty. She was bigger than all of us, but she wasn't fat. She is what men would call thick and curvy with a flat stomach. Her beauty is what landed her a plus-sized modeling contract.

This is probably another reason why Shay and Piper clashed; they worked in the same industry. Piper was a makeup artist to the stars.

"Don't speak to me then, wanna be black, bitch." Shay picked her stuff up and moved even further way from Piper, sitting in the back of the bus.

"Be cordial or keep the distance. Either way is cool with me. Just don't ruin the trip for everyone else." I sighed in relief, glad that I was able to calm these two hotheads down before they came to blows.

"Hey, Vanity."

"Hey, Lyric." I hugged her. She was sitting next to Piper. "Damn, you're pregnant too?"

Lyric gave me a sad look. "Not like I planned it. As usual, I got one more mouth to feed." She sighed. "It's a lot on me right now."

"I know," I said, giving her another hug. Everyone always thought Lyric was my sister too. That's how much we looked alike. The only difference was she had blue eyes and blonde streaked hair.

"Lyric, I'm not going to give you a hard time. Just try to enjoy yourself, ok?" I stared into her big blue eyes and then hugged her again. "Everything's going to be alright."

"Ok, I'll try," she said, quietly sitting back down.

Lyric had the worse luck with men. She was the true definition of unlucky in love. Seeing her pregnant made me wonder if she had finally found the right guy. However, this wasn't the time or place for me to get into all that. I knew she was dating someone. I just hoped it wasn't like all her other relationships. She never told me what happened. All I know is it hasn't been good. If anyone deserved happiness, it was definitely Lyric. My heart really went out to her.

Looking out the window, I saw a Cadillac limousine pulling up. My cousins Natalia and Karen stepped out. Damn. Both of them were pregnant too, looking like they were going to go into labor any minute now. This trip is getting more fucked up by the minute. How the hell are we supposed to turn up when everyone is knocked up? This shit was pissing me off. They should have cancelled. I didn't book a trip to do maternity shit.

Marcel made his way onto the bus. He was holding onto Natalia as she waddled down the aisle.

"Hey, girl," she said, hugging me. I couldn't even get a good squeeze because her big belly was all in the way.

Natalia had to be the most beautiful pregnant woman I'd ever seen. Some women were just meant to have a lot of babies. I think Natalia is one of those women. She looked radiant. Not to mention, she pushed those kids out and snatched her shape right back. Probably another reason why Marcel can't stay off of her. Natalia, Karen, Piper, and Cookie all had killer bodies.

"What is Marcel doing here?" I asked, giving him the stank face.

Natalia gave a bashful look. "Girl, you know he wasn't going to let me come alone. Not while I'm pregnant."

Shit, that'll be never then. "Um, this was supposed to be an all girl's trip. That's why I didn't invite Ivan," I sighed in disgust.

"I'm so sorry. Please, don't be pissed at me. I told him not to come."

I rolled my eyes. I hope this trip doesn't suck. "Whatever. Here's your seat right here." I had assigned seating. Some people just didn't need to sit by each other. Like Shay and Piper.

I stepped to Marcel, looking up at him with my hands on my hips. "I like how you crashed my trip. You know you weren't invited."

"Don't get mad at me." Marcel put his hands up in the air, signaling that he didn't want no problems. "This was all Cash's idea."

"What? He's here too?"

"Damn right, I am," Cash said, getting on the bus with Karen. "Stop complaining. We family too. Where's my damn seat at?"

"Shut up." I playfully nudged him as he moved pass me. "It's right there. Have several."

He laughed loudly. "Oh, that was cute, girl." He put his hand on his hip, mimicking me. Then, he dropped the charade.

"This ain't over." He pointed his pinky finger at me. "I got my eye on you."

"Shut up." I fell out laughing. "Get the hell outta here. You got that from a damn movie. Biting ass."

Cash fell out laughing too. We always joked around like that. Cash and Marcel were like brothers to me and Pebbles.

I rubbed Karen's belly, speaking baby talk. "Aww, wooky at you, big girl."

"Hey." Karen smiled. "You look pretty."

I put my hand on my hip, striking a home girl pose. "Making it do what it do, baby."

Karen grinned. "You about as crazy as Cash and Marcel. I see why they call you their little sister."

We shared a laugh as I made my way back over to Natalia and Marcel. "Now, back to you," I said to Marcel while he was putting the carry-on in the overhead compartment. "How many babies y'all gonna have?"

"Eight," he said, like that response was normal.

"No we're not either," Natalia interjected. "This is it." She pointed to her stomach. "We're done after this."

"Eight," Marcel repeated confidently, looking directly at me.

"Well, damn, this is baby number what?" I eyed Natalia's belly. "You're pregnant every time I see you. I'm confused."

"Number six and the last damn one." Natalia shifted around in her seat trying to get comfortable. "I'm sick of not seeing my damn feet. That's ok. If I do get pregnant again I'm leaving you with all them kids. And I'm taking half."

Marcel gave a dramatic gasp like he was offended. "Y'all are my witnesses," he said, looking around at everyone on the bus. "You heard her say she was taking half? I didn't imagine it, right?"

"Shut the hell up, Marcel. You damn right I'm taking half. I deserve it all for being pregnant this many times. You get on my damn nerves."

Marcel gave her a wide smile, aggravating her even more. “So, you’re going to leave me?” He didn’t look the least bit bothered by her accusation.

“Yep. You can have all the kids you want. I’m out.”

“I’m never going to let you go. I’ll be looking for you in the daylight with a flashlight.” Marcel used a pen to demonstrate how goofy he would look trying to find out where Natalia was. We all busted up when this fool said, “Natalia, where you at. Baby, I can’t find you.” She was standing literally right in front of him.

Natalia rolled her eyes really hard. “You so damn stupid sometimes.”

Marcel stood before her as if he had no idea why she was mad. I could tell that was pissing her off too. “When are you leaving me? I just want to make sure I have enough flashlights. Maybe I can catch a sale or something. You know, they might be sold out when I go.”

“Ugh!” Natalia sighed in disgust, sitting down looking out the window, ignoring Marcel. “Stupid ass.”

She wasn’t fooling nobody. Natalia wasn’t going nowhere. She loved everything about Marcel, including having all of his babies.

“You want eight babies?” I asked Marcel. “So, are you going to take care of eight babies? Not just financially either. With that many kids she needs more than just money. She needs your support.”

“No doubt,” Marcel said strongly. “I’m going to always be by her side. As long as I got air in my lungs.”

“Not all the time. You went missing before,” I quickly reminded him, giving him a stare down.

“That’s a long time ago. I’ve been with her consistently since I found out about baby number three.”

“Ummm-hummm. And what does that mean?”

“That’s right Vanity. Get him.” Natalia turned back around, all in our conversation.

Marcel wrapped his arm around me. “Let me holler at you, little pit bull in a skirt.” He was right. I could be brutal when I wanted to be. "I love your cousin. You know that. You were at the wedding. You practically live at my house. She got everything she asked for then and I'm still giving it to her now. Nata-Natalia gets anything she wants."

I thought about their wedding. It was absolutely fabulous. I never got the exact figure but it had to be at least a million dollars or more. No expense was spared. "Ok, go ahead, I'm listening."

"You love your baby cousins, right?"

"Of course. Go 'head."

Marcel leaned in closer as if he had a secret to tell. "Well, I'm trying to make my own singing group. Like the Jacksons."

I looked at him like he had lost his mind completely. "Boy, get the fuck outta here."

He cracked up laughing. "I had you going, didn't I?"

I laughed too, shaking my head. "You stupid." I was starting to see Natalia's point.

"Nah, but seriously. I just want a big family. I feel like when God brings two people together in union and they have a loving relationship, they are blessed. Babies are a blessing. "

I couldn't argue with that. He had a point. I felt the same way.

"And I mean, we can afford it. Natalia isn't stressed out. She has nannies. Plus, I keep up with the kids too."

Did he say nannies? As in plural. "Even the late night feedings? And what about when they are sick?"

"Yes, all of that."

I looked over at Natalia. "He does all that?"

Natalia nodded her head. "Yes, he's Mr. Mom. I have no complaints about him with the kids or money."

"What's the problem then?" Now, she had me looking at her crazy. "What you complaining for?"

"See, Vanity, I thought you were on my side."

"Girl, please. You better give this man his damn singing group." The whole bus started laughing. "He's fine, rich, and as much as you stay pregnant, he got to be putting it down. Shit, you know how hard it is to find a good man? And you got all of the above. Girl, bye. Have several seats."

Marcel and Cash started cracking up.

Natalia rolled her eyes at me. "Never mind. I thought you were helping me out."

"Well, I was, but you don't have a valid point. I can't be defending no nonsense. Bye, Felicia."

"Whatever, Vanity."

"Real talk, you better have all the babies he wants. Keep playing and somebody like Shay is going to steal your man."

Everyone cracked up again.

"I heard that," Shay said. "I would never do that to Natalia."

I turned around looking at the back of the bus. "Yeah, right. You are known for stealing someone's man and sleeping with someone's husband. I love you but I have to keep it one hundred."

"Cuz she's a skank ass hoe," I heard Piper mumble. Thank goodness Shay didn't hear it.

Shay's face turned pale. "See, Vanity that was so uncalled for. You know that was way back in the day. I would never do nothing like that now."

I gave her the screw face. "But it's true though."

Marcel interjected, "Excuse me. I'm not going to be stolen by nobody. I love my wife. The only way I'm leaving her is in a casket. Until death do us part." Marcel looked back at Shay. "And, um, no disrespect, Shay, but ain't no dayum way in hell. I'm just saying."

The bus laughed again. Piper laughed so hard, you could hear her cackle louder than everyone else.

Shay mean mugged Marcel. "See, Marcel, you ain't even right. Big girls need love too."

Marcel put his arm around Natalia. "This ain't got nothing to do with your size. That's not what I was referring to."

"That big ass mouth," Piper mumbled. I gave her a look, mouthing, be quiet.

"Whatever, Marcel. Get on my damn nerves." Shay took her seat, putting her earbuds in, tuning us all out.

Cash stood up, facing me. "Sit your little troublemaking ass down."

"I know you not talking. I learned it from you. Shit starter is your last name."

Cash grinned. "I can't help it if I know all the tea."

"Don't be so full of yourself. And since I'm on you, how many babies do you plan to have? A church full just like Marcel?"

Cash stopped laughing. "Hell the fuck no! We have a boy and Karen is pregnant with a girl. I'm done. I will get snipped, cut, burned, and tied before I have six screaming kids in my damn house, driving me insane. Marcel can have all that shit."

"And what are you having?" I asked Natalia.

"A girl. Number six. And that's why I said I wasn't having anymore. I fulfilled my wifely obligation." She looked at Marcel. "I'm done."

Marcel got all in her face. "You're not done until I say you're done. I own you. If I want you to have six more, you better spread your legs and have them."

The whole bus paused when Marcel said that. Even me. He had enough money to buy all of our broke asses. I wasn't saying a damn thing else to defend her. She was on her own.

"Sike!" Marcel yelled, making everyone laugh again. "Just kidding."

Natalia mushed him. "Show out if you want to. Don't let these people see you get fucked up."

"Don't beat me," Marcel said in a slave voice.

I laughed. "Shoot, you might as well face it. Marcel has an agenda. You're about to be pregnant for the rest of your life."

Natalia smacked her lips. "Don't say that. You trying to get him taken out in his sleep."

"Girl, it's true. Think about it. You been pregnant for the last five years." The twins, Cellie and Celina were four. Rio was three. Harlem was two. Bronx just made one. The new baby girl's name was going to be Brooklyn.

Cash cracked up laughing. "I think I'm siding with Vanity. If you sit next to Marcel, you're pregnant."

"Shut up, Cash," Natalia said. "Keep your ass over there."

"Y'all ain't shit," Karen said, taking up for Natalia. "Marcel stop stressing her out. You said you were done after this baby."

I left them bickering over that. I can't talk about that no more. The conversation was never-ending.

I made my way back to my seat about to sit down when I noticed someone was sitting in it. "Aw, hell naw!"

Cash rushed over to me. He must've known I was about to snap. "Wait a minute, Vanity. I forgot to tell you that I invited my brother too."

I sighed. First off, this was an all girls trip. It was bad enough that Marcel and Cash crashed the trip. Then he invited his brother too. What the hell? I hated sharing the seat next to me. I liked to stretch out and get comfortable. Now I had this nicca all in my space. I paused finally taking a good look at who his brother was. A blast from my past.

Cash misunderstood the look on my face, interjecting immediately. "Hold up, I know what you're thinking, but this is not Emerald. It's my brother—."

"Keystone," I said, finishing Cash's sentence while staring at his brother. I'm sure the color must've drained from my face. "I know exactly who he is."

"I go by Stoney now," he said, staring back at me.

"Well, my job is done," Cash said, walking away, realizing that he was no longer needed to diffuse the situation.

I eyed Stoney as he stood up, giving me an enticing hug. He favored Emerald but I knew the difference. He was my second love. Ivan being my first. Keystone took my virginity. Something Ivan never knew. He always thought I gave myself to him.

Keystone was the boy crush that I never got over. "You look exactly the same. Well sorta." I giggled. "You're all grown up now."

He had a lot more sex appeal. I mean sex was dripping off of him like a second skin. Keystone had always been really cute. Now, he was all man and super handsome. His boyish cuteness turned straight into pure masculine appeal.

Keystone held my gaze with the most beautiful hazel eyes that changed colors from amber to various shades of green. Back in the day, his eyes looked more light brown rather than green. Looking at him now, green seemed to be the dominant color.

"You don't look the same." He let out a sexy snicker, twirling me around so he could get a better view. "You've filled out a lot. No more skin and bones."

I playfully smacked him. "I wasn't that skinny."

"I'm just messing around." He looked at my body like it was a cold glass of water on a scorching hot day. "You looked good then and even better now." He licked his lips.

"Well, it's so nice to see you again, Keystone, I mean, Stoney." He had me so nervous, throwing my game all off.

"The pleasure is all mine." He licked his lips again, seductively. "I hope we get real acquainted on this trip." His pretty eyes skimmed my body, taking in every curve, inch by inch, as if he wanted to sex me all night long.

"Likewise," I said, trying not to drool.

I looked away, hoping that he didn't notice my extreme attraction to him. He had my panties super moist just like back in the day. I've never felt that way about no other man, not even my husband and I loved him very, very much. There was just something about Stoney—not sure what. Just a feeling that I was always meant to be with him. Even now, ten years later, it felt like no time was lost between us. Like we were going to pick up right where we left off. The last time I saw him, he sexed me so good that I still had fantasies about it.

Looking down at my roster, I saw Stoney's name listed next to Karen and Cash. I have no idea why I didn't see it before. But this is what I can expect when Shay helps me out. We get men tagging along on our girl's trip.

I looked back at Stoney, trying to keep calm. "Well, the bus is full so you'll have to sit next to me."

"I wouldn't think of sitting anywhere else." Even his damn voice was sexy. Shit, I'm in trouble. "Listen, I hope I'm not intruding. Cash said it was ok for me to come."

I let out a silly girl giggle. "No, you're fine."

"So you've noticed," he said, purposely licking his lips once more.

"I mean there was one seat left anyway. It's yours now." Get it together, girl. Don't let this sexy man trip you up.

"Did you want the window or the aisle?" he asked politely, but I caught him secretly checking me out.

I was so lost in him that I didn't hear a word he said. He was breathtaking to say the least. I could see his chiseled stomach through his designer wife beater. "Um, what did you ask me?" I asked, playing in my hair. I always did that when I got nervous.

He pointed to my hair. "Don't be nervous. We're old friends. Window or aisle?"

How did he remember that? I gave off a nervous giggle. "Oh, window, of course." I smiled.

He smiled back. His eyes landed on my breasts then they dropped down to my stomach and then a little lower as if he had x-ray vision, seeing my soaked crotch. He stared me down before putting his carry on into the overhead next to mine and then taking his seat.

I found myself staring at him too, longing to kiss his full lips. He was an awesome kisser with succulent lips. The more I stared, the wetter I got. What the hell was wrong with me? Out of all the people to show up on this trip, it would have to be an old flame. I was about to be on this beautiful island where everyone would be half-naked, including me, paired up with the one I felt got away. I said a silent prayer because I was going to need it.

The ironic thing about all this is, nobody knew about my relationship with Stoney. Our affair was a secret. In high school, I was creeping with him while in a relationship with my then boyfriend turned husband, Ivan. Well, technically, we were on a break. He was a football star. All the girls were crazy about him including a super hoe named Lila. Rumor had it that he messed around on me with her because I wouldn't give it up.

Just like most men, Ivan denied it. He couldn't fool me though; I knew it was true. That's what pushed me right into the arms of Mr. Charming himself, Stoney. I had no problems handing my virginity over to him as revenge. My rebound plan turned into months of steamy hot sex, beautiful love-making, and an awesome friendship. It was like I could tell Stoney anything. For some reason, he just got me, for who I was, and what I was all about.

As if life had come full circle, Ivan and I were having problems once again and out of the blue, Stoney appears.

I cleared my throat and looked back at my roster. Now, where was I before Stoney knocked me off my square? Oh, I know, roll call. Going down my list, I called out everyone's name until they were all accounted for. Everyone except for Pebbles and Juicy.

"Has anyone heard from Pebbles or Juicy?"

They had ten minutes.

Everyone spoke at the same time concluding what I already knew. They were missing in action as usual. Without hesitation, I called Pebbles phone. No answer. So, I called Juicy. Her phone went straight to voicemail. It was probably dead, but knowing Juicy, it could be cut off. She never paid the damn bill.

I'ma give these two little tricks a little while longer and then I'm going to tell the bus driver to leave their asses. I don't understand why they can never get anywhere on time. Works my fuckin nerves.

While I was waiting for their slow asses, I handed out everyone's itinerary, explained the arrival and departure times, and announced the roommate situations. I wanted them to have all the information just in case they wanted to go their separate ways and not hang out with the group.

Also, I emphasized that everything was all-inclusive. They didn't have to pay for anything regarding the hotel, food, or beverages. However, alcohol was not included. And those who paid for activities, it will show on their itinerary.

Time was ticking.

By the time I finished with my speech, fifteen minutes had passed. Still no sign of Pebbles or Juicy. They were just irresponsible.

"I can't wait much longer," the bus driver said.

"That's cool. They'll just be left. Can you give me a few seconds to pray first?"

"Sure, Mrs. Vanity," he said politely.

"Everyone, can I get your attention, please?" I was standing at the front of the bus, waving my itinerary for them to quiet down. "We are about to take off, but I want to say a quick prayer first. Can everyone bow their heads, please?"

Everyone on the bus stopped talking, quickly bowing their heads.

"Dear Heavenly Father, I'm coming to You in the Mighty Name of Jesus Christ. I'm asking that you bless each and every one of us on this trip. Bless the bus, the driver, all the passengers, and the family members boarding on the Westside. Bless us going and coming, Father. Bless the people we are leaving behind. Bless all the kids, parents, family, and friends. Give us all a spirit of joy, peace, and love as we partake on this vacation together as a family. It's in Your Son's Precious Name that we pray. Amen!"

Everyone chimed in. "AMEN!"

Chapter 4

Pebbles

I jumped out of Chip's car and threw the keys at him. He caught them and quickly followed after me. He was still trying to get back together and I wasn't having it.

When I walked inside of his house, I expected Juicy to be ready to go. Instead, I see her ass in the air riding his roommate's dick. She could be such a slut at times.

"Ah fuck yeah!" Juicy hollered. "Get this pussy. Yeah, baby, get it."

"You like that shit, huh?" Dino said, pulling her long hair.

"Hell yeah, I do, nicca. I love me some good dick."

"See you always fucking around. I'm going to leave your ass," I said, bypassing their moans and groans on the living room couch.

Juicy stopped momentarily. "Just let me bust one more nut. Ssssss. Ah fuck, nicca. Then, I'll be ready."

"You got five minutes. Vanity ain't going to be pissed off with me because of you. We still have to swing back by the crib and grab our bags."

"Ah, shit, this dick is good. I swear!" I heard Juicy moan as I stormed into Chip's bedroom, gathering my things. Chip lingered behind, watching them like they were porn, before he joined me in his room. Easing up behind me, he wrapped his arms around my waist and lined his dick up against my ass. "Let me get some before you go."

"No. You must be crazy. I'm about to leave even if that means Juicy stays here with y'all."

Chip looked at the time. "I can make us both cum in five minutes and still get you to the bus before it takes off."

I didn't want to admit it, but hearing Juicy and his boy Dino, get down like that was turning me on. That's why I wanted to get the hell outta here before I was busting it open wide too.

Light kisses traced my neck. I felt myself getting weak. "Stop it, Chip."

"Stop what?" He started playing with my nipples through the thin shirt.

I leaned back against him, enjoying the close feel of his warm, hard body.

"Let me do it right quick," Chip begged, slowly grinding against me. "I promise, I'll make you feel real good." His hands dropped to my thighs caressing them gently before raising my skirt. His hands were touching my pussy before I knew it.

"Where are your panties?" he asked me, nibbling on my neck.

I opened my legs wider so his finger could freely touch my clit. "I don't know. I couldn't find them after you took them off."

"Commando is sexy." He unfastened his pants whipping his huge dick out. I mean, when I said huge, his dick was long and big. It took me awhile to get used to it too. Sometimes, it still hurt.

I rested on his dresser with my ass upright, giving him easy access to slide right in. I was surprised when he just put the tip in, working it slowly at the entrance of my vagina. This felt amazing. I didn't know if I was just attracted to Chip or if he was just that skilled, either way, I found myself pushing my ass back trying to take him all in.

"Slow down," he told me, gripping my breasts with both hands, caressing them as he rocked back and forth. "Let me do my job and make you explode."

Being hot natured, it didn't take much for me to cum. Fucking was my stress reliever. I had no problems getting my freak on. Whenever. However. Whomever.

Looking in the mirror, our eyes met. Chip stared at me with intensity while his dick was barely inside of me. "You want more?"

"Yeeeeessss," I begged. We never did have a problem in the bedroom. Great sex has always been our thing. "Give me that big ass dick." I bucked back harder, feeling his dick slide in a little more. "Damn, you make me so hot."

"I love this pussy," Chip moaned, dipping all the way in to the hilt. He wasted no time grinding deep inside of me.

"Shit! I'm about to cum." My body trembled.

"I'm about to cum too."

"Yes! Yes! Yes! Yes!" I cried out in ecstasy. "Oh my God Chip! Fuck Meeeeeeeeeee!"

Chip let go of my breasts, fingering my clit. I was already about to cum, but when he did that, I really let loose. Arching my spine, I pushed back against him hard and fast, doggy riding his dick until white sticky juice came down.

"Damn, baby," Chip moaned on the verge of cumming. His eyes were shut tight. His hands held my ass steady. "I'm about to nut," Chip said, shooting out hot cum. "I promise, your pussy is the best."

I laughed and he laughed too.

"Well, well, well. Look who decided to get her fuck on too," Juicy was standing in the doorway dressed in the club clothes from the night before. "And you made me rush my fuckin nut and you in here getting you one."

"Shut the hell up and get your stuff."

She cut her eyes at me. "It's funny how it's good for you, but it's not good enough for me."

"Worry about your shit, not mine." I walked over slamming the door in her face. "Help me find my damn panties so we can go," I told Chip.

Chip tucked his Python dick away, scanning the room. "Did you look under the bed?"

"Yes."

Chip bent down, lifting the bed skirt. "Not good enough," he said, twirling my panties in the air.

"Whatever." At this point I didn't care who the fuck found my underwear. I just needed to slip them on my ass and roll out before I missed a free trip to the Bahamas.

"Let's go!" I yelled at Juicy who was stretched out on the couch, looking like she was about to go to sleep. "We already late and you still bullshitting."

"Girl, please," she replied sluggishly, getting off the couch. "You tripping."

"You got all your shit? Cuz we not coming back. If you leave something, it's just left."

Juicy was short and petite like me. About the same size—B cup breasts, very tiny waist, a regular plump ass, and tattooed makeup. We were both half white with slanted almond eyes, petite noses, and full oval lips. However, I was light with long curly hair, that I dyed red, and any other color of the rainbow that I liked. Juicy was light brown with medium-length jet-black permed hair that was streaked light brown, honey blonde and dirty blonde.

It's a shame because Juicy was too pretty to have such low standards. She looked up to the reality TV stars, imitating their ways and emulating their ratchetness. At eighteen, she loved being a THOT. On her to-do-list was to appear on the Bad Girls Club. Brainwashed by society, she thought this behavior was cute. This low mentality is the reason why she dropped out of school in her senior year.

As soon as her parents found out, they tossed her stupid ass in the street. Now, she's staying with me. I'm trying to help her get her life together so she doesn't end up a statistic. That seems real hard sometimes. She was cramping my damn style, trying to tell me what to do.

Chip jumped behind the wheel. I hopped in the passenger's seat. And in true Juicy fashion, she hopped in the back on Dino's lap.

"I'm feeling you, girl." Dino said to her with his hand rested on her butt. "I can't wait to hook up when you get back."

Juicy giggled. "I can't wait either."

Ugh! I turned up the music to drown them out.

Juicy leaned against my seat. "Can we stop by the L first?"

"We don't have time for that," I told her without turning my head around.

"Girl, boo. It ain't gonna take that long. I'ma need me a drank to get on this plane. You know I ain't never flew before."

I sighed. I loved Juicy, but she was on my last nerve already and it wasn't even six am yet. "And that's why you need to get your ass back in school, finish your senior year, and broaden your horizons."

"How you gonna tell me what to do when you do the same things?"

"Because I'm grown, little girl. I graduated from college and I'm living in my own shit. Holla at me when you get on my level."

"I'll stop at one close to your place," Chip said, trying to make peace. "And I promise, you'll make your bus too."

"You making a lot of promises." I sat back in my seat getting comfortable. "I hope you can keep them."

"Oh, I can and I will. I can back everything up," Chip said, playfully grabbing his crotch.

I laughed. "That's about all you working with too. The rest of you sucks." Chip knew I was just playing with him.

He bobbed his head to the music. "My game is tight. Watch and see."

I perched my lips. "Humph. I'll believe it when I see it."

After we stopped at the liquor store and got some tequila, vodka, papaya, and pineapple juice, before we pulled up to my spot.

"Sexy, sexy," Rondo said. "Where you been?"

"Heeey," I said with a flirty undertone. "Clubbin. You know how I do."

Rondo was the maintenance man who lived across the hall. We met right after I broke up with Chip. I was so lonely, and in need of some serious dick, so I hooked up with him. I've been seeing him for a couple years now. We had an understanding. He just fell back and played his position until I was ready to hand my pussy over to him again. It wasn't like I kicked it with that many dudes anyway. Only three including Rondo. I'd been with Chip majority of my life so it was hard to move on.

"Heeey," Juicy said, imitating me.

"What's up?" he said, never looking her way. His eyes were directly on me. "Anything you need?"

My body warmed a little. Chip might be my best, but Rondo was definitely a contender. This man had skills. "Not right now. But maybe when I come back. I might need to be tightened up then."

"Cool. Where you going?"

"To the Bahamas. Remember? I told you."

"Yeah. Yeah. I just forgot. I've been working too hard." He licked his sexy lips. "Well, have a good time. I'll watch your place while you're gone."

I grinned, thinking about our last time. "Thanks, Rondo."

He hugged me, copping a feel on my booty. "My pleasure sexy," he whispered in my ear.

I blushed. Rondo and I had some sweet late nights.

"Uh-Hmmmm." Juicy acted like she was clearing her throat. "I'm still standing here waiting to get in."

"Where's your key?"

"I left it."

I dug in my pocket, handing her mine. "I'll meet you inside."

"We have a flight to catch or did you forget?"

I shooed her away like a fly. "I didn't forget. I'm the one who reminded you, remember?"

"Yeah well, don't take too long. CHIP AND DINO are still in the car waiting on US."

I sucked in air, staring at her. She was trying to blow up my spot. "You don't think I know that? Get out of my damn business."

"Well, sexy, I better let you go." Rondo checked me out once more. "I'll see you when you return."

"Ok," I said, salty that Juicy opened her big mouth.

I was about to start in on Juicy when I saw the time. "Oh, fuck! We need to get our shit and roll out as fast as we can. Or we really aren't going to make this flight."

Juicy poked her head out of her bedroom. "That's what I was saying while you were grinning up all in Roooooondo's face."

"Girl, stop talking to me and get your bags together."

I showered right quick and threw everything I could into two suitcases. One of them was so stuffed that I had to sit on it to close it. I was hoping that it didn't weigh over the limit. If it did, I didn't have no money so Vanity would have to be pissed and come out of her pocket. She can afford it. Her and Ivan make good money.

"You ready?" I asked Juicy, struggling with my heavy suitcases, wheeling them to the door.

"I was born ready," she said, waltzing out of the bathroom in a change of clothes.

"I hope you washed your ass." I put my shades on. "Grab your luggage and let's go."

Chip and Dino got out of the car when they saw us barely making it with our luggage. They carried our bags to the car.

Chip slammed the trunk. "We really don't have that much time now."

"Well, drive like your mama is on fire then."

We both laughed. Dino and Juicy looked at us strange. I didn't care. It was an inside joke. Something we used to say all the time when we were silly kids.

Chip hauled ass on the Dan Ryan from Chatham, trying to make it to 95th. Meanwhile, Juicy done cracked open the liquor mixing up a drink in a juice bottle.

"You're going to be sick."

"No, I'm not."

"Yes, you are. You should have waited until you ate something first."

"I got this," she said, taking a sip. "I'm a pro at this shit."

"We'll see about that in about an hour, hard-headed ass. Is that the bus pulling off?" I asked Chip when he got off on 95th street.

"Looks like it," he said, scoping out traffic.

"That is them," Juicy said. "I see Vanity looking out the window at us."

Sure enough as the bus was riding pass us at the light, Vanity had her eyes dead on the car. "Oh, we're fucked now."

"No, you're not." Chip bust an illegal U-turn in the middle of the street, almost causing a few accidents. "I got this."

The bus went through the light and Chip was right on its tail.

I got really frustrated because they were still riding. "They about to get on the E-way, Chip."

Juicy sighed. "Either they don't see us or they don't care."

"I hope you're prepared to follow that bus to the airport," I told Chip.

"I'll take you if I have too, but he's going to stop. Believe that."

Sure enough, the bus looped back around and pulled into the bus terminal. Vanity got out with the meanest mug I'd ever seen in my life, holding a clipboard.

"Don't just sit in the damn car! After you fuckin flagged us down!" she yelled. "Get your asses out before you really do get left. Let's go!"

All four of us jumped out of the car, scrambling. I grabbed my carry on while Chip got my luggage handing it to the bus driver to put under the bus.

"I'm sorry," I told my sister trying to smooth things over. "It's not my fault." The last thing I wanted was for her to be upset with me the whole trip. I didn't need that kinda stress in my life.

"It never is, Pebbles. You don't take the blame for anything. That's the problem. Maybe one of these days you'll grow up and take ownership of your shit, and stop trying to pass the buck."

"But fa real, this time. I would have been here."

She looked at me with disgust. "I'm not in the mood. Just get your shit and get the fuck on the bus."

Chip walked up, taking me into his arms. "Bae, think about what I said."

"Um-hmm, I will." He was crazy if he thinks I'm giving him any thought on this trip. I'm going to get me some island dick or get dicked down on the island. No matter how I said it, dick was my main focus. I paid attention to Chip's wants and needs for way too long.

"I can't wait until you come back so I can suck on your pussy." I loved when Chip talked dirty to me. It made my nature rise instantly, putting me in the mood.

"Bye." I gave him a kiss and got on the bus.

Dino smacked Juicy on the ass. "I'm going to miss you, Juicy Booty."

"I'ma miss you too, boo."

Dino tongued Juicy down and she got on the bus sitting next to me.

I glanced over at my sister across the aisle. She looked at me with daggers. I turned up my lip and gave her the same funky look right back. She was such a control freak. Always got her panties stuck up her ass.

I sat back in my seat, trying to relax. I couldn't. "Where that drink at?" I asked Juicy.

"I got you," she said, handing me a juice already mixed with alcohol. "I knew you were going to need one when we got on the bus so I hooked you one up in the car."

"Thanks, Juicy." I took a sip and thought about my relationship with my sister. Man, it was bumpy.

We were four years apart. But we looked like we could be twins. In fact, both of my sisters looked just like me. People confused us all the time. And we were constantly being complimented on our beauty. That was as far as it goes. Vanity and I were like night and day.

Vanity was always grown acting, even when we were kids. She didn't mess up like normal kids did. She was always responsible and motherly; punctual and doing the right thing. Me, on the other hand, I was the wild child, a free spirited, a go with the flow type of chick. I had no problem showing off my body and expressing my sexual needs.

I'll admit I have a hard time keeping a job. It's just that I haven't found out what I really wanted to do yet. Thank goodness for my parents. Because of them, I never went without. If they didn't help me, some man was always throwing money at me.

Men were always offering to pay my bills, buy me gifts, and fight for my attention. And yes, I let them. I had no problem with them spending money on me. That means I can keep my money in my pocket.

Vanity frowned upon my lifestyle. She thought I was a gold digger. But frankly, I didn't give a damn what she thought. If I wasn't asking her to pay my bills, then she shouldn't have shit to say.

Chapter 5

Vanity

Once the bus got going, people were finally settled in. Some were watching the movie playing. Others were reading. Some were whispering conversations back and forth. Others were sleep.

I sat next to the window trying to sit as far away from Stoney as I could. This man had my coochie throbbing. I had the feeling that if he accidently brushed up against me, my juices were going to gush out everywhere. Besides, I was still trying to process the feelings that I had for him. I had a feeling that he was doing the same.

The bus was freezing. It was so cold my teeth were chattering. I tucked my arms in my pink hoodie, but my legs were still cold. I don't know why I dressed in this cute summer outfit when it was cold as hell here in Chicago. Yeah, it was nearly a hundred degrees in the Bahamas, but we hadn't made it there yet. I called myself dressing for where we were going since it would be blazing hot the moment we arrived.

"If you're cold, you can borrow my jacket," Stoney offered, looking me over with a sexy gaze.

I quickly looked out the window. I didn't even want to look at his fine ass. "Nope, I'm good," I lied.

"No, you're not." He reached over and touched my thigh. I almost had an orgasm. "You're freezing."

"It's ok," I said as my teeth kept chattering. Who was I fooling? Nobody.

"Hold on, I got you." He stood up, reaching into the overhead bin. All I saw was the imprint of his big dick. Shit! I was really messed up now.

He reached inside, pulling out a blanket before sitting back down. He unfolded it, leaning over, rubbing his warm body next to mine. Gently, he placed the blanket over me. "Is that better?" he asked, staring me right in my face. And the way his eyes kept traveling to my lips, I was sure he was going to kiss me.

"Yeah, much better," I replied, hoping he didn't see the little rocks my nipples had turned to.

He smiled, leaning in even closer, whispering in my ear. "You know, that blanket is big enough for the both of us. I might get cold too. Then, we'd have to share."

Oh damn! When he said that all I could imagine is his face buried between my legs, eating me out. I blinked a couple of times to get rid of those images. "Um, sure, that'll be ok," I said, wondering why in the hell was I inviting the temptation.

He licked his sexy lips. "Don't be surprised if I take you up on that offer."

I couldn't say another word. I had already done way too much. I used part of the blanket to curl up against the window making a pillow. I closed my eyes so I didn't have to look at him anymore, quickly falling asleep.

*****

I felt a nudge. I'm not sure how long I was knocked out. Slightly opening my eyes, I saw that everyone was exiting the bus. My spot felt so comfy. Nice and warm. It didn't feel this nice before I drifted off. At this point, I didn't even want to get up and go nowhere.

Just then it dawned on me that I was snuggled-up under the blanket with Keystone. How the hell did I get so close to him while I was sleep? The smell of his cologne mixed with his masculine body scent had my hormones raging. His arm was around my shoulder. I was nuzzled in his armpit. My head rested on his chest. His other hand was on my thigh, nearly under my skirt, too close to my vagina. All I could think about was his fingers moving a little higher touching my clit.

After coming to my senses, I rose up and scooted away from him, sitting back in my seat. "Sorry. I'm so used to being curled up next to my husband. Old habits die hard." I gave him a faint smile and tried not to get lost in his pretty eyes again. Damn, did this nicca put a root on me? Why couldn't I stay away from him?

Stoney gave me a warm smile. "It's okay. I always hold my fiancée the same way."

I was so disgusted with myself. "I don't even remember moving next to you."

"Me either," Stoney openly admitted. "I went to stretch and realized you were there. So, I held you close, keeping you warm." He caressed my thigh. "Your legs were cold."

I didn't want to, but I removed his hand. "Thanks again. I don't know what came over me. I didn't get very much sleep last night," I lied. Girl, you need to pull yourself together. Like right now.

Subconsciously, I must've moved closer to him because of those wild thoughts I had before I dozed off. I was doing my best not to think like that, but secretly, I wanted him to beat it up.

"Where are we?" I asked.

"At the rest stop on the Westside."

I stood up, stretching. Stoney's eyes traveled down my body, lingering on my tank and then my mini skirt. I wondered where my pink hoodie was. And why the fuck did I take it off if I was so cold? This man got me losing my damn mind. I'm doing one dumbass thing after another.

Reaching back in the seat, I removed the blanket and saw my hoodie buried underneath. Quickly, I put it back on. From the corner of my eye, I noticed Stoney staring at my breasts before meeting my gaze. This time he didn't even try to hide that he was checking me out. His gaze caused heat to radiate throughout my body. I must've had the same effect on him too. A lump formed in his pants again.

I got to pull myself together. This is ridiculous. I haven't seen this man in ten years. And my pussy was ready to jump ship and throw away years of marriage for a quick fuck.

Stoney stood to his feet, stretching in the center aisle. "I'll be back. Do you want anything?"

"Oh, I'm getting off too, but thank you."

"No problem," he said, brushing past me, making sure I felt his erection.

I was ready to bend over, hike up my skirt, and spread my legs, letting Stoney have his way with me. I fantasized what if—instead of moving past, he came up behind me, resting his erection against my backside. His warm breath on my shoulder. Giving me luscious kisses while tugging on my thong. My body would shudder as the head of his penis slid pass my ass cheeks, near the opening of my slick, wet hole. Slowly, he would enter me, going deeper, connecting with my hidden treasure. His dick would feel like the best.

Arching my back, I would buck against him ready to reach a much-needed climax. Oh Stoney!

"Are you sure you don't need anything?" Stoney asked, snapping me out of my sexual visualization of him. I hope I wasn't acting it out before him.

"What? Oh, um, that's ok. Nah, I'm good. Really."

He gave me a lingering stare. "Ok, but if there is anything. I mean, anything, let me know."

"Ok, I will," I replied, watching him walk off the bus.

I stood there lost in thought. I didn't know what was happening between us. Whatever it was, it was forbidden. I was married. I wasn't happily married, but I was madly in love with my husband. We were just going through a rough patch. That's all. And Stoney admitted that he was engaged. We both had someone. The challenging part was neither one of them were on this trip. And the sexual tension between us was bananas. Even if I managed to block my lustful thoughts out of my mind, I was sure that we would end up somewhere alone, making out. Just like a few minutes ago. It was obvious that he was flirting with me. And it was obvious that I liked every bit of it.

After getting my thoughts together, I finally got off the bus, making my way to the bathroom.

"What the fuck is that smell?" The pungent odor of throw-up hit me in the face as soon as I walked into the public restroom. If I didn't have to pee so bad I would have ran the fuck back out.

Juicy was on the dirty bathroom floor, on her knees hugging the toilet while Pebbles held her hair out of the way.

I must've come in on the end because Juicy was just dry-heaving. "Why the hell is Juicy throwing up? Please don't tell me she's pregnant."

Pebbles rolled her eyes. "Aren't you one to talk? No, she's drunk."

"Drunk? Who gave this little girl some liquor?"

Pebbles turned up her lips and gave me another nasty look. "Vanity don't come in here all high and mighty like you wasn't partying and drinking when you were eighteen. Let's not forget how wild you were back then. You were supposed to be babysitting me when I walked in on you fucking Ivan against the wall while Mommy and Daddy were out on date night. How soon we seem to forget our own shit."

At that moment, I wanted to ring my sister's neck. "How dare you make this about me? I'm not sprawled out on the floor kissing the porcelain."

Pebbles turned her back on me. "Let it go for once."

"I will not. You're a bad influence on her."

"Just like you were a bad influence on me. You got married and think you're Mother Theresa. Pul-leeze."

"What does that have to do with Juicy's ass being out on this nasty bathroom floor?"

"Everything. Because you act like your shit don't stink, Mrs. Goody Two Shoes. Well, I'm here to tell you, your shit smells like fifty farts."

"I never said my shit don't stink, you did. So, stop trying to turn this around on me."

"No, but you act like it. You're quick to point out everyone else's faults, judging us, but what about yours? Your skeletons are piling up in a closet somewhere just waiting to fall out. And I'm going to be the first one to say, I told you so."

I was two seconds from putting my hands on my sister. She was begging for me to fuck her up. Before this trip was over with, I'm sure I was going to make good on it, beating her ass. "What the hell did you drink, Juicy?" I asked her when she finally stood to her feet.

"Vodka and Tequila," she said still looking queasy.

"Now, you know better than that, Juicy." Pebbles rolled her eyes at me and walked over to the sink, washing her hands. "I don't know what your problem is with me," I said unable to ignore her stank attitude. "If you got something you want to get off your chest, do so. I'm right here."

"I will when I feel like it. Right now, you're not worth my time."

I shook my head. She was such a spoiled brat. "Did you eat anything, Juicy?"

"No," she said, looking like she wanted to throw up again.

"Girl, you know you can't be drinking and you haven't eaten anything. And why are you drinking this early in the morning anyway?"

"Don't answer that," Pebbles interjected. "It's a set-up. As soon as you say why, she's going to lecture you on something else. Just agree to the shit."

"You need to check yourself. Obviously, you knew she was drinking on an empty stomach and you didn't seem to care."

"Chile, please. I'm not Juicy's keeper. She is grown. I can't tell her ass what to do. I mean, I try to, but she barely listens to me."

I gave Pebbles the side eye. "Really? That's all you got."

"What do you want me to do?"

"Something bad could've happened to her. Did that ever cross your mind?"

I gave her the, you should know better look.

She dropped the sour face. "Ok, I'll try to do better."

"That's all I'm asking."

After scolding Juicy, I insisted that she rinse her mouth out and get rid of the liquor on the bus. She walked out of the bathroom with her head hung low. Reaching in my purse, I sprayed some body mist to freshen up the bathroom because the stench was profound. It was so stank that I had to hold my pee for a hot second. My stomach was bubbling and it felt like I had to throw up too. Using my hoodie to cover my nose, I rushed into the furthest stall and squatted over the toilet, doing my business.

Pebbles was still in the mirror when I came out of the stall, finally relieved. "So, who was that dude you were curled up with?"

I reached for the paper towel to dry my hands. "You all in mine. Why?"

She whipped around looking at me with her hand on her hips. "Cause he didn't look like your husband to me."

I avoided her accusing stare. "Girl, please, he's Cash's brother. No big deal."

"Yeah, okay. Does he know that you're married?"

"Yes, he does," I said getting defensive.

She looked me up and down as if she could see the guilt on me. "Well, don't fuck up your marriage for a cute face, nice body, and a big dick. It's not worth it."

"Stay the fuck outta my business."

Pebbles stood in my way. "I know we don't see eye to eye, but I'm serious. Ivan loves you. And you don't know this dude from a can of paint. He just wants some ass. I know you not that blind."

"Like I said, mind your fuckin business." I bumped Pebbles hard, hurrying out of the bathroom. She was the last person that needed to give me advice, as messy as her life was. Besides, what did she know about Ivan? Only what Chip told her. Because she sure as hell hadn't asked me a damn thing. If she did, she would know that we were having major problems. I was on the verge of leaving him. Yep, just packing all my shit and walking the fuck out.

Coincidently, I walked right into Stoney as I made my way out of the bathroom. He was leaving the men's room.

Chapter 6

Pebbles

I wanted to run up, grab my sister by her hair, and sling her to the ground, pouncing on her like a wild animal. She always pressed the wrong buttons. She better be glad I wasn't trying to make a fool of myself by whipping her ass. That would mess up the trip before it got started. Instead of following after her, I stayed behind in the bathroom, taking in deep breaths until I calmed myself down.

My pressure rose right back up the moment I exited the bathroom. Vanity was walking towards the bus. And guess who just so happened to be walking beside her? Cash's no-good ass brother. I observed the way his eyes swept over her. It was obvious that he lusted after her. And by the silly way she was acting, she was lusting after him too. This makes a lot of sense. It explains why she was so defensive. She didn't want me to know.

Vanity's marital problems were a lot worse than what I thought if she was openly getting close to another man. I knew her and Ivan were going through something. Every once in a while Vanity would slip up and say something that made me realize that there was trouble in paradise. I assumed it was small. I figured, if it were something serious, one of them would have mentioned it. I guess I was wrong.

For as long as I could remember, Vanity's world rose and set on Ivan. She's never mentioned another man. Never even looked at another man. Never entertained the idea of having another man. Her loyalty was to Ivan. So how did this nicca slip right in? I can't stand her ass half the time, but I knew my sister. She wasn't a cheater. And this behavior was way out of character for her.

I purposely waited for them to get on the bus first. That way when I got on, I could observe them first hand. Sure enough, by the time I boarded the bus, I saw the extra friendly, flirtatious conversation between them. I couldn't hold back anymore. I had to say something.

"I know you not getting on this bus again without greeting me," Cash said, blocking my path.

Oh damn. Does he have a sixth sense or something? Some kind of brother intuition. Where they know to telepathically help each other out. "My bad, I was in a rush the first time."

"What about now?" Cash asked before he embraced me in a bear hug, kissing my cheeks like he always did. Somehow, Cash and Marcel adopted me as their little sister, which meant I couldn't even piss without them interrogating me about it.

"Stop it, Cash!" I squealed. "You make me so sick with all that mushy stuff. What's wrong with you?"

"Look at you all grown up. I remember when you were still in high school, begging for a ride."

Cash picked with me every time he saw me. "You can't be treating me like no baby anymore. I'm twenty-one."

Cash laughed. "You'll always be a kid to me."

I smacked my lips. "See, that's the problem. You're stuck in the past." I glanced over at my sister. "I didn't know you were bringing your brother along."

"Oh, it was last minute. He really needed this vacation."

"Alright, so what can you tell me about him? Because he's mighty friendly with my sister."

Cash took a swig of water. "I know how protective you can be. But Stoney—"

"Stoney? What kinda player name is that?"

"Well, his real name is Keystone, but—"

"Oh, never mind." All of them had crazy ass names. What was their mother smoking? "Why is he talking to my sister? All in her face."

Cash chuckled. "You sound jealous."

"Nah, never that."

"Why don't you ask him?"

"True. I'll talk to you later," I said walking away from Cash, approaching his brother. "Hi," I said, interrupting their chummy conversation. "I don't think we've met yet. My name is Pebbles. I'm Vanity's sister." I extended my hand past my sister's angry stare, greeting him.

"Keystone, but you can call me Stoney." He shook my hand while looking me over.

"Nice to meet you Stoney." I smiled at him, but gave my sister a knowing look that said, if you know what's good for you, you'd switch your damn seat before Ivan fucks your ass up.

"How'd you get stuck sitting with my sister, the grouch? She's usually alone when her husband doesn't travel with us."

Vanity kicked my foot.

I mean mugged her.

Sex was written all over his body language. He was leaned in towards her. His hand rested on her upper thigh and he looked like he wanted to rip her clothes off and lick her from head to toe.

"Your sister's not that bad. She's actually really sweet." He smiled at Vanity and then at me. "All the seats were taken so she got stuck with me."

"Well, you can switch with me if you like," I said trying to run interference.

"No thanks," Vanity protested. "He doesn't want to sit next to throw up Juicy."

"Hold up. She threw up?" Stoney asked, rising from his seat, looking over at Juicy.

I waved at him to sit down. "Wow, could you be any more obvious? Geez. What happened to subtle?"

He laughed. Even his laugh was sexy. "My bad. It's a natural reaction to look. I'll try to be more discreet next time."

"Next time? What next time?" I had to laugh too. "It better not be a next time. I didn't sign up for all that."

He laughed harder and so did I. "Yeah, I guess you're right. Who wants to throw up again? So, let me cancel that."

I smiled at Stoney seeing why my sister was so hypnotized by him. I found myself captivated by him too. He was quite charming and super cute. Not to mention sex oozed from his pores. "You know, you're cool with me, Mr. Stoney."

"Likewise, Ms. Pebbles," he said with wanton.

"Well, let me take my seat and leave you two kids alone."

"Aww, whatever," my sister said while Stoney grinned at me.

I glanced at him one last time before walking over to my seat. He was definitely looking back. I couldn't blame my sister for being mesmerized. He had me mesmerized too. If given the chance, I'd be all in his face too. But then again, I wasn't married. That's the issue I had with her. She told Ivan he couldn't come because it was a girl's trip, but she's all up in Stoney's face. Not a good look.

*****

We were finally at O'Hare International Airport. It seemed like it took forever to get here. Maybe because I was up majority of the night. I'm not sure, but I was more than ready to put on my bikini and soak up some sun. We couldn't get to the Bahamas quick enough.

After checking in our luggage, getting our boarding passes, and going through security, everyone made their way to the food courts near our terminal.

"What you gonna eat?" I asked Juicy.

"I got a taste for some chili."

"No, the hell you don't either. You're sitting next to me. I'll be dammed if I smell fart all the way to the Bahamas. You better find a taste for something else. Real quick."

Juicy cracked up laughing. "That would be foul, huh?"

"Literally."

"Ok, then, I'll just have what you're having."

I glanced around trying to decide. I'm going to get something light. My stomach always gets queasy when I fly. I don't want to be jacked up when we arrive."

"Yeah, I better do the same. I'm still not one-hundred after what happened earlier."

"I know you not either. You puked your guts out." I was still looking around trying to decide. "Ok, I think I'm going to have Starbucks. That way I can get a delicious breakfast sandwich and a caramel macchiato."

"I'ma have a seat."

"You alright?"

"Feeling a little weak. I think I'll feel better when I eat something. Can you get me the same sandwich and a hot Chai tea?"

"Sure."

Juicy walked off and I went and got in line.

"Hello beautiful," someone behind me said.

I turned around, looking in the man's face. He wasn't bad looking. Not as cute as I preferred. I would have found him more attractive if he didn't have this nerdy flare about him. The glasses, fitted polo shirt, and cargo shorts with loafers. Yuck! Yuck! Yuck! There was nothing sexy about what he had on. And he spoke like a nerd too. Super proper and boarding school like.

"My name is Jayson."

My face contorted as if he had shit on his tongue. "Not interested." I turned back around just in time to place my order. "Can I get a caramel macchiato, hot Chai tea, and two bacon and gouda breakfast sandwiches?"

"Will that be all?"

"Yes," I said, digging in my pocket for my money.

"I got it," Jayson said, stepping forward, handing the lady a fifty. "Also, can I get a spinach and feta wrap and a white chocolate mocha?"

"Thanks," I said while we waited for our orders.

"You're welcome." He stared at me like I was on stage at a beauty pageant. "Am I worthy enough to get your name now?"

I shrugged. "You act like you paid my car note or something. What you dropped, I could have dropped myself."

"Ouch. You don't give brothers no breaks, do you?"

The lady handed me my order and I walk away from Jayson, wandering into the bookstore. He came across as a straight up lame. I didn't have time. My fingers scanned over a few urban books. I loved a good read. I didn't think I would have much time to read on this trip, nonetheless, I forgot to bring a book just in case. Whenever I traveled, I always had one. I picked up a few, looked at them, reading the back cover before putting them down, walking out.

As I made my way back towards the terminal, someone came up behind me, nudging me.

"Here you go," the familiar voice said.

I turned around. It was bug-a-boo ass Jayson, handing me a bag with three books in it. "Thanks." I politely took the bag out of his hand, about to walk away.

"Can I at least get your name?"

I stopped and turned back around in a cutesy way. "Pebbles."

He stepped up, closing the gap between us. "Pebbles," he repeated. "A pretty name for a pretty woman. I knew you would have a unique name."

I sighed. Why was this man in my damn face? "Listen, um, um…"

"Jayson."

"Yeah, what do you want?"

"I want to get to know you," he said, staring at me with goo-goo eyes. "Can I have your number? I have a lot more things I'd love to buy for you."

I thought about it for a minute. Jayson's boring ass might come in handy. When I get back, my car note is due. If I can't pay it, then I would be hitting his ass up. "Ok."

His eyes lit up like shiny stars.

I pulled out my phone and gave it to him so he could punch in his number. After entering his number, he quickly called himself from my phone, trying to be slick.

Before I knew it, I'd popped him twice in the head before taking my phone back.

He ducked for cover, slightly backing away from me. "What did I do wrong?'

"I didn't say I wanted you to have my number, jackass. I said I'd take yours."

"Oh, I'm sorry. I didn't know. I'll erase it if you want me to."

I had wasted enough time with this clown. "Forget it. Even if you erase it, I'll be in your call history and on your bill, genius. Just know that if you call me too much, I'm blocking your dumb ass."

Finally, I ditched Jayson, making my way over to Juicy with our food. She snatched her bag like a homeless person.

"Um, a thank you would be nice," I said, looking at her like she was crazy.

"Thank you," she said, tearing open her sandwich, attacking it, taking a huge bite. "It feels like I haven't eaten shit in weeks. I'm hungry as hell."

"You look like it too."

We laughed.

I stopped laughing, turning up my nose like I smelled fart when Jayson went trotting by, sitting a few rows away. Aw, hell naw. He's going to the Bahamas too?

Chapter 7

Vanity

I was seated on the plane having a deep conversation with Stoney when my phone started vibrating. I noticed that I had two missed calls and a text from Ivan. I wondered what he wanted. He hated to text. He only did it because of me. I looked at the time and assumed that he was at work by now.

Lately, we had been fighting like cats and dogs. We didn't see anything eye to eye anymore. It was like I woke up one day and we just grew apart. I suggest counseling and Ivan refused.

None of my friends or family knew just how bad things were between us. To save face, I sugar coated the arguments that nearly turned physical. I just wanted things to work out. I cared deeply for him. That's why I booked this all girls trip. I needed a getaway so I could clear my head from all of Ivan's angry rants. He'd become so critical about everything. Yelling at me for the littlest things.

My phone blinked, indicating I had another text.

Ivan: Hey, babe. You're probably high in the sky by now. I wish you were here with me. Why do you have to travel so much? I miss you.

I smiled bright, texting him back.

Me: Heeeey baby. I miss you too. I loved my morning workout. Tee hee. I wanted to lay back down next to you and catch a few more zzz's. LOL.

Ivan: You wouldn't have to catch more zzzz's or leave if you kept your ass at home like we discussed. That's one of our biggest issues. You leaving all the fuckin time. You act like I don't make enough money. Like I can't take care of you. Like you want to be the man in this relationship. Do you have a dick? Stop trying to wear the fuckin pants and let me handle this shit. Learn your place, woman.

I frowned while responding to his text.

Me: Here you go. Please, don't start that shit again. I'm not quitting my job. If anyone should know me, it should be you. I'm not a stay at home type chick. Stop trying to change me. Accept me for who I am or else.

Ivan: Or else what? You gonna leave? Stop playing with me. Don't make me act a damn fool. For real.

Me: I don't want to argue. I'm sick of that. Let's talk about this later.

Ivan: But you brought this bullshit up. Not me. Stop bringing shit up you don't want to talk about.

Me: Can you just see my point of view for once? Think about how I feel.

Ivan: See, that's the problem, you're so worried about you that you forgot about me. Your husband! Remember? Oh, how could you when your ass is never at home. The shit really pisses me off, Vee.

Stoney immediately picked up on my change in behavior. "Did you get some bad news?"

I sighed, practically in tears. "No, I'm just texting with my stupid ass husband. Get on my fuckin nerves."

"Oh," Stoney said, sensing my frustration. "Everything will be ok once we get to the Bahamas, have a few drinks, and get our party on." He patted my knee for comfort.

I smiled. "Yes, I could use that drink right now."

"Did you want me to order you one?" He looked around for the stewardess. "I'll find out what they got."

Stoney has always been attentive. One of the things I always liked about him. "No. But thank you very much. You're so kind."

He leaned over, whispering in my ear. “Anything for you, beautiful,” he said, kissing me on the cheek. “You’re too pretty to be stressed out.”

I had to admit. It felt good to be desired by Stoney. Something that I was missing at home. Sure Ivan and I had scrumptious sex, but the romance was out the window and down the street. Right along with our relationship. Ivan had me stressed the hell out, walking on pins and needles.

Ivan: Why haven’t you responded yet? Whatever. My break is over. Call me when you get checked in so I know you landed safely. That’s if you have enough time for me then. What am I talking about? You don’t have time for me when you’re here. Ain’t no way I’ll get your time while you’re on vacation. Your family is always more important. I’m sure you don’t even miss me like you say you do. If you did, you would’ve let me come. Must be some other reason why you didn’t want me there. And you say I’m the one messing us up. I go above and beyond for you and all you do is want more and more. What about me?

This nicca had me heated. What the fuck is his stupid ass talking about? I’m glad he didn’t come if he was going to have this sour ass attitude. I texted him back.

Me: Fuck you. You’re an asshole.

Something had to change. I can’t keep going on like this. Ivan has been taking me for granted for two years. Talking to me crazy. Taking his frustrations out on me. I’m at my last straw with him and this marriage. Expressing my concern to him has gotten old. Either he was going to agree to counseling and start treating me better or I’m out.

Before I knew it, tears came to my eyes. Ivan and I used to be so happy. What went wrong? It seemed like the only time I enjoyed his presence was when his dick was deep inside of me. The moment he bust a nut, he was back to his pissy ass attitude.

“C’mere,” Stoney advised, motioning with his finger for me to turn my back to him. “Let me massage the tension away.”

I don’t know how he sensed it, but I was super-duper stressed out. Without hesitation, I turned around in my seat with my back to him. Like magic, his hands began to knead my flesh.

I never did ask him what he did for a living, but if I had to guess, a personal masseuse would definitely come to mind.

"How does that feel?" he whispered in my ear.

"Mmmmmmmm." I closed my eyes, feeling a tingle down below. "Your hands are incredible."

"I know how to please a woman," he replied seductively. "I would love to please you. What you like that?"

"Yeeeeessssss," I said before I knew it. I couldn't help it. I was curious. What was he going to do next?

His hands moved further down, rubbing near my shoulder blades. Then pass my bra strap to my lower back.

I looked over my shoulder, across the aisle. Pebbles and Juicy were both knocked out, sleeping on top of each other. Then, I looked around to see if anyone was paying attention to us. No, they weren't. Nobody cared.

I felt his lips grazed my neck. "Let me please you during this trip too?" he asked, appealing to my desire. "I want to suck your nipples, your clit, and your toes."

It was chilly on the plane but I was starting to get really hot. I knew I was wrong. I was so pissed off at Ivan that I didn't want Stoney to stop. He was making me feel good, just like he said he would.

Stoney took the blanket that covered me and pulled it over the both of us. He scooted really close to me. "I need you to be really quiet, ok?"

"Ok," I agreed, nodding my head. My heart was racing, anticipating his next move.

His hand landed on my thigh, moving under my skirt. Instinctively, I opened my legs wider and his hand traveled even further, reaching my thong. Gently, he touched the thin fabric, causing another tingle between my legs.

"I can stop if you want me to." His lips touched mine. "But I have to admit, I've wanted you since I laid eyes on you again."

The attraction was mutual. "I wanted you too," I said, breathing even harder.

Stoney kissed me passionately while his fingers massaged my clit. I was so excited that I was about to cum as soon as he touched me. I don't know if it was because I was on an airplane, or the fact that the people around us had no idea, or because Stoney was forbidden. I wanted to lean my seat all the way back, rip my skirt and panties off, and allow him to fuck me high in the sky.

I began rocking back and forth against his fingers.

"That's it," he said in a hushed voice. "Let me take away all of your stress."

I humped faster against his hand, indulging a little more by grabbing the bulge in his shorts. Stoney used his other hand to open his shorts. I slid my hand inside of his boxers freeing his thick erection. Wow! He's even bigger than what I remembered. He was just as worked up as I was, already leaking precum.

I couldn't believe that I was on a plane with my family, jerking him off while he played with my clit. I'd be lying if I said that I wasn't extremely turned on. I wanted to really get loose and straddle his lap, but that would be pushing it.

Sensing that I was at my peak, Stoney put his head under the cover and popped out one of my breasts, sucking on it. I continue to jerk his meat as my body stiffened. Just as I was about to scream with pleasure, Stoney covered my mouth with his, quietly moaning as he shot a hot load of cum in my hand. My body shuddered going into a frenzy. I kicked the seat in front of me during my pleasurable fit.

When I stopped convulsing, Stoney released my body, fixed his clothes, and moved back into his seat as if nothing happened. We were both stunned when the stewardess came out of nowhere, as if on cue, offering us snacks. Like she was waiting for us to get finished.

Neither one of us made eye contact with her. The moment she left, Stoney went to the bathroom. I assumed to freshen up. I didn't want to make it obvious but I needed to do the same thing. I had cum oozing out of my hand, sliding between my fingers, onto my thigh.

"Here," Stoney said, handing me a travel-size pack of wet wipes.

I jumped out of my seat and rushed to the bathroom as quick as possible. The first thing I did was wash my cum-stained hand. The next thing I did was use the wet wipes to clean up my kitty. I still couldn't believe I did something so freaky with a man who wasn't my husband. Guilt started to settle in. Now I had regret about the amazing experience.

As I traveled back to my seat, it felt like all eyes were on me. Like everyone knew what I had just done. I couldn't actually tell if I was being paranoid or if they really knew. The joy that I just experienced turned to sadness by the time I flopped down next to Stoney.

"What's wrong?" he asked, immediately picking up that my mood was off.

I shook my head, staring out the window. "Nothing." He moved closer and I pushed him away.

"Don't tell me nothing. I can tell you're upset again. Look at me." I wouldn't face him. "Look at me," he said sternly.

Finally, I turned around, facing him with sad eyes.

"Are you still stressed?"

"What?"

"I asked, are you still stressed? Because not that long ago you looked like you were about to pop a vein out the side of your neck."

Thinking about what we just did made me grin. "No. Not anymore."

"That's what I want you to remember. How great your climax was. Even your skin is glowing." His hand lightly stroked my hair. "You're amazing."

I blushed, loving how his compliments made me feel.

"I can't lie. I look forward to making love to you on this beautiful island."

I looked pass him at Pebbles who stretched, looking directly at us. At first I thought she had seen something. I knew I was in the clear when she stuck her tongue out, snuggling back up with her travel pillow.

Stoney leaned back in his seat, closing his eyes.

I curled up next to the window, drifting off into a peaceful sleep.

*****

"Bitch! We about to have a blast," my older sister Joseline aka Joss said, looking at the beautiful island as we waited to be checked in by customs. This was her first time coming to the island. She was ready to get all the way turned up.

Biologically, Joss was a man. Her birth name was Joel. For as long as I could remember, she always went by Joss. I mean all the way back to being a toddler playing dress up. At eighteen, as a graduation present, my parents paid for her sex change. I was glad because after spending two seconds with her, you knew that she was definitely a girl. Nothing about her was manly. Unless you were really familiar with sexual reassignment surgery or that lifestyle, you wouldn't have a clue. And even then, she was drop-dead gorgeous, being as pretty as me and Pebbles, if not prettier. She had the same petite curves, breasts, booty, and a vagina too. Men went crazy over Joss. Simply, they adored her over the top personality.

I couldn't help but laugh. "Why you got to act crazy everywhere we go?"

"Hunny, cuz that's how I do. If I ain't the life of the party, then I'm dead. Somebody has to show you girls how to have a good ass time." She puckered her lips, blowing air kisses and twerking at the same time. "It might as well be me," she said snapping her fingers in my face. "Who do we have here?" She dropped her shades, eyeing Stoney as he made his way over to us.

"Here's your luggage," he said, sitting them down next to me.

"Thanks, boo" I said in a flirty manner. I smiled at him and he smiled back.

"I'm going to talk to my brother. I'll see you in a bit."

"Ok, boo," I said, watching Stoney walk away. He shook his head and laughed. And I did too.

"Bitch! Who in the hell is that?"

"Shhhhh," I said, hushing her. "Why are you so loud?"

She curled her lips, batting her eyelashes. "Now, you know better than to shush me. Who the hell is that?" she asked in a quieter voice.

"Cash's brother Stoney."

"Damn! He is all kinds of fine. God himself dropped this man straight from the sky. Good grief. I'd pay top coins to be his woman. Or give a kidney if I didn't have enough." She laughed, twerking again.

"Joss, hunny, he's not that type of man."

"Dammit. All the fine ones are straight." She took another look at Stoney. "Shit, he is delicious. You think he would know the difference?" She pushed up her C cup breasts, bunching up the itty-bitty shirt she had on.

"Yes, he would. And even if he didn't, he's not into all that extra that you're packing."

"You seem so sure. How would you know?" Joss stared deep into my eyes. "Oh my God! Did you fuck him? You did. I know it. I can tell."

All I could do is smile. My silence told it all.

"Bitch! You been holding out on me." She dramatically stomped away and then came right back like she was walking the runway. "Hell naw. I ain't know you had that much freak in you. Was it good?" She looked back at Stoney. "Humph. Humph. Humph. I know it was good. It just had to be."

I blushed.

"He looks like he got some scrumptious dick." She stomped her foot. "He should have been gay. I'm so jealous right now."

We laughed.

"How big is it?"

"I never said I did it." I was praying that she didn't know what we did on the plane.

"Shut the fuck up. It's written all over your face," she sang. "You don't have to say a woooorrrrrd."

"You're speculating. You know nothing."

"I know that if you haven't tapped that, you will be. This island is uber sexy. He's uber sexy. You're uber sexy. He's alone. You're alone. And he don't look like the type that you can spend time with and not fuck. Some love is going to be made. Ah, I just wish it was me trading places with you."

I laughed at her theory to hide how true she was. "What about you? What's up with your love life?"

"Bitch. Nothing. Ever since me and Art broke up, I'm having a nasty time trying to get over him. That's why I needed this trip right here. To meet me a sexy island man who knows how to do a girl right." She threw her long curly hair over her shoulder and shook her hips. "I need him to work all these curves, hunny. Work it so good that I forget my own name. Yes, Gawd!"

I started shaking my hips too. "Girl, they not ready."

"They sho'll the hell ain't."

After getting our luggage, we had to go through another checkpoint before being allowed on the island. I did a roll call while we made our way through customs, accounting for all my family members. This has become a part of my routine ever since we lost one of my baby cousins. I told my aunt not to bring her small children, but she didn't listen. The baby wandered off and we didn't find his little ass until three hours later. That mishap nearly blew the whole damn trip. No more kids were allowed to come after that.

I think I'm going to have to band pregnant people too. This trip is populated with them. All these baby bumps are killing my vibe. I just saw my cousin Cookie. She's expecting too. This would be her and her husband Travis' first child.

I truly don't understand their relationship. And how they met was really weird too. She was hired by his best friend to have sex with him for his birthday, as a gift. A foursome. Cookie is a triplet. From what I was told, her sister's Sugar and Spice were delivered in a gigantic birthday cake on his porch. They all had sex with Travis at the same time. Somehow, Travis fell for Cookie. While Sugar and Spice moved on with their lives.

I waited outside in the heat for the rest of my group to make their way through customs.

"Is this our bus?" Pebbles asked, approaching me with her luggage. "Cuz I'm hot as shit."

"Yeah, I think so."

"Well let's find out cuz I'm ready to sit in the air. I'm sweating my damn edges out."

I tapped on the air-conditioned bus door. "Are you Malic?"

"Yes, I am," he said, getting up from his seat walking off the bus to greet us. I showed him the voucher for the bus, which had all of our names on it.

"Can we wait for our group on the bus?"

Pebbles fanned herself. "Yeah cuz it's hot enough to fry an egg out here."

"Sure," he said, quickly taking our luggage, loading it on the back of the bus.

With such a large group of people, there were several buses that pulled up to take us to our hotel. I arranged for the buses by itinerary. Everyone was grouped by the things they choose to do on the trip. Each person had a roommate. Pebbles and I were sharing a room. Juicy and Shay. Lyric and Piper. Joss and Cookie. Marcel and Natalia. Karen and Cash. And Keystone had a room by himself. Not sure how that happened.

After being off the plane for over an hour, we were ready to check in to our hotel rooms. I don't know about anyone else, but I was ready to freshen up. After having fun with Stoney on the plane, I felt dirty. Not to mention it was hotter than Africa on this island. The last thing I wanted to do was stank.

Everyone got in line with their roommates.

Pebbles and I stood in line behind Stoney.

Pebbles sighed loudly. "I can't do one more damn line. This shit is ridiculous. We're never going to have any fun," she said, sounding like a bratty kid.

I shook my head at her. "You're so impatient."

She sighed loudly, once again.

I ignored her this time, concentrating on Stoney. I couldn't help but notice his swag. He has always had major presence. I wondered what his angle was. Did he just want some booty? Or was he really feeling me, like he always says? And what did that really mean? One more reason why I felt like he was taboo. My life was complicated enough. I can't handle the nicca I got. Then add cool ass, smooth-talking, never break a sweat Stoney to the mix.

My eyes stayed on him as he stood at the counter. Something about him just drew me in. His mannerisms. How attentive he was. Everything I was missing from Ivan. He used to be so loving and not snap out all the time.

Stoney grinned when he caught me staring at him. I tried to look away, but it didn't happen fast enough. I had no choice but to smile back. He purposefully walked back to where I was and told me how beautiful my smile was. That made me blush once again. He winked at me and then walked away.

Pebbles stood by my side with her arms folded across her chest. "Stoney got you wide open."

I returned the attitude. "Girl, bye. Shows how much you know. I got him wide open."

Pebbles smacked her lips. "Yeah, ok. Let's see who's right."

"I got this," I said, hoping to convince her. Truth is things could go either way at this point.

"Yeah, ok. I hope so. Something tells me that you don't got this."

I didn't want to admit it, but she might be right. Stoney had always had an extreme effect on me. Just his stare alone made me wet and tingly. Back in the day, we might have been kids, but what we shared was as real as it came. Most people would call it puppy love. I beg to differ. That bond, connection, or whatever it's called was real. Oddly enough, if Stoney never disappeared, I might have married him instead of Ivan.

Pebbles nudged me, hard. I took two steps forward, stumbling. "Stop daydreaming about Stoney and step up to the damn counter. We been in this line long enough. I'm ready to check in."

Embarrassed, I immediately stepped up with our hotel information. After getting our key cards, Pebbles and I strolled through the hotel amenities with our suitcases, sightseeing as we looked for our room. Walking down the hall, who do we see—Stoney shirtless, holding an ice bucket.

"Here comes trouble," Pebbles mumbled. "Why does he have to be shirtless? He is doing way too much."

I giggled. He looked damn good shirtless. "I'll meet you inside," I told her.

"Don't do nothing I wouldn't do."

"I'm not doing anything." Actually, I was kinda shocked that his room was right across from ours.

"Yeah, right. Is that what they call booty calls now? Anything." Pebbles opened the hotel door, wheeling her luggage inside.

Stoney stopped right in front of me, looking as sexy as he wanted to be. "Humph. This is convenient."

I laughed. "If I didn't know any better, I'd say you were stalking me."

He chuckled. "You might be stalking me because I got my room first," he said pointing across the hall.

I stepped closer to him. "Aye, can we keep things between us? About you know what. I don't want everyone to know."

Stoney squinted his eyes, shaking his head. "Whatever you say."

"Oh, and just to make things clear, we're not together. It's just sex. I didn't want any miscommunication about that."

He was still shaking his head. "If that's how you want it. You're calling the shots. I'm just a squirrel in your world trying to get a nut."

He stuck his key card in the door while I stood there looking stupid, wondering if I just made the right move.

Pebbles walked back into the hallway. "Pick your face up. He's gone. I'm going to find Juicy."

Chapter 8

Pebbles

The welcoming party was off the hook. It was an outdoor festival that consisted of the local residents selling food and souvenirs, a parade, and contests. Native people welcomed us to the island by putting handmade necklaces around our necks. We watched in awe as the marching band performed like it was half time. There was acrobatics with kids doing flips and all kinds of stunts and also, African and exotic belly dancing.

I felt right at home with the half-naked people partying in the streets. Because I was half-naked too. My body was tight so I showed it off every chance I got. I had on a string bikini top and the smallest cut off shorts I could find. I wore my fashionable shorts with the zipper undone and turned down, showing off my flat stomach and part of my string bikini bottom.

This look got me all kinds of attention. And I loved it. Men couldn't take their eyes off me. I smiled and flirted, definitely enjoying the moment. Juicy wasn't too far behind, copying after me. I couldn't be mad at her, if she was going to get her sexy on, she might as well learn from the best. Nobody on this trip knew how to be as sexy as I did. Well, maybe Joss.

I was truly enjoying myself while the pregnant women were struggling. Natalia's feet were swollen. She looked like she couldn't take another step. Karen kept rubbing her belly, groaning, because she ate too much. Lyric just looked hot and bothered.

Piper and Cookie seemed to be getting around pretty well for two knocked-up chicks. They were sporting sexy clothes and shoes. I guess they weren't going to let being pregnant stop them from getting their sexy on. Can't say I'd blame them. And men were hitting on them too. They both had all kind of trinkets from men trying to buy their time.

The stage behind us lit up. A spotlight shined on the main stage while a live band played some hot Reggaeton in the background. A Hispanic man approached the stage and started rapping in Spanish. The atmosphere was already sexy, but this sensual music kicked it up a notch. Everybody started getting loose, winding and grinding.

I found myself swaying to the music. Naturally, Juicy joined in rocking her hips too. I was surprised to see Piper and Cookie shaking their big bellies, getting loose as well. They were dancing pretty good to be carrying another life. Two dudes joined them. The party really got started then. A crowd formed around us, and before long, we were all partnered up dipping it and doing it.

Everyone stopped dancing and began clapping when the rapper ended his freestyle. He took a bow and left the stage. Next, a young woman and man walked up, welcoming us to the Bahamas. "Do you know what time it is?" the guy said in a thick Bahamian accent. "Contest time!"

Everyone in the crowd cheered.

The lady smiled and stepped forward with a similar accent. "That means we will be picking people from the crowd and giving away prizes to the winners. So, show me what you got!"

Everyone cheered again.

"The first contest will be salsa. The prize will be dinner for two at any restaurant of your choice. Do I have some volunteers?"

Everyone screamed.

The woman looked around in the crowd, picking a young white couple first. They looked really excited to go up there, but

I seriously doubted if they could salsa. She picked another white couple and two black couples before she ended up picking Vanity and Stoney.

My heart almost dropped when she pointed to them. Vanity looked at me and I looked at her. I don't want to go up there, she mouthed.

Stoney looked ready. "C'mon, let's go. It'll be fun."

"Noooo. I can't Salsa." Vanity looked scared. She should be. Dancing wasn't her strong suit. She can twerk a little and do enough to look hot in the club, but that's as far she went.

"But I can," Stoney said, confidently. "It'll be easy. I'll guide you."

"Stop being a chicken and go up there," I told her. "You're here to have fun. Loosen up, tight ass."

Vanity stared me down while the crowd cheered her on with cash and Marcel being her biggest supporters chanting her name louder than everyone. She looked at all of us like she wanted to fight.

I turned to Stoney. "Just drag her up there. She's not going to resist too much."

Stoney picked Vanity up caveman style. Her body was thrown over his shoulder with her booty in the air. He carried her on stage before putting her down beside him. They stood in line with the other couples, ready to compete.

"Get that frown off your face," I hollered. "And shake something."

The announcers gave them a few minutes to practice. Just like I thought the first couple was horrible. They danced like they had two left feet. The other couples weren't that bad. But Stoney was up there looking like he was the salsa king. He danced so good that he made Vanity look good too. His dancing skills helped them to win first place. After accepting their gift certificate, Stoney picked Vanity up carrying her off the stage the same way they went on.

I cracked up. Vanity was putting up a front, but I know she liked every bit of Stoney's affection. She kept giving him side looks, trying not to be obvious, but I saw it. And I saw the way he rocked his hips too. I bet he got a mean stroke.

"Let's give all of our couples a hand," the woman on stage said. "Who's ready for our next contest?" She pointed the mic towards the audience. We erupted with cheer. "I'm going to need brave people for this one. Nobody shy. Do I have any volunteers?"

People started screaming. Juicy standing to my left started jumping up and down with her hand in the air. "Me! Me! Pick me!" she yelled.

The lady looked down making eye contact with her. "You right here. Come on up."

Juicy practically ran up on stage.

"Now, I'm giving away fifty dollars for this next contest." More roars from the crowd. "Wait a minute. You all haven't heard what I'm going to do."

"I don't care what it is for fifty dollars," Juicy said.

The other two girls up there looked around wondering what they had to do.

"I'll bet the anticipation is killing you," she announced. "Let's not wait any longer. A wet T-shirt contest."

All the men in the crowd went crazy.

"You got to be kidding me," Natalia groaned.

"I don't want to see this shit," Karen added.

"But that's not it. You have to give me your best Flashdance impression while being sprayed with water." She demonstrated the move that they'd have to do. "I want you to do something like that, but put your own twist to it."

Juicy began cracking her knuckles and jumping around like she was warming up for a fight.

Juicy was a natural when it came to dancing. Nobody up on that stage was going to beat her. I couldn't wait for her turn. She was going to dust all them chicks. The first girl to dance was shy and timid. She barely moved, looking as if she was scared to get wet. Her performance was so bad that she got booed. The second girl, she tried. She moved pretty good. Even though, she almost slipped and fell in the water. But at least she put in the effort.

When Juicy hit the stage, not only did she command our attention, she hit those moves like she was the lead in the movie. She ended the scene with a high kick in mid-air, landing on her back like the professionals do. The crowd went wild. Just like I predicted, Juicy won.

The guy moved to the edge of the stage. "This is our last and final contest. Any volunteers?"

"Pebbles!" Vanity yelled out, pointing to me. "Right here." She mouthed to me, payback.

"Girl, what you doing?" I asked her. She done lost her mind.

"Don't be a chicken. Ain't that what you told me?"

"Yeah, but they up there doing some crazy stuff now. You got off easy. I'm not about to be showing off my tits and ass for no damn money. That's THOT shit."

Vanity turned around to the family. "Don't y'all want to see Pebbles up there? Let's point to her and chant her name."

I don't know why in the hell they all listened to her. Doing exactly as she asked, causing a great amount of attention to be placed on me.

"You right here," the guy on stage said, pointing at me. "Come up here."

"What am I doing?" I yelled. Cuz he had me fucked up if he thought I was about to degrade myself.

"It's a dance contest."

I stared him down, approaching the stage. "It better be. I'm not in for the foolery."

"It is, pretty lady," he said. "Don't be so feisty." He smiled and winked at me.

After recruiting all the girls, a total of six of us, he gave the rules to the dance contest.

"It's gonna be a big booty dance off."

"A whaaaaat?" I put my hand on my hip. "See, you trippin. That's not what you said."

"Calm down, feisty one. It won't be that bad."

Everyone laughed.

"This some bullshit. But you got me up here now. Let's go."

"Ok, ladies, here are the rules. When the music starts playing, I want all of you to shake what ya Mama gave ya. Then the best two will do a dance off for the hundred dollar prize."

I sized up my competition. I was the smallest one with the smallest booty. But that wasn't going to stop me from getting busy. I had some freak nasty moves that would put all these chicks to shame. From what I can tell, I'm the most limber. I'll use that to my advantage.

As soon as the music dropped, I made my presence known by twerking the hell out of my little booty. It wasn't that my booty was real little. I was working with a nice package. It's just that these girls were working with some donkeys. I didn't have no donkey. I had a donk. But you couldn't tell me that. I worked my booty like it was the biggest booty on Earth. I popped so hard that my damn earring fell off while making my cheeks jump.

Then, I incorporated stripper moves. I got real low while twerking, and then came back up, and I was still twerking. Only to go back down to the floor twerking even harder. I'm sure that I out twerked them. Especially when I put in a few of those belly dancing moves that I saw earlier.

When the music stopped, we all were breathing hard.

"Give these ladies an applause!" The Bahamian announcer kept staring at me, smiling. "I've seen a lot of booty contests, but this has to be one of the best. Now, when I point to each girl, I want you to cheer loudly so I can pick the final two for the dance off."

The first girl, with the biggest booty, she got a lot of cheers. I knew she would. She needed another planet just for her ass. The cheers became less and less until he pointed to me. That's when the crowd started cheering like mad. Most of them were probably from my family, but I didn't care.

"You," the guy said pointing to Planet Booty. "And you," he said, pointing to me. "It's time for a face off. There will be two rounds. One of you will dance to the music. The music will stop. Then the other will dance. The music will stop again. It will be one more round and then the winner will be picked by the crowd. Are you ready?" he asked looking at us both.

"I been ready," I said, not even fazed by my competition. There was no way she could out dance me. I was the queen of this shit right here. She would be bowing down when I finished. Believe that.

"I want you girls to bring it," he said, making the crowd scream.

I gave him a head nod, ready to get down to business. This was my shit. It's what I lived for. Competitions. Especially dance. Nobody could fade me with this. I used be in the number one dance group in Chicago called Metro. We went all over the country battling, winning almost all of our competitions.

"Get ready. Get set. Go!"

When the music dropped I expected to hear some more Reggaeton. But they came hard, kicking this thing off with some Chicago flavor. One of those dope house music beats.

Ol girl was first. She started popping really hard, bouncing her breasts and booty to the rhythm of the beat. The crowd backed her up cheering her on. I'll admit she was doing her thing.

But I wasn't the least bit intimidated. As soon as the music dropped for me, I did the same move she did while holding one leg in the air, popping my ass from left to right. Then I switched legs, turned around and did the same move just a little faster from left to right. The crowd got real hyped. Taking it one step further, I threw some Footwork in on her ass. As big as her titties were, I know she couldn't bust those moves.

"I see we have a battle for real," the guy said. "These ladies aren't playing. One more round. Leeegggoo!"

I guess she saw I meant business and came out the gate with a split. She bounced in the split and then made her ass clap, making everyone cheer for her.

I just watched waiting for my turn. I had something for that ass. I couldn't wait for the music to drop. When it did, I did the same mid-air kick that Juicy did, which she stole from me anyway, and landed on my back with one leg straight out and the other leg underneath me. In a roundhouse twirl, I grabbed the leg that was underneath me. Lifting it high in the air, I twisted my body until I fell into the same split that ol girl did, twerking. I bounced in it a few times, before I leaped to my feet, and did the same thing all over again with the opposite leg. When I was done this time, I just finished by staying in the split twerk-bouncing.

The crowd went completely bananas.

It was a wrap. I won.

The announcer didn't even ask the crowd who won. He just walked past ol girl, straight to me, handing me my money.

"You killed that shit!" Cash said, running up to me as I walked off stage, towards my family. "That chick didn't know what the fuck hit her. She still standing up there looking goofy."

"I have to give you your props," Marcel cosigned. "That was real live. You did your thing."

Juicy ran up to me all hyped. "That bitch didn't have a chance. You mopped the stage with her ass. Straight bomb. I mean, it wasn't nothing but bits and pieces when you walked away."

"Cuz that's what the fuck I do," I gloated. "Thinking she was going to see me," I said, patting my chest. "Fuck outta here."

Chapter 9

Pebbles

The welcoming party was over. The crowd began to scatter. Marcel, Natalia, Karen, Cash, and Lyric left. The boring pregnant women were tired. Marcel and Cash looked like they wanted to hang out but left out of respect for their wives.

Vanity said she was calling it a night too and Stoney tagged behind her. I doubted if they were going to turn in. At least not separately.

That just left me, Juicy, Shay, Piper, Joss and Cookie. Enough people to still have a good ass time.

"So, what y'all want to do?"

"Bitch! We want to go shopping on your ass," my sister said.

I smiled, waving my winnings in her face. "Wishful thinking, but um, that's not going to happen, hunny."

"You the one that just won all that money. Shit, you need to be treating all of us."

"Juicy won some money too," I said to her, trying to deflect the conversation. "Ain't nobody hitting her up. What about her?"

Juicy smacked her lips. "Don't be all in my pockets just cuz people counting your paper. That money is already spent. So, don't nobody even ask."

"Ok. Ok," Piper said. "Let's just go shopping. The more I stand still, the more my damn feet hurt. And I'm way too cute to have hurt feet."

Her and Cookie hi-fived. "I know that's right girl. Me too."

We started walking further down the street, exploring the vendor booths set up with items for sale.

"Oh, I have to have that." Shay stopped to look at the display of sarongs. "I've wanted one of these since forever. And every time I visit, I keep forgetting to buy one."

"Me too," Joss said raising her shades to get a better look. She picked one up, holding it next to her body. "This would be too cute on me."

"I'll buy that for you," some white man said to Shay.

"Thank you." Shay smiled at him. I could have sworn I saw dollar signs in her eyes. "Well, you know I'm not done shopping yet. Are you going to buy those items too?" Well, look at Shay work it.

He handed his credit card to the Bahamian lady behind the cash register. "Charge whatever the pretty lady wants."

"I think we're going to be best friends, boo," Shay said, searching for her next item.

"You are stunning," the man's friend said to Joss.

She batted her long eyelashes and played with her hair. "Thank you. You're not so bad yourself, Mister."

"I can't stop staring at you. You're a natural beauty. I'm sure you get men hitting on you all the time."

That's all Joss needed to hear before she was arm in arm with this man, getting him to trick off his money too.

I watched Joss and Shay wander off with their newfound friends. I hope he has a lot of money. Joss is about to run them pockets.

Piper and Cookie were hungry so we stopped at one of the food joints. They got a shrimp and fish dinner.

I was hungry too but I didn't even want that until I smelled theirs. "Let me get a piece."

I reached my hand in Piper's plate and she smacked it. "Back up. You know I don't play about my food. You should have bought you some." She gave me the evil eye.

"See that's foul." I looked at Cookie and she turned her back to me, still chomping away. "You too, huh?"

Cookie turned back around with an attitude. "Here! And don't take all my food either." She rolled her eyes when I snatched a large shrimp, a piece of fish, and a few fries. "That's it. Buy you some."

She yanked her plate back so fast I almost dropped the few crumbs she gave me. "Dang. Thank you. Y'all pregnant women are a trip."

"Now, what you won't do is, eat my food and then talk about me. Don't make me come out these heels. Cuz you know I'll do it."

I reached over and hugged her. "Thank you, cousin Cookie."

"That's more like it."

I must admit, that was the best seafood I'd ever had. I thought about going to get me some, but the line was around the corner now.

I heard Juicy's stomach growl. "Was that your stomach?" I asked, laughing.

"Hell yeah. I'm hungry. I haven't eaten since we were at the airport."

"Why don't you go and stand in line for us?" I said, pointing to the people who just lined up for the fresh seafood.

"You got a deal if you go and stand in the ice cream line for me."

"Deal. I'll meet you over there."

I strolled further down where people were standing around an outdoor ice cream parlor. The design was a really unique cone shape and the tables and chairs looked like sundaes.

I walked back over to where they were, approaching Cookie and Piper. "Prego One and Prego Two, while you two stand here feeding your fat faces, you can sit down if you walk back over here with me. I'm about to get some ice cream.

Piper's food was gone. She was wiping her face with a napkin. "Did you say ice cream? Yeah, I'm in. I want two scoops of chocolate." Just greedy.

I stood in line for ice cream looking for the prices and the two pregnant chicks had a seat. The line was kinda long, but it moved fast. I was placing my order before I knew it. I already knew what Juicy wanted. She always got the same thing, a banana split. Piper already told me what she wanted and I wanted a turtle pecan cluster.

"That'll be twenty dollars."

Damn! They were expensive. That's why they don't have prices listed. I reached in my pocket, and got the money out, about to hand it over, when this dude came out of nowhere bumping me.

"Excuse me, Miss, I got it."

I was about to cuss his stupid fuckin ass out when he pulled out a twenty handing it to the man, paying for my order.

"Thank you, even though you did bump the hell out of me," I said, retrieving the carton that carried all three of our treats.

"Sorry about that. I just wanted to get your attention. Let me get that for you." He took the carton out of my hand.

I stopped giving him a hard time, finally looking at him. He was cute. Beautiful bronze skin, standing before me in swim trunks, tank, and flip-flops, He had muscles, neat brownish blonde dreads, and a nice package from what I could see. Definitely my type. I could see myself having a freaky nightcap with him.

I smiled. "That's nice of you."

"Oh, I don't mind."

"What's your name, cutie?"

"Tre. What's yours?"

"Pebbles."

I walked over to Piper and Cookie, handing Piper her ice cream. She took it and stared at Tre. "We send you to go and get ice cream and you come back with a fine piece of dick."

We all busted up laughing, even Tre.

"Um, thank you, I think," he said with a bashful smile.

"Trust me," Piper said, stuffing her face full of ice cream. "That was a compliment. I know cute when I see it." She took him all in. "And baby, you sexy as fuck."

"Calm down," I told her, knowing she can get buck wild. "You're pregnant and married."

"I know. You don't have to remind me. Shit. I can still look. There's no crime in that."

"Well, look and don't say nothing."

She sighed. "Alright. Damn. You can be a prude just like your sister sometimes."

If she only knew that Vanity wasn't as much of a prude as she thought. She was probably somewhere getting her freak on with Stoney.

Just then, Juicy walked up with our food and three more handsome guys joined us. Tre introduced them as his cousins, Adam, Scott, and Tony. We pushed two tables together and sat down. Juicy and I ate our food while delighting in a conversation with the guys.

Afterwards, Tre suggested that we all walked over to the man-made beach. Basically, it looked just like a regular beach with sand and water. It just wasn't a large body of water because someone created it. However, it had the most beautiful glow under the moonlight.

"I saw you up there on stage," Tre said, sitting down next to me on the side of the pier. "You did your thing."

"Thanks," I said, staring at his sexy body. I couldn't wait to see him wet.

I took off my shorts. I wanted Tre to be turned on so he would get turned up. Just like me, Juicy was half-naked too. Cookie had on a bikini with a fishnet cover up that left nothing for the imagination. Piper removed her Sarong revealing a two-piece and a tiny baby bump.

"Let's play truth or dare," Juicy suggests, snuggling up with Tre's cousin Tony.

"We can't play that with Cookie and Piper," I said.

"Yes we can too," Cookie said. "I'm all in."

"Me too," Piper said. "Just don't get too crazy. I am married with child."

"You're all in," Scott asked, moving closer to Cookie. If I didn't know any better, I'd say that he was hitting on her. "How is that so?"

She turned towards him. "Just like I said."

"But aren't you married too?"

"I am. But my husband and I have an open marriage. I'm free to do whomever I want."

Scott's eyes lit up like a Christmas tree. "Word?"

She looked him up and down with a sexy smile. "Word."

"I'd love to get to know you then."

Cookie leaned back with I got you wrapped around my finger smile on her face. "Depends. We'll see."

"I don't know what it depends on, but I'm down," he said, looking like a dog in heat. Thirsty.

"Calm down, man," Tony said. "You look like you ain't never seen a pregnant woman before."

"I can't help it," Scott confessed. "You know I have a thing for pregnant women."

I could tell by the way Cookie looked at him that she was about to wear his young butt out. "Can you rub my feet?"

Scott jumped down into the water, standing before Cookie like a slave. "You're so fucking beautiful. I'll do anything you want me to."

"Damn," Piper exclaimed. "You're making me hot and bothered." She fanned herself with her hand.

"I'll cool you off," Adam suggested, moving close to Piper like Scott did Cookie.

"Like hell you will. My marriage ain't open. And my husband is a detective. He'll chew you up and spit you out. Trust me, you don't want none."

Adam backed up a little. "Oh, ok. I don't want no problems."

We all laughed at the silly look on his face.

"So, I got a question for you Cookie, before we get started. Um, you said your marriage is open, so does that mean that what I heard about you and your sisters having a foursome with your husband is true?"

Cookie smiled at me with no shame. "Yes, it's true."

"Wait, what?" Juicy asked. "What had happen?"

"Me and my sisters had a foursome with my husband," Cookie said as if it were nothing. "It was before I was married though."

Everyone kinda just stared at her. I had more questions but I decided to ask them later.

"Are we going to get this game started or what?" Cookie asked.

Piper stood to her feet. "You know what, I'm out." She picked up her Sarong and began to walk away.

"At least let me walk you back to your hotel," Adam offered.

"Ok, but you better not try anything. Don't think I won't beat your ass."

"I promise. I won't. I just want to make sure you get there safely."

"Ok, let's get this started!" Juicy screamed. "I wanna go first." She looked at everyone. Her eyes settled on Scott. "Truth or Dare?"

"Dare," he said boldly.

"I dare you to kiss Cookie."

Dang, Juicy wasn't playing. She was ready to get things poppin for real. Scott leaned over, carefully, cradling Cookie's body. He kissed her so sweet that he made my panties wet. I bet Cookie saw him in a whole new light now. After that kiss he laid on her, she was probably ready to jump his bones right in front of us.

"Well, well, well," Juicy said, prancing around. "That's how you kick things off. Scott, it's your turn."

Scott stares at Juicy. "Truth or dare?"

She looked at him as if he should have known the answer. "Boy please. Dare."

Scott thought for a moment. "I dare you to go skinny dipping."

Juicy stared at him boldly. "It ain't nothing to it, but to do it," she said, stripping out of her bikini top and bottoms. She slowly walked into the water until it was up to her neck. She did a back flip and then walked back out, seductively putting her bikini back on.

"Wow!" Scott exclaimed. "You didn't even hesitate."

"Nope. Never that," she said with sheer confidence. "It's my turn again." She glanced at all of us. Our eyes met. I looked at her like you better not pick me for none of that crazy shit. "Tre, truth or dare?"

Tre poked is chest out. "Let me mix things up a bit. Truth."

"When's the last time you had sex?"

"Last night," he spat.

Scott and Tony stared cracking up laughing. I mean, they were laughing so hard until they both fell over holding their sides.

"Aw, wait a minute. What's so damn funny?" Juicy asked. "You must be lying, Tre."

A smirk came across his face. I knew he was lying too. "Ok, maybe it wasn't last night."

"Or never," Scott said, still laughing.

I looked from Tre to Scott. "What does that mean?"

Scott looked at me with a straight face. "Tre's a virgin."

"Aw, c'mon, man. You didn't have to tell her," Tre said, obviously feeling some kinda way.

"Reaaaalllly?" I looked at Tre. Virgin?

He looked embarrassed. "Go ahead and laugh. It's ok. I can take it."

"I'm not going to laugh," I said honestly. "Actually, I think it's sexy." Scott and Tony both looked at me like I lost my mind. "Makes you hotter as far as I'm concerned."

Tre blushed again. "Really?"

If he only knew how turned on I was. "Yes."

"Excuse me," Juicy said, snapping her fingers at us. "Um, Mr. Virgin lied. That means he owes me a dare."

"Ok. What you want me to do?" Tre asked.

"The same thing I just did, boo. Get them buns in the water. Leegggooo!"

I thought Tre was going to be shy about taking off his clothes, being a virgin and all, but he was very sure of himself.

When he took off his trunks, I saw why. He had a scrumptious dick. I creamed in my bikini bottoms as he strutted into the water.

"Dayum!" Cookie and Juicy both said at the same time.

"Back the hell up," I told them. "Virgin boy is all mine."

"You're going to take his virginity, for real?" Scott asked me.

"Hell yeah. If he lets me."

"He'll let you. He's been staring at you all night. You know, since you were up on stage."

"Is that right?" I asked, licking my lips as Tre got out of the water walking towards me. He stood right in front of me with water dripping all over his body, slowly stepping back into his trunks. Oh, yeah, I can't wait to get a piece of that virgin dick.

Juicy, Cookie, and I followed Tre's movement with our eyes as he sat down beside me.

"Shit, I'm done. I'm ready to go fuck now," Juicy said, grabbing her stuff.

Scott helped Cookie up. She gave him a naughty smile. "You can come to my room if you want."

Juicy and Tony went in one direction. Cookie and Scott went in another direction. That left me and Tre sitting alone on this beautiful beach.

"So, what do you want to do?"

I leaned back, lying flat, staring up at him with lust. "I want you to do me."

He stared down at me. "Are you sure? We can just sit here and talk, if you want."

"Now, you know you don't want to just sit and talk to me." I grabbed him by his erection, pulling him closer to me.

Tre took the hint, climbing on top of me, kissing me. I thought that because he was a virgin that he'd be a sloppy kisser. Surprisingly, he wasn't. His kisses were real nice.

I slid my hands down his trunks, grabbing a handful of his tight ass. I loved a man with a nice ass. Something I could hold onto when we fucked. He undid my bikini top, freeing my breasts, sucking on them. I ran my fingers through his neatly groomed dreads.

"Let's move to the other side," he suggested. "It's darker over there. That way we won't be seen."

We strolled over to the other side of the beach holding hands. Tre admitted that he saw me on the plane. He said he was dying to get to know me. I let him know, I wasn't trying to do all that. I'm just trying to fuck.

Tre kneeled before me, untying my bikini bottoms, pulling the fabric from my body. He looked at me under the moonlight admiring my nude curves. His hands explored my inner thighs before he kissed them. Shivers went up and down my spine when he finally spread my fleshy folds and his tongue connected with my clit.

Gasping for air, I threw my head all the way back, holding his head steady between my legs. "Yeah, baby, lick it just like that." His licks were driving me bonkers.

His tongue vibrated against my clit. It felt so good that I wanted to just lean back and float in mid-air.

Stopping briefly, Tre backed me up, gently pushing me into the lounge chair. "Put your knees up to your chest," he whispered.

I did exactly like he said, spreading my vagina in front of him like a buffet.

"Pretty," he mumbled, tracing my outer lips with his finger before slurping on my waxed pussy again. He licked, sucked, and slurped until I couldn't take it anymore, leaking cum onto his tongue.

"Hmmm, you taste good," he said, wiping his lips with the back of his hand. Standing, he straddled the chair, positioning his pelvis in front of me, sliding his dick up and down my wet slit. The teasing was really turning me on.

Chip did this to me all the time so it wasn't new. But the fact that I was on this beautiful island with a complete stranger, who was finer than a muthafucka, with my legs open for the world to see, had me feeling extra sexy.

Tre knew he had me when I started bucking my pussy at him. "Super wet. Just how I like it."

He slid a condom on and leaned the lounge chair back so that my body was flat. He opened my legs wider, holding them steady in the crook of his arms as he climbed on top of me, shoving his dick in.

"It feel good to you, baby?" he asked, kissing my, lips, face, and neck.

"Oooooooooh. Yeeeesssss. Real, real good."

Tre has some skills to be a virgin. His stroke was nice. He rocked his hips with hard calculated thrusts. Every time he pumped inside of me, I felt like he took my body to new heights. I loved how snug his dick was inside of me.

He kissed me tenderly, thrusting harder and deeper.

"Oh, that's it right there, Tre."

"You like that, baby?"

"Yeeeessss," I cooed, arching my back and grabbing his ass, making him go even deeper.

Tre wasn't fucking me like no virgin. He was beating my pussy up like a pro. He probably lied just to get some. At this point, the dick was so good that I didn't even care if he lied.

He hid his face in my chest, nibbling on my breast. I wiggled my hips underneath him, concentrating on my third orgasm. I was bucking so hard that the flimsy chair we were in felt like it was about to break. I wouldn't care if it did. I would fall to the ground and still work to get this nut.

Tre kissed my lips. "You feel awesome."

"You do too."

"I can't hold back any longer."

"Me either," I confessed.

"Ssssssssss. Fuuuuuck!" Tre screamed. "I'm about to cum," he exclaimed, humping me wild and crazy.

My body jerked like a fish out of water as I came right along with him. I locked my arms around him and we held each other, rocking back and forth.

Tre stood to his feet. He stretched and then began to look for his trunks.

I rose to my feet and began putting back on my bikini. "You lied. You weren't no virgin. You better be glad your sex was on point or I'd be pissed off at you right now."

Tre slipped his trunks on. "I didn't lie. I was a virgin. I swear."

I twisted my lips. "How'd you get so good then?"

"I guess I got experience from porn and practicing on blow-up dolls."

Did this nicca say blow-up dolls? I busted out laughing. "Are you serious?"

"I'm dead ass."

I was still laughing. "Well, those dolls did you some good."

"You got jokes. What hotel are you in?"

I was still in orgasmic bliss and unable to think of the name so I pointed to it.

"Ok, me too."

Tre held my hand as we walked in silence back to the hotel. I wasn't sure why he was quiet. I was quiet because he just fucked my brains out. I was tired and ready to go to bed.

"Well, this is it," I said as he leaned back against his room door. "I guess I'll see you around." I yawned.

He reached out, pulling me into his arms. "Stay the night with me?"

I yawned again. "Huh?" Normally, I would cuss a man out if he asked me something like this at three o'clock in the morning. Since we already fucked, what would be the point? "Look, Tre, what we did was spur of the moment fun."

"Yeah, yeah, I know," he said casually. "I just want some more of you."

"But I'm tired," I whined.

"Don't you want some more?" he asked, pinching my nipples through my bikini top. "I know you do."

Damn, how did he know me so well? As soon as he began touching my nipples, I got aroused all over again. "Oh-kay."

"Besides, that lawn chair was mad uncomfortable. I can't wait to be in the bed this time."

"You ain't kidding. I thought it was going to break."

We laughed as he unlocked the door, retreating to the shower. We both smelled like beach water and sand was all over us. I stripped out of my bikini and hopped in the shower first. Seconds later, Tre joined me, washing my body all over. My body came to life. I was aroused all over again.

I took the sponge from him and began to wash his body. While using my soapy hand, I stroked his penis until it was fully erect again. We continued to kiss each other using the soap as foreplay.

Finally retreating to the bed, Tre asked me to lay on my back. He spread my legs wide and started munching me out once again. "How do you want it this time?"

"Surprise me."

Chapter 10

Vanity

I decided to leave the Welcome Party as soon as it was over. Being up on the salsa stage dancing with Stoney confirmed just how attracted I was to him. That's why I needed to get to my room as quickly as possible.

Stoney didn't get the hint. The moment I walked away, he did too. I promised myself that I was going to steer clear of him after seeing some of Ivan's social media posts. He was really tripping. The last thing I needed was to raise more suspicion. He already thought I was on this trip just to get away from him.

"Will you slow down?" Stoney said finally catching up to me.

"Leave me alone!" I shouted.

"Why? What's wrong with you?"

I began to walk even faster hoping that he would be left in my dust. "Just go away."

"What's wrong? What happened?"

I refused to look at him. Afraid that I might change my mind and give in to my desires. Being mean to him was the only way I could stand to be in his presence and not want to make love to him. "I said, GO AWAY!"

"Vanity, I can't. It's dark. I don't want you walking back to the hotel alone. At least let me see you safely inside of your room. Then, I'll leave you alone if you want me to."

Why was he making this so hard for me? "Fine. Try and keep up," I said, continuing to power walk.

I stayed one step ahead as we made our way to my hotel room. "Well, this is it. Thanks for walking me. Talk to you later," I said without giving him a chance to respond, slamming the door in his face.

Making my way to the bed, I sat down but I had a feeling that Stoney hadn't left yet. That he was still on the other side of the door. Quietly, I walked back over and looked out of the peephole, only to see him still standing there just like I thought.

Why was he still standing there? What the hell did he want? I started to ask him and then changed my mind, making my way to the shower. A cold shower would do me good right now. Shedding my clothes, I got into the shower hoping the water would clear my mind and set me straight.

It was so hot outside. Taking a cold shower was actually refreshing. I stood under the showerhead and let the water run over my face and down my body, hoping that it would rinse all the lust away. I took my time washing my body and enjoying the moment. I guess a little too much because I got even more aroused.

Naked images of Ivan penetrated my thoughts. It made me yearn to be fucked. Pinching my nipples with one hand and toying with my clit with the other hand, I imagined that Ivan was in the shower with me. Something that we did numerous times on numerous occasions. The more I teased my clit, the hornier I got.

And then, something happened. No longer was my mind fixed on images of Ivan. Somehow I had drifted back in time when Stoney and I was on the plane—when his hand was rubbing my clit. I could still hear him quietly moaning in my ear while I caressed his big dick. I remember thinking how badly I wanted to feel him inside of me.

I spread my legs wider, rubbing faster, still thinking about Stoney's sexy ass and how badly I wanted him. I imagined him putting me in every position possible, even being lifted up and down in the air. From the way he tossed me around the salsa stage, I'm sure that he could make that happen with no problem. That was one of the positives of being small and petite.

When I finally realized that my horny imagination went from Ivan to Stoney, I was thoroughly disgusted with myself. Even though I was still horny as ever, I wouldn't allow myself to orgasm, quickly getting out of the shower.

I dried off, put on my panties and tank, and got in the bed. It felt good to lay down. The bed hugged my body. I closed my eyes, hoping to fall asleep, but that never happened. I tossed and turned until my throat became dry. Getting up out of my comfortable bed, I made my way to the small refrigerator by the door. That's when I noticed a note underneath. I picked it up, wondering who it was from.

I know how you feel about me. You can't hide it. I feel the same way. My dick stays hard and I can't stop thinking about you. Come chill with me in the hot tub. I promise I don't bite. Well, maybe a little. But I'm sure you'll like it. Stoney.

Temptation was a bitch.

I was doing everything I could not to think about Stoney. I had finally got my mind off of him and now I had dick on the brain once again. Going back to sleep was out of the question. The only thing I could do was join Stoney at the hot tub. But I wasn't going there to chill with him. I needed to talk to him, taking a stand against this fiery flame between us.

I slid into my bikini, sheer cover up, and thong sandals. Snatching the note off the nightstand, I proceeded to the hot tub to give him a piece of my mind.

The hot tub was way off in the cut. I passed by three pools and two bars before I made my way to the large hot tub area. And the way it was shaped. It looked like it was specifically designed for couples to have privacy while they got their freak on. The gigantic hot tub was sectioned off in to a lot of private, secluded, romantic areas.

"Looking for me?" Stoney asked, walking up behind me. He was dripping wet, looking like a sexy surfer. His trunks were clinging to his body, outlining the imprint of his big dick.

Immediately, I realized this wasn't a good idea. All these damn people on the island and nobody was in the hot tub. We had the whole damn place to ourselves. I just shook my head at the irony. "Yes, I came to give you this note back."

Stoney cracked up laughing. "You got to be kidding me, right? You didn't come here for that." He laughed at me some more.

I was so attracted to him. He had me flustered with my own thoughts. "No! What I'm trying to say is, I wanted to talk to you about the note."

He walked up on me and my nipples got hard as rocks. "Talk to me about it in the hot tub."

I backed up into the large palm tree behind me, trying to get away from him. "See, this is what I want to talk to you…you…you about," I stuttered.

"Why are you stuttering?" he asked me, all up on me.

"I didn't come to stay," I said, sweating bullets. This man had me nervous. Because I knew at any minute, I was going to rip off my bikini and jump into the hot tub with him.

"Yes, you did," he said, pinching my nipple. "Why else would you come out here looking sexy in that tiny bikini?"

He had a point. That was stupid. "Whatever."

I turned to walk away, and he picked me up like I was a small child, and jumped into the hot tub. My arms flailed in every direction as if I was drowning.

While Stoney rested on an underwater bench, watching me make a complete ass out of myself. "You're doing way too much right now," he said, still laughing at my expense. "The water's not even that deep."

Finally I stopped screaming and stood up, feeling like a real jackass because he was right. I realized that the water only came to my shoulders. I guess I thought it was much deeper because I was dunked in.

"That's not funny." I was so pissed. I wanted to slap his face.

"C'mere," he said, still playing around.

"Go on." I swatted him away. "Get on my nerves."

He laughed at me again, sitting back on the bench. "So, what did you want to talk about?"

I took a seat on the bench next to him. "This thing or whatever it is we have between us, it has to stop."

He looked at me as if I had just spoken a foreign language. "Yeah, you told me that already."

"Then why are you looking at me as if you don't care?"

"Because I don't. At least I don't care about that topic."

I sighed. "You're making this real hard for me. You know I'm married.'

"True. But I like what I see. And I know you're not happy with him. That's real clear."

"So, he is still my husband."

"That has absolutely nothing to do with me."

"You're an ass. You know that?"

"I've been called worse."

We stared at each other with lust.

"So what do you want me to do?" he asked. "You want me to say I'm going to leave you alone? That I don't want you? That I'm not attracted to you?"

"No, I want you to stop acting on it."

"Then, I want you to stop acting on it too. Stop seducing me. Stop flirting with me. Stop being half-naked around me. Bending over and getting me all worked up. You're just as guilty as I am, if not more."

I guess he had a good point. I had sexual thoughts of him constantly. I guess I was flaunting before him without knowing.

"That's what I mean. Stop looking at me like that. Biting your lip as if you want to jump on my dick."

I didn't even realize I was biting my lip. "Sorry. I guess I'm guilty too."

"Look, I can't lie to you, I feel like we started something back in the day that we never got to finish. And it's not just sex either. I've been feeling this way since I saw your picture."

"My picture?"

"Yeah, Karen and Natalia have tons of pictures of you and they're always mentioning you."

My eyes got widen, thinking that maybe they spilled my secret. "Wha-what did they say?"

"Calm down. Nothing while I was around. I just heard your name a lot. I can tell you're close to them."

Now, he had my attention. "So, you were stalking me. I was just joking earlier, but it's mighty convenient that you're on this trip with me right now. "

He slid close to me, touching my leg underwater. "Don't flatter yourself. I think you're hot as fuck, but look at me? Do I look like I need to stalk anybody?"

I sucked my teeth, moving his hand away. "Oh, cocky, aren't we?"

"No, baby, just confident."

"Well it doesn't matter. I'm not cheating on my husband with you." I smiled at him, feeling good about standing my ground.

He put his hand back on my leg, moving up to my thigh, closer to my crotch. "I have a question for you."

"Shoot."

"So, you wouldn't call what we did on the plane cheating?" He stared me down with those sexy green bedroom eyes. "Because I'm pretty sure that your husband would definitely consider another man making his wife cum, cheating."

My jaw dropped. What was I thinking? Damn, I thought I had this all figured out. He was right. I was only thinking about penetration. Not the fact that I kissed another man. That I'd been fanaticizing about another man. That I jerked another man off and had his cum in my hand. I was trying not to fuck up and I had already fucked up. "I need a drink."

"Oh, that's not all. There's more."

How the fuck could there be more? "I can't right now. Tell me later. Get me a drink."

Stoney didn't question me again. He hopped out of the hot tub, ready to fulfill my request. "What do you want?"

"Anything with Tequila in it. Make it strong."

"I'll be right back."

I leaned back, closing my eyes, enjoying the bubbles beating against my skin. My shit was always so crisp. I can't believe I got myself in such a sticky situation. No matter what I do from this point on, I've already fucked up. Whether I fuck Stoney or not is irrelevant, because if Ivan ever found out the little bit that I did do, he's still going to lose his mind.

"Here you go." Stoney got back in the hot tub handing me a mixed drink.

I took a sip. "This is good." I took another sip while looking at the tray he brought back. "What's up with the bottle of Tequila?"

Stoney snickered. "I'm not sure. The bartender was packing up when I went over there. She made your drink and mine and put the half empty bottle of Tequila on there too. And told me it's all on the house and left."

I took another sip. "Wow. I see I'm not the only one lusting after you."

He knocked his drink back. "Yeah, but, I'm lusting after you."

I polished off my drink too. "Pour me some Tequila."

Stoney grabbed the bottle and poured a little in my glass. I took that to the head and asked for more. "So, that's how you plan on dealing with this? Getting drunk, again? I never thought you'd be that type."

Again? What the fuck is he talking about? He must have me mistaken. "You don't even know me well enough to say what type I am."

"I know you more than you think I do."

"What's that's supposed to mean?"

"We'll talk about it later. You can't right now, remember?"

"Aww, let me out this muthafucka." Obviously, he had me mistaken with some other chick.

Before I could stand, he scooped me up in his arms, kissing me. I relaxed, wrapping my legs around his waist. Within seconds, Stony moved my bottom to the side, entering me.

"Aaaah, you feel so good inside of me," I said, riding the shit out of him.

"You do too," he mumbled in between kisses, holding me close.

"Oh. Oh. Oh. Oh. Oh. Oh. Oh. I'm about to cum." I continued to ride his dick like a jockey as spasms took over my body. "OHMYGOD! I'M CUMMMMMMMMING!"

Stoney lifted me up and brought me back down on his dick making my toes curl and my body shake even more.

"Sit on the bench," I told him, breathing heavy.

"You think you can handle some more?"

"Boy please, don't act like you don't know. I'm just getting started."

Stoney grinned as he held onto me, floating back in the hot tub, scooting on to the bench. He was still inside of me when I landed in his lap. Now that I'd busted a good nut, I was ready to seduce him. He'd been begging for the pussy. I was about to give him the ride of his life.

Grabbing the sides of the hot tub behind his head, I stretched my thighs out making my hips widen and my pussy more flexible. I stared deep into his eyes as my body rose all the way up until it felt like the tip was going to fall out and then I slammed down extra hard pushing him far up inside of me.

Stoney wrapped his arms around my waist, slowing my thrusts down. I went from an up and down movement to a slow circular rocking motion.

"Why'd you stop me?"

"Because you're splashing water everywhere."

"If it's good to you, then water splashing should be the last thing on your mind."

"It is good to me. But you're faking it. I don't need you doing porn star moves, trying to seduce me."

Damn, how'd he know? "What do you want then?"

He grabbed both of my hands, taking them into his, kissing them. "I want what you want. How do you like it?"

"I like to be made love to."

"Then, let me make love to you. Instead of you putting on a show trying to impress me."

Stoney was asking for a lot. I was trying my best to have sex with him and not get my heart involved. Maybe that was easy for some women, but I never mastered that. "Making love is intimate. I'm not sure if I want to go there. I'd rather just fuck."

"You're too pretty to be fucked."

I sighed. Not understanding where he was going with all this.

"Close your eyes." I closed them. "And don't open them back up. Just concentrate on what you feel."

He let go of my hands squeezing my bottom while sucking on my breasts. With my eyes closed, I had no choice but to think about what he was doing to me in that moment.

Stoney began to grind his pelvis with mine, creating a special rhythm. He lifted my legs up, resting my feet against the sides of the hot tub. His hands were underneath me so I didn't fall back into the water. The position was very awkward, but at the same time, it was so pleasurable. Because of the way he held me, the water bubbles were dancing on my clit while his dick pressed against my prized possession. I gripped at his arms, thrusting my hips upward, actively seeking my climax.

"You're so damn sexy," he whispered. "And your pussy is to die for."

"Oh Gawd!" He was in so deep. "I'm about to cum."

"Mmmmmm. I love to hear you say that. That's what turns me on." He kissed my legs and the insides of my thigh. "Let it all go, baby."

"Oh!" I was right there. "Oh!" I bounced as hard as I could. "Aaaaaah! Ssssss! Aaaaaaah! Sssssss! Aaaaaaaah!"

"That's it."

My eyes rolled into the back of my head and my body trembled violently as I kept on bouncing. Stoney felt so good, I couldn't stop.

"I got you, baby. I'm not going to let you fall. Get this dick how you want to."

My body went into a convulsive fit. Twisting, jerking, and shaking uncontrollably for nearly a minute before I came off my sexual high.

“Did you cum?” I asked wiping water from my face.

He gave me a devilish grin. “A little bit both times. But I’m ready to bust a big one.”

“Men can do that?”

Stoney ignored my question. “C’mon. I’m ready to take this back to my room.”

He got out of the hot tub, grabbed the bottle of Tequila, and then helped me out. I stood on the side of the hot tub and nearly lost my balance, falling back in.

Stoney laughed. “I see somebody had a great nut.” He kneeled before me. “Hop on.”

I climbed on his back and he carried me to his room, laying me down on his bed.

“Now, I’m ready to get this pussy how I want it,” he said, removing my bikini top and bottom. I lay on my back before him totally nude while he admired my body.

“Niiiice,” he exclaimed, running his hand up and down my smooth skin. The way he was staring at me made me feel like the most beautiful woman in the world. By the look on his face, I could tell that he truly loved what he saw. “You don’t even know how much you turn me on.”

“I feel the same way.”

“Do you?” He positioned himself between my legs, entering me.

I gasped from the pleasure I felt. “Yeeeeessss.”

“Huh, do you?” he asked me again.

“Yeeeeeessss.’

“Don’t lie to me, Vanity,” he said, sliding out of me, putting his face between my legs, sucking on my clit like pussy was a sport.

“Ooooooooooh!” This man was about to have me addicted. “I promise I feel the same way.”

“You like this tongue on your clit?”

“Aaaahhh! Yeeeesss!”

Spreading my legs wide, he licked from my ass to my clit before flicking his tongue gently against my pearl and then slurped on it like a neck bone. The shit he was doing had me floating on cloud nine.

"Is this my pussy?"

"Yeeeeeessss." His tongue was so damn good I would have agreed to give him a kidney if he asked me to.

"Are you sure?" he asked again, sticking two fingers inside of me while lapping at my clit. "Does this pussy belong to me?"

"Oh my God! Yeeeeesssss!" Stoney was mind-fucking me. He was so damn good at it that I didn't give a shit what he asked me as long as he didn't stop.

Stoney got back on his knees, lifting my ass off the bed, entering me. He had one hand on my clit, the other hand on my breast while sucking on my toes and beating the hell out of my coochie. I was getting pleasure in so many places that by the time I did cum, I didn't know what had hit me.

"You cumming, baby?" Stoney asked me when I started screaming loudly.

"Yessss! Yessss! Yesss! Yesss! Yesss!"

"Yeah, that's the sound I love to hear," he grunted, jerking my hips toward him, forcefully. "I'm about to cum too."

He let go of my legs, climbing on top of me, humping me hard and fast until he released. "Aaaaaaaaah! Fuuuuuuukkkkk!"

We were both breathing hard like we just ran a race.

"Girl, that shit was amazing."

"Yes, it was. Just like old times."

"No, I think that was next level."

I giggled. "True. But it was incredible back then too."

Stoney put his arm around me, holding me close. "I never stopped thinking about you."

I snuggled up next to him. "I never stopped thinking about you too."

We fell asleep curled up.

*****

Buzzzzz. Bzzzzzz. Bzzzzz. Bzzzzz.

With my eyes closed, I blindly reached for my phone on the charger. "Hello."

"WHY THE FUCK YOU DIDN'T CALL ME YESTERDAY LIKE I ASKED YOUR ASS TO?" Ivan screamed through the phone. "TO LET ME KNOW YOU FUCKIN MADE IT SAFELY. YOU MUST BE UP TO NO GOOD IF YOU CAN'T MAKE A FUCKIN PHONE CALL TO YOUR HUSBAND. DON'T MAKE ME COME TO THAT MUTHAFUCKA AND SET SHIT OFF IN THAT BITCH!"

I was half-asleep before I answered. Now, I was fully awake after Ivan nearly busted my eardrum, screaming. "Why are you yelling?" I yawned. "My phone was dead."

"Because I asked your ass to call me when you got there. You said ok. I ain't heard shit from you since. And why the fuck are you still sleep? I'm starting to think that you took this trip because you're hiding some shit from me."

I tossed the cover off of me, moving from under Stoney, sitting on the edge of the bed. "What the hell is your problem?" I whispered.

"Baby, where you going?" Stoney asked, pulling me back into his arms, snuggling his body close to mine.

"Is that another nicca I hear?" Ivan asked.

"No. I mean, yes. I'm in the hallway."

He sighed loudly. "Doing what?"

"Getting ice."

"That's some bullshit. How the fuck you sound? You must think I'm a damn fool. You were sleep before I called. Yawning all in my ear and shit. Now, your ass is getting some ice. The lies just keep on coming with your ass."

I was so tired I couldn't even think straight. I pulled away from Stoney again. "I'm not lying."

"Yes, you are." I could hear the hurt in Ivan's voice. "Do you still love me?"

Stoney pulled me back in the bed next to him. His arms around my body. This time I couldn't get away. He had me practically pinned down.

"ANSWER ME!" Ivan screamed. "WHY THE FUCK DO I HEAR CRICKETS? FUCK IS UP WITH YOU?"

Before I could answer, Stoney took my phone out of my hand ending the call. I tried to reach for it, but he held it high in the air out of my reach, pressing the power button until it was completely turned off. Then he tossed it across the room. It landed in the chair in the corner.

"Fuck you do that for?" I asked with tears in my eyes, still trying to move away.

"Lower your tone," he said, snuggling up next to me again, trying to go back to sleep. "Lay down."

"No!" I screamed, fighting to get away from him.

He calmly held onto me while I tired myself out. "Are you done?"

"No," I said, feeling the effects of being up all night. I sighed. "Why'd you do that?"

"Because you're with me on vacation and this nicca is stressing you out. Deal with him when you get back."

I threw myself back onto my pillow, silently crying. I was so mad I didn't know what to do. "You just made everything worse."

"Well, let me make everything better." He began kissing my neck and shoulder. He was about to move to my breasts when I turned over on my side, facing the opposite direction. "Leave me alone."

Stoney paid me no attention, kissing my shoulder down my back. His warm body moved next to mine with his erection resting against my bare ass.

"I'm not in the mood."

"You're not?" Stoney asked, spreading my cheeks, sliding right inside of my soaked pussy.

His strokes were deliberately slow hitting my spot immediately, making my clit throb. I laid there teary eyed as if he wasn't affecting me. His hand slipped under my arm, holding my left boob while grinding deep inside of me. It felt good too. Before I knew it, I was pushing my ass back against him, grinding my hips too.

"That's right. Give me that platinum pussy."

"Oh Gawd!" Stoney was definitely a beast in the bedroom. I couldn't believe that I was already on the verge of cumming.

"That's right. Let Daddy take all that stress away."

"Oooooh. Yeeeeeeesss," I said, pushing back even harder.

Still deep inside of me, Stoney rolled us into a new position. He was on his back. I was on top of him, laying on my back too. Both of my legs straddled his legs with my clit in the air, fully exposed. Holding onto both of my breasts, Stoney began to pump upward towards the ceiling, pounding my pussy deep. I'd been in this position before but it never felt like this. Stoney had me aroused to the max.

"You know this is my pussy, right?"

I bounced harder. "Yes! Yes! Oh my God, yes!"

His thrusts sped up. "Don't hold back. I want you to squirt."

"Yeah! Yeah! Yeah! Yeah! I can feel it. I'm about to cum."

"I'm about to cum too," Stoney said in a husky voice. His right hand moved from my right tit to my clit.

"Aaaaaaah! I'm there. Almost there."

"That's right," he said through clenched teeth. "Give it to me so I can cum with you."

I threw my head back against his chest as my juices gushed out, like a shaken can of pop. I've squirted before, but nothing even close to this magnitude.

"EEEEEEEEEEEEEEEE!" I screamed at the top of my lungs. I know the whole floor heard me cumming in octaves.

"I'm about to release mine too, baby," Stoney grunted. He stopped rubbing my clit, taking hold of my thighs, fucking me with a sexual body roll.

All I could do was lay unresponsive on top of him and go along for the ride. My body remained limp while pleasure exploded between my legs over and over and over again, sending me into an orgasmic coma.

"I'm convinced you know magic. The things you do to me." I giggled, thinking how amazing he is in bed.

"I do." Stoney smacked my ass. "We need to get up if we're going to make it to breakfast."

"Ugh, I'm even more tired now," I said, rolling off him, back on my side. "I need at least one more hour of sleep. You have officially worn me the hell out."

Stoney laughed, rolling over spooning me. "I can't get enough of that good pussy."

"Aren't you tired?"

He yawned. "Yeah, a little bit."

"A little bit? You should be beat too."

There was silence. I turned my head to see if he was sleep. His eyes were wide open, staring at the ceiling, deep in thought.

"What's on your mind?"

He looked at me, melting my heart. "I was just thinking—never mind. It's going to sound stupid."

"No, I want to hear it," I said, turning around to face him. "I want to know."

He sighed. "Have you ever felt like what was going on in your life wasn't what was supposed to go on in your life."

"Yeah. Lately, I've been feeling like that every day."

"It's just that—the way I am with you, I've never been like that with no other woman." He thought for a moment. "Well, kinda sorta, I have. But even then, it wasn't the same."

"Your fiancée? You've never had sex like that with her?"

"Naw, never. I mean sex with her is great. Nothing for me to complain about, but not like it is with you. Things have always been special between us."

"Funny you said that because I was kinda feeling the same way. Ivan is an incredible lover. So I found myself comparing you to him and—you're just better. It's like you know my body better than he does, which doesn't even seem possible. He'd kill me if he ever heard me say that."

"I feel the exact same way."

We both exhaled.

"Do you think we would be good together? I mean, if we weren't already taken? Or we'd still end up being each other's secret?"

"Yeah," I said, quietly, pondering over everything that he just said. "I do. I think that we'd have a great relationship."

I turned back over on my side, allowing him to spoon me again. "Well, let's just enjoy each other while we can."

I laid there thinking if there was a reason why I reconnected with Stoney. Was it a sign to make me end my marriage? Since it was on the rocks anyway. Or did he come into my life to make me appreciate what I have at home? To bring Ivan and I closer together.

We slept for about an hour before getting up.

Stoney went to shower and I walked across the hall to my hotel room. I needed to call Ivan back. But at this point, I didn't know what to say. Clearly, he was pissed off, way before he even heard Stoney's voice. Nothing I could say would make things better. He wasn't even rational when he got this angry.

Plus, I didn't feel like arguing. I'd have to deal with Ivan later. Right now, I agreed with Stoney. I wanted to enjoy our fling. Soon enough, I'd have to deal with the backlash.

"Where the hell have you been?" Pebbles asked me, walking out of the bathroom with a towel around her.

"Where the hell have you been?" I fired back.

"Oh, no, don't even try it. I was out all night, but my husband didn't call you because he couldn't reach me."

"What did you tell him?" I asked, stepping out of my bikini.

"Nothing. I didn't know where you were." She eyed me suspiciously. "Although, I have a sneaky suspicion that you were across the hall with Stoney all night."

I gathered my stuff for the shower. "I'll talk to Ivan later."

"You're not going to call him now? That really makes you look suspicious. I mean, if you're going to fuck Stoney as least try to play it off with Ivan. One day this vacation is going to be over. And you'll have to go home to him."

I sighed. She was right. I just didn't feel like dealing with it. "I'll text him then. And if he calls you, just tell him to contact me."

"I sure will because I don't want to be in your mess. Ivan gets real stupid when it comes to you. When the shit hits the fan, I don't want to be anywhere around."

Pebbles was saying all this right now, but the minute something popped off, she was going to be right by my side, ready to throw down in the trenches with me.

Chapter 11

Pebbles

"C'mon, Juicy!" I yelled at the bathroom. "You better not fuck around and make me miss breakfast."

"I'm coming! I just need to slick up my hair, dang!"

"You should have been done that. What the hell you been doing all morning? Ain't nobody got time for this shit." I see I'm going to have to leave Juicy's ass.

"Oh-kaaaay!" she said stepping out of the bathroom.

"You look cute," I said, liking the way she cleaned herself up. She was a hot mess before this. I don't know what her and Tony did all night, well I kinda have an idea, but she was hella busted this morning.

Her hair was slicked up into a cute up do with large hoop earrings. She had on a fitted pastel romper with matching wedges.

"You look cute too," she replied, grabbing her purse.

"I know," I said, standing up, twirling around modeling. I knew I was cute. I had on a sexy baby doll flare mini dress. Most of my back was out and there was a diamond cut out in the front that showed my cleavage. I had my curls pinned up in an elegant bun.

"Ok, I'm ready."

"About time."

We walked into the restaurant where the rest of our family was eating breakfast. Karen, Cash, Stoney and Vanity sat on one side of the table. Across from them was Natalia, Marcel, me, and Juicy.

"Well, don't you two look cute," Juicy pointed across the table at Vanity. Then she looked back at me and smiled. She knew that type of shit got on my nerves. I hated being compared to Vanity.

I frowned. Vanity and I had on matching outfits. Her dress was white and mine was beige. We both had on the same matching shoes and earrings. Granted, this has happened many times before. We share the same taste in clothes. But I surely didn't expect it to happen while we were on vacation. I wanted to go up to her and call her a copycat, yanking her curls out of her head. However, there is no way she knew what I was going to put on. She was in the shower when I got dressed and left.

I ordered my breakfast and made my way over to the table. "So, what did y'all do last night?" I asked Cash, sitting down across from Vanity and Stoney.

"Well after Marcel and I got the Preggers to sleep."

Karen whacked him with her napkin. "Don't start with that mess, Cash."

Everyone laughed. They were always clowning.

"Like I said, after the two Hippos went to sleep. Me and Marcel hit the club."

I couldn't wait to club on the island. "That's what I'm talking about. What club did y'all go to?"

"The one down the street."

"What is hot?"

Cash looked across the table at Marcel who was sitting next to me. They gave each other a look and then laughed.

"I know what that look means. Y'all had a good time. Next time take me."

Karen and Natalia, who were wearing maternity shorts and tank shirts with comfortable sandals, looked at their husbands like they wanted to jump on them.

"Y'all better not had too good of a time," Natalia said with an attitude. "Not while you got me knocked up carrying another baby. I could have been at the club too. Instead of housing your sixth offspring, Marcel," she said emphasizing his name.

"Awww, baby, you know I only got eyes for you," Marcel said, turning on the charm. He put his arm around her, pecking her lips. "We just hung out and drank and people watched mostly. That's it," he said, rubbing her belly.

"Don't get these Bahama bitches fucked up," Natalia said, picking up the fork on her plate, threatening to use it.

"Oh, man, don't get her started," I said, looking over Marcel's shoulder at Natalia. "She'll fuck around and have us all locked up over you."

Marcel looked back at me and chuckled then he gave Natalia his attention. "Baby, you know you get a little psycho while you're pregnant. Nothing happened. We were just enjoying the club atmosphere. But if it makes you feel better, next time you can come. I only stepped out because you and Karen were sleep. And me and Cash were bored." He gave her the sad, puppy dog-face. "Honey, we're on vacation too."

Natalia put the fork down. "You have a point. I'm sorry. Maybe I overreacted. I trust you. Besides, these hoes are ugly anyway."

Her and her pregnancy hormones. I sighed. Geesh. "Where's everyone else at?"

Karen took a sip of her iced tea. "Girl, they were still sleep when I called them. I'm not even sure if they are going to make it shopping with us."

"Fuck that. I can sleep at home. I'ma be turned up while I'm here. I'm trying to do any and every thing."

Juicy gave me a hi-five. "That's what I'm talking about. Getting my party on. And breaking these island nicca's pockets."

"And I've seen a few fine men that I'd like to do."

"Hell yeah. Me too."

"Don't follow her lead, Juicy" Vanity said, staring at me. "I thought you were trying to be a better example for her."

"Like you were for me? Be a good example by keeping it real. Tell me where you were last night?"

She stared me down and I gave her the same ice-cold stare, not backing down.

Vanity turned beet red. "I was sleep."

"Like hell you were. If you were sleep, so was I."

She was always meddling in my business. I liked giving her a taste of what she dished out. "You asked me what happened to Stoney last night, Cash. Did you ever find him?"

Cash's eyes darted across the table at Marcel. They shared a secret moment, nonverbally communicating. "Yeah, where did you go last night, Stoney?" Cash smiled from ear to ear.

Stoney gave Cash the side-eye not even entertaining his brother's question. He just kept on eating his breakfast as if nothing had been said. I can't even front, he was smooth about it too. But Cash didn't seem to like it too much. He pulled out his phone playing around with it for a minute before sliding it across the table for Stoney to see.

Stoney took one look at it. He gave Cash a really foul look, picking up the phone. It looked like he was about to erase whatever it was. I snatched the phone out of his hand. I wanted to see it. I had a sneaky suspicion that it involved Vanity. And sure enough, it did. I was watching Stoney and Vanity in the hot tub having scandalous sex.

Damn, Stoney had a big dick! And he could fuck too. He had my sister suspended in the air doing dick push-ups with her pussy. "I guess this video answers my question."

"Hell naw!" Juicy leaned over getting a closer look at the video. "You putting it down like that?" Juicy asked Stoney. "Have mercy, you got some serious skills. Damn." She started fanning herself with her hand.

I mushed her. "Shut the hell up, Juicy."

"What's on there?" Vanity asked.

I was about to hand her the phone when Stoney snatched it out of my hand. "Nothing," he said about to erase it.

"No, I want to see what was on there. Obviously it has something to do with me."

He eyed her. "I don't think that's a good idea."

"Just give me the damn phone!" Vanity yelled.

Stoney shook his head, handing it to her.

"I want to see." Natalia jumped out of her seat. She was moving pretty fast for a pregnant chick.

"Me too," Karen said, moving just as fast, waddling.

They both gasped when they saw what was on the phone.

Tears filled Vanity's eyes as she watched the video. She dropped the phone, balling.

Karen sighed. "Cash, you recorded this?"

"Yeah, we kid around like this all the time on tour."

"Oh really," Karen said, giving her husband the you know better than that look. "You kid around like this with other bitches? I'ma about to fuck your ass up."

"Um, honey, not bitches. I meant recording each other and playing pranks. All of us do it." He looked at Marcel for help. Marcel quickly looked up at the ceiling, pretending like he didn't know what was going on.

"All of y'all, Marcel?" Natalia asked, storming towards him, moving empty chairs out of her way.

"Noooo," he said, shaking his head like a kid in trouble. He looked at Cash, like shut your ass up. "Baby," Marcel said. "I don't know what Cash is talking about. All I do is sing and dance." He got up doing an old school dance from the 70's. "That's it. I don't even breathe unless you know about it."

Natalia cut her eyes at him. "You think I'm stupid don't you? Don't make me cut your dick off." She had a butter knife in her hand. "Cuz I will. Just try me."

Marcel looked like all the blood drained from his face, grabbing his jewels. "No, baby not my manhood." He slowly backed away from her. "Why are you threatening me? You're mad at Cash, remember? Not me. Focus, baby, focus." Marcel pointed at Cash. "Get 'em. He recorded the video."

"Why'd you do something stupid like this, Cash?" Karen said, leaning over him, ready to get all in his ass."

Cash looked like a little boy being scolded. "It was supposed to be a joke."

"On who?" It was obvious Karen was beyond pissed off.

"Stoney's slick ass. He's always lying."

Stoney picked the phone back up. He typed in a few things. I assumed erasing it. Then he handed Cash back his phone. "You play too damn much. While you were trying to get at me, you hurt Vanity in the process."

"I—I didn't mean to do that." Cash got out of his seat, approaching Vanity. "I was going to erase it. None of this was about you. I was just playing around with my brother. Guess I wasn't thinking. Sorry." He hung his head low.

"I looked like a whore," Vanity said, raising her face from her hands. Her makeup was smeared. Mascara was running down, giving her the appearance of a raccoon. She looked around at all of us and then got up racing off towards the bathroom.

"Vanity!" Stoney yelled about to go after her.

I stopped him. "I got it."

"Can you tell her that I didn't have nothing to do with that shit Cash pulled?"

"I know you didn't. I'll tell her. You handle your brother. I'll handle my sister. And when you get a chance, I want to talk to you in private."

He stared at me for a hot minute. "Yeah, sure, we can talk whenever you want."

I went into the bathroom. I didn't see Vanity at first. I assumed that she was in one of the stalls. Luckily the bathroom was empty. I found her posted up in the handicapped stall. "You can't stay in here forever, you know?"

She wiped her nose with tissue. "Says who?"

Me and my sister had our issues, but I couldn't stand to see her in pain. "Look, I can't say I know how you feel, because I don't. But what I do know is Stoney didn't have nothing to do with that. And I don't think Cash was thinking straight when he did it. You know he's silly like that. Besides, he's family."

Vanity stared at the floor. "It doesn't even matter. Everyone knows that I'm a cheating whore." More tears dripped down her cheeks.

"Is that how you really feel? I mean, you might have cheated, but I don't think you're a whore. Where is that coming from?"

She shrugged her shoulders as fresh tears streamed down her face.

I'd never seen my sister so pitiful. And something told me this was about more than just a sex tape. "What's really going on?"

She looked up at me with tears and then went back to staring at the floor.

"I know we aren't the coolest sometimes, but we're sisters. You know no matter what I'm going to have your back. Talk to me," I said, starting to get emotional too.

"Ivan and I have been having some serious problems for months now. Maybe even years. I went to see a divorce lawyer before we came here. I don't think we're going to make it."

"Whoa! I knew y'all were having some issues. I didn't know it was this serious. Everything makes perfect sense now. I should have known something was up. Your behavior has been way over the top lately. So, you want to be with Stoney? I mean, if you do, I'd understand. He's sexy as fuck. Fine. Dress nice. Nice rebound dick for sure."

Vanity wiped her tears. "I don't know. I can't tell if this is just vacation dick, if I'm on the rebound, or if I really want to leave Ivan."

"Do you love him?"

"Who?"

"The fact that you don't know who I'm talking about means there is something more going on between you and Stoney. Because you've never hesitated about your love for Ivan. At least I've never seen it."

"I love Ivan, Pebbles, but there is something sweet between me and Stoney too."

I think he was sweet on her too. Also, I noticed all those lustful looks that he kept giving me too.

There was a knock on the door. "Vanity, are you ok?" Stoney asked.

"Yeah, I'll be out in a minute."

The door closed.

I hugged my sister. "It'll be ok. You're among family. Let me reapply your makeup."

While I was beating her face, I asked a question I was dying to know. "Whose better Ivan or Stoney?"

Vanity grinned. "Who do you think?"

"Shit, from the looks of that video, it has to be Stoney. He was wearing your pussy out."

Vanity giggled. "Peb, it was so damn good too. It felt like he made love to my soul."

"Girl, that's some deep shit."

We laughed together.

"Listen, if Stoney makes you happy, then you should divorce Ivan. This is your life. The only person that needs to be happy is you. Not me or anyone else. Just you. And don't worry about what people think. If you sit around analyzing their thoughts you'll really be fucked up then."

"Since when did you get so wise? I'm the big sister."

It was my turn to grin. Hearing her say that I was wise meant a lot. All I ever heard her say were things like irresponsible, lazy, gold digger, and other mean words.

Vanity and I walked out of the bathroom hand-in-hand. I wasn't sure what everyone thought, but one thing I knew for sure, I wasn't going to allow them to dog my sister. Fuck that.

"I'm sorry," Cash said again, hugging Vanity. "Forgive me?"

She hugged him tight. "Of course, I forgive you. We're family."

"Yeah, but I really screwed up. I want to do something nice for you to make up for this mess I created. I'll talk to you later about it."

Stoney pulled Vanity away from Cash, into his arms. "Are you ok? If not, we can leave now," he said, staring into her eyes.

Vanity stared back. "Yes, I'm fine."

"Are you sure?" he asked still holding on to her, tight.

She looked like she was holding back tears. She nodded her head, being strong. She sat back in her seat and Stoney sat next to her with her hand in his.

Yeah, he was definitely feeling her. I wasn't sure what she should do because she had a long history with Ivan. But if any man could knock Ivan out the picture it would be Stoney's fine, sexy ass.

"Please don't tell Ivan." Vanity looked at each one of us. "Our marriage is on the rocks. I'm not sure if I'm ready to give up just yet." She looked down avoiding our stares. "I know this probably isn't what you want to hear, Stoney."

"No pressure here. I want whatever you want. Whatever is meant to be, will be, regardless."

Karen leaned forward, looking over at Vanity. "Look, I just want to say what just happened was very unfortunate." She looked at Cash like she wanted to kill him. "And childish, but we're your family. We're Team Vanity. There's no loyalty to Ivan up in here."

"I don't even like his ass," Juicy admitted. I kicked her foot under the table. "Ouch! Well, I don't. Shoot."

"Yeah, I agree with Karen," Natalia chimed in. "Ivan who?"

Marcel leaned forward, looking at Vanity. "Ivan is a cool dude, but I'm Team Stoney. He's like my little brother. I want whatever he wants."

"Me too," Cash added.

Vanity smiled. "Thanks y'all. For not judging me."

Karen pushed her empty plate away. "Girl, please. I can't judge nobody. You know how jacked up my marriage was with Maurice. That bastard. I didn't even know we were having problems. This low down dirty nicca invited me to lunch and whipped out divorce papers. I was so gone after that stunt he pulled I nearly killed myself stepping into ongoing traffic. If Cash hadn't come to my rescue I would be road kill right now."

"Is that how you two met?" Vanity asked.

"Yeah, this crazy storm came out of nowhere right after he saved me and he invited me back to his place. The rest is history."

"That's her version." Cash grinned. "What I remember is the storm knocked out the power and we were stuck in the elevator. To pass the time, I was knocking the lining out of that pussy."

Karen reached over and punched Cash. He moved quickly so her blow landed on his thigh. "Ow! That hurt."

"It should have, with your stupid ass. You better be glad I didn't knock you out."

Stoney shook his head at Cash. "You don't ever learn. I think you like misery."

Natalia got Vanity's attention by placing her hand on the table, flashing that expensive wedding ring.

"Girl, move your hand back, you're blinding us," I said, giggling. "Where my shades at?"

Natalia smiled admiring her ring finger for a moment. "Relationships are hard, Vanity. You know the troubles that Marcel and I had."

Vanity nodded her head.

"Aw, shit, here we go again." Marcel threw his head back with disgust. "Yo, I'm never going to live this bullshit down. I made one damn mistake."

Everyone laughed.

Natalia playfully hit his arm. "You damn right you're not. I'm going to keep reminding you because I went through hell. You try carrying two babies everywhere while your baby daddy is on tour with a bunch of groupie bitches."

"But I redeemed myself. I stepped up. I'm a great father and the best husband ever. I eat, breathe, and sleep just for you."

Natalia leaned over kissing Marcel. "I know, baby. You did. It's my hormones again. I'm sorry."

Stoney looked at Natalia. "I was on tour with him during those nine months. There weren't any girls around him. In fact, he moped in his room every night."

"You ain't got to lie, Stoney," Natalia said. "Taking up for your boy and all."

"Oh, I'm not. It's the truth."

"You sing?" I asked Stoney. This nicca is full of surprises.

"Yeah, I do backgrounds for Marcel. Just depends on my work schedule. But most of the time I fill in when he's in a jam. And usually, I go on tour."

"Impressive. You got video?"

"No, but I'm sure nosey does," Stoney said, cutting his eyes at Cash.

Cash started searching through his phone, immediately. "Let me find it right quick."

"So where did you come from?" I asked Stoney. "Because I've known Cash for many years. I don't remember you. I've never heard your name until now. It's like you magically appeared out of thin air. In fact, I don't think I've ever seen pictures of you either."

"There's pictures of me at home. You just probably thought they were Emerald like most people do."

"Ok, maybe so. But it seems like you just popped up out of nowhere."

"It's a long story," Stoney said. I could tell he didn't want to talk about it. But he was going to tell me something if he was going to be messing around with my sister. I needed the tea on this situation.

"Well give me the cliff note version then."

"I grew up in a separate house with different parents. My parents died in a car accident."

"But I thought you two were brothers. So, you're not blood brothers?"

"Yes, we're blood brothers," Cash said.

Stoney sighed. "I told you it's a long story."

I wasn't letting up. I needed to know a little bit more. "So do you have a different parent, Cash? Because Stoney and Emerald look alike."

"No," Cash said. "Me and Emerald have the same parents."

"Aw, fuck it. I'm so damn confused. Never mind."

"That's how I feel," Stoney admitted. "I grew up with my father and mother."

Cash corrected him. "No, your mother is my mother."

Stoney sighed. "I'll break it all down for you some other time. It's a touchy subject. And Cash and I are still working some things out because of it."

"I understand. I was just wondering. That's all."

I pushed the cold plate of food out of my way when Cash handed me his phone with the clip of Marcel's last performance. Sure enough, Stoney was behind him, killing it. I wanted to see for myself if he was any good. "Nice," I said to him, handing Cash back his phone. "And your ass needs your recording feature disabled. I'm going to keep my damn eye on you whenever you're around."

Cash smirked at me.

I gave him the finger.

Juicy adjusted her seat, sitting on her leg. "What I want to know is how you stood there recording them? Cuz that was a long ass video. You had to be horny. I'm just saying."

I laughed. "Yeah, Cash, that was some freak nasty shit. Did you watch it?"

Cash cracked up laughing. He glanced at Stoney before looking at me and Juicy. "C'mon, you know I watched that shit."

We all busted out laughing including Vanity, who seemed to be in better spirits.

Cash waved his hands, getting our attention. "But hold up!" We were all still laughing. "Nah, but hold up! It gets better." Everyone quieted down. "Marcel was with me!"

"Oooooooh!" we all screamed.

Cash grinned. "While y'all talking about me that makes his ass freak nasty too."

"Damn, Marcel." I looked over at him, pointing and laughing. "You were peeping right along with Cash? That's a bad look, homie."

Marcel shrugged his shoulders, cheesing. "I admit I'm a freak. The shit was hot." He chuckled. "Sorry, Vanity, no offense." He picked up a piece of cold toast from my plate, throwing it at Cash. "You suck ass. You know that right?"

Cash dodged the toast. It landed on the floor behind him. "I don't suck as much as you do right now. Marcel The Peeping Tom." Cash got up imitating one of Marcel's famous dances in a really silly way, cracking us up even more.

"Shut the fuck up, Cash. Throwing me under the bus. You supposed to have my back." Marcel was still laughing. "I can't stand your fraud ass."

Cash raced around the table, trying to hug Marcel. "What you want, Mr. Peeping Tom? A huggy wuggy," he said, talking baby talk to him.

Marcel was rolling. "Get the hell away from me," he said, pushing Cash back. "I'm not speaking to your fraud ass."

Vanity smiled. "It's all good. I don't care anymore. It's out in the open and off my chest. I'm just glad I don't have to hide it anymore. But don't tell the others. They can't keep a secret to save their lives."

She got that right. "Nope. None of them. Shay's got the biggest mouth in the Midwest."

"The United States," Juicy said.

I nodded my head. "She can't keep nothing. She'll have your shit on CNN. Joss won't even pretend to keep it. The whole damn island would know within one hour of her knowing. And Lyric was just weak. Cookie is cool sometimes, but nah. Not something this important."

Vanity looked at me. "I can trust Piper, though. I'll tell her later. We're deuce like that. And Lyric is weak, but I can trust her too. I just don't want to put anything extra on her. She's so fragile right now. Cookie, she has her moments. So you might be right about her. I don't know."

I agreed. "Yeah, I forgot about Piper. She's cool as hell. Knowing her, she'd probably be happy because she can't stand Ivan's guts."

"I can't stand his ass either," Juicy mumbled. I kicked her foot again. "Ow! I'm just keeping it real. Dang."

I tapped Marcel on the shoulder. “So what y’all doing while we go shopping?”

“Golfing.”

I turned up my lip. “Umph. Sounds boring.”

“That’s because it’s a man’s sport,” Marcel said, pinching my cheek. “Not for little girls, like you.”

“I’m definitely ready to go now. Y’all about to start that little girl shit. I ain’t got time.”

Everyone laughed at me as I stood to my feet.

Chapter 12

Pebbles

"Ugh! What's up with the long faces?" Shay asked when we got in the minivan cab. "Shopping is supposed to be fun and y'all bitches look like someone died."

None of us said a word, taking our seats.

Joss analyzed us too. "What the fuck happened? What did I miss?" She got up and sat next to Juicy. "I know you know with your little nosey ass."

"I'm no nosier than you!" Juicy spat.

Joss moved over to me. "C'mon, Peb, we're tight. Let a bitch in on what happened."

"Nothing to tell," I said, putting my Prima Donna shades over my eyes.

Joss looked at all of us, taking her seat. "Y'all already know I'm going to find the shit out."

"Yeah, something happened," Shay cosigned. "The vibe is way off."

"Who gives a fuck?" Piper got up and sat next to me. "I wouldn't tell y'all big mouth bitches shit either."

Shay sucked her teeth. "See, wasn't nobody even talking to you."

I jumped up before Piper could, making sure she stayed in her seat. "Whoa! We're on vacation. Chill out."

Piper turned all the way around, facing Shay. "One day I'm going to see you, bitch. Believe that shit."

"See me then, bitch. I don't give a fuck."

This shit don't make no sense. I sat back down next to Piper. "Why you let her get to you like that?" I whispered.

"Cuz I hate fake ass, man-stealing hoes. She keeps coming at me because she's jealous. But when I floor her ass, she'll be satisfied then. All this back and forth shit ain't me. I'm action. I beat bitches asses."

I laughed inside. Shay didn't want to see Piper. She fought like a dude. I've seen her whip ass before. Even being pregnant, she'd still put a hurting on her. Shay was a lot of mouth. She couldn't fight though.

As soon as we got to the shopping area, I headed to the nearest food spot to get me something to eat. My stomach was touching my back. If I didn't eat something soon, I was going to eat one of them. I found this one little spot still serving breakfast and ordered the works. Bacon, sausage, eggs, grits, and pancakes with orange juice. I ate every last bit of it. Not a crumb was left.

Now that my tummy was full, I decided to get my shopping on. I had no idea which direction my family went in but I was sure that if I kept walking past booths, I'd run right into them.

Strolling on my hunt to find them, an array of beautiful handmade necklaces caught my eye. I had to stop at this particular booth and get me one.

"How much?" I asked the guy bending down behind some boxes. It looked like he was restocking or something. I wasn't sure. His back was to me. He had a killer body and a real nice ass.

"How much for these?" I asked again, impatiently. Was he deaf?

"Three dollars for those," he said in a slight Bahamian accent, pointing at the necklaces that I was referring to. "And five dollars for those." He pointed to another set of equally as beautiful necklaces.

I wasn't even thinking about the necklaces anymore. This man standing in front of me was all kinds of hotness. Drop dead gorgeous. Tall with a golden brown island complexion and the sexiest light brown bedroom eyes ever. Just looking at this exotic specimen made my coochie drip.

For some odd reason he reminded me of a Bahamian Stoney with the same type of let me fuck your brains out sexiness. They favored a lot. Same height, built, and similar features.

"I'm sorry, what did you say?" I couldn't remember nothing he just said to me. I was too busy concentrating on the fire burning between my legs.

He smiled and politely repeated himself. "These are three dollars and those are five."

"Oh," I said, suddenly more interested in him than the jewelry. "Are you from here? Because you don't really sound like it. Your accent isn't as thick as most people that live here." His accent was sexy as fuck, making me lust after him even more. If he kept talking to me, my panties were going to fall off.

"I was born here, but as soon as I turned eighteen I left, moving to Chicago in search of my father."

"Shut the hell up," I said, shoving him in excitement. I quickly straightened up when he looked at me strange. "Oh, my bad. That's where I'm from too." I giggled. "Sorry. Old habits die hard."

He continued to stare at me, smiling. "It's ok. I've been living in the United States for the last ten years so I'm familiar with a few things."

I caught him drooling over my body. "So, um, what's your name?"

"Pebbles. Yours?"

"Gabriel."

"If you live in the States, what are you doing here?"

"Visiting. I'm filling in for my mother so she can take the day off."

"That's really nice of you," I said, still checking him out. "I bet you have plenty of women here and back home. International player."

He grinned moving a little closer to me with desire in his eyes. "No, not at all. I was hoping that I could spend some time with you. I'd like it if you came to a party with me tonight."

"Can my family come too?"

"Sure. You all can be my guests."

"Ok. That's what's up."

I turned my back to him walking further inside of the booth, getting a closer look at the necklaces. I still wanted to buy a few, after I jumped his bones. "I'll take these six," I said, purposely bending over right in front of him, exposing my ass cheeks underneath my short mini dress.

I turned around and looked over my shoulder, giving him a sexy wink while shaking my ass. He stood there for a moment admiring the view before he walked up behind me, pinning my body up against the table.

My breath caught in my throat. Beads of sweat gathered on my forehead. His aggressiveness really turned me on. He grabbed my breasts feeling me up through my clothes. I stood there enjoying the touch of his hands as they moved from my thighs up underneath my dress.

"I want you," he moaned, grinding up against me.

"I want you too. Let the covering down." No shame in my game. I was on vacation. I needed a piece of this ridiculously fine man.

While Gabriel closed the plastic covering, I took off my outfit so it wouldn't get dirty and struck a pose in my bra, thong, and heels.

"I find you very attractive," he said, kneeling before me. "Can I taste you first?"

I pulled my thong aside, exposing my pretty pussy. "It's all yours, baby. Eat as much as you want."

He slipped my thong off and dived in face first, lapping at my vagina.

"Oh, that feels sooooo good," I moaned, throwing my head back, spreading my outer lips.

"Put your legs over my shoulder," he said with his face still buried in my coochie.

I put one leg over his shoulder. He palmed my ass lifting the other leg over his shoulder too. For support, I balanced myself on my hands with the table behind me.

"You taste so sweet."

"Oh shit! Your tongue is so sweet."

"I want you to cum on my face."

"Oooooooh shit!" I cried out, coating his face with plenty of juice.

"Mmmmm, I love your pussy," he moaned loudly with his face still in my crotch. "Cum again for me. Just like that."

He didn't have to ask me twice, I started throwing it at his face, moving every which way I could. I was rocking so hard that we were both starting to lose our balance. Lifting me up in the air with my crotch still in his face, Gabriel stuck his tongue deep inside of me, bouncing my petite body up and down on his face.

I ain't never had it like this before.

After a few tongue thrusts I was creaming all over his face again. "Oh shit! Oh shit! Oh shit! Oh shit!" I screamed. Gabriel held me steady as powerful ripples overtook my body. "That was the best orgasm ever."

I was still breathing heavily when he carried me over to an empty table, laying me down. I watched in anticipation as he undid his pants and pulled his dick out of his briefs. It was the perfect size. Just the way I liked it.

"Let me get it doggy style," he said, motioning for me to turn around.

I slid off the table standing to my feet, positioning myself with my ass in the air. He grabbed my hips, jerking my body towards him. Opening my legs wider, he rammed his dick in me.

"Ung! Ung! Ung! Ung! Ung!" He gripped my breasts, pounding me fast and hard. "Ah! You feel as sweet as you taste."

I bent over slightly arching my back, pushing off of the table, clapping my ass on his dick.

"Oh! Right there," I said, feeling tingles in my vagina. Ah! This man had me so worked up.

Gabriel was almost there too. Picking up speed, he pounded even harder. "I'm about to cum in this sweet pussy."

I rubbed my clit vigorously, cumming instantly. I fell forward onto the table, vibrating the necklaces with my orgasm. Gabriel came wildly too. His body landed on top of me as he let off a huge nut.

"Real sweet pussy," he whispered while kissing my neck and back. "You don't know how much I needed that."

"I have to go," I said, feeling some kinda way about him. "My family is somewhere around here, probably looking for me."

Gabriel rose up and pulled out of me, fixing his clothes. I slipped back into my dress and put my thong in my purse, ready to leave. It was so weird for me to feel more than a sexual attraction to him. I had no idea why. This only happened one time before with Chip, which was understandable. Was the sex so good that I was catching feelings? I needed to get my damn life, quickly before I spazzed out on this dude, making myself look real crazy.

He grabbed my hand. "I'm going to see you later, right?" His sexy eyes searched mine, intensifying my attraction to him even more. "You're still coming to the party?"

"I don't know." And I didn't. I got what I wanted—a good hard fuck. There was no use of us shooting the shit.

"I hope you reconsider. I want to see you again."

"Why? Because of my sweet pussy?" I asked sarcastically. All of a sudden, I was irritated as hell. "Don't pretend. There's no need for anything more. We both got what we wanted. It was great." I bit my bottom lip thinking that it was more than great. It was magnificent. "Let's move on, aight?"

He held my hand, staring at me as if he was trying to think of the right words to say. "Look, I don't normally do this, but I invited you to the party because I want to get to know you. I mean, really get to know you."

I rolled my eyes. Why is he trying to hang on? Is he trying to make this awkward? "I'll think about it." I sighed and rolled my eyes again. "Where's this party going to be at anyway?"

"At the dock." He let go of my hand, picking up a pen, writing down a name and a number. "This is the host of the party. Just tell him that I invited you and your guests."

"Ok," I said, walking away again when he grabbed my hand once more.

I was about to swing on him when he kissed it. "Until then, gorgeous."

I turned up my lip. "Until then," I replied with an attitude.

Yes, I was flattered. He wanted to get to know me. Whoopty Doo. Niccas say that shit all the time and don't mean it. I'm a realist. I know that because I gave up my pussy the way I just did, that I shouldn't expect nothing more. Some international player dick is what I got.

As soon as I left Gabriel's booth, I went straight to the bathroom, wet a paper towel, and wiped myself down there. It was too hot outside for me to be walking around with sticky nut between my legs. That's a sure fire way to be stanking in no time.

Once I freshened up, I left the bathroom trying to find out where everyone went. It's like they disappeared or something. I didn't have to look too far because I heard Juicy's ass big mouth nearby. She was standing on the outside of one of the larger booths while everyone else was inside shopping.

"Hey, where you been?"

I smiled thinking about how good Gabriel just sexed me. "Looking for y'all."

"Oh." She eyed me suspiciously trying to tell if I was lying or not. "Well, we're almost done shopping now. Unless you want to look at some things."

Dang! I left my necklaces. "Naw, I'm tired. Tell them I went back to the hotel. This heat is kicking my ass. I need a nap."

"Ok, I will."

I hailed the taxi that was waiting nearby, going back to the hotel. On my way to my room, I saw Cookie give Scott a goodbye kiss. He spoke to me as he walked by.

"What the hell?" She was standing in the doorway with a towel covering her pregnant body. "He's been in there with you since last night?"

Cookie grinned. "What can I say? It was damn good. I couldn't get enough."

I cracked up. "I ain't mad at you. Good dick is hard as hell to find."

"Is everyone mad at me for missing breakfast?"

"Naw, girl, we kept it moving. You weren't the only one who didn't show up for breakfast."

"Where's everyone else at now?"

"Shopping. You better not miss the cruise though."

"Oh, I'm not. I'm going to take me a nap right quick. Then, I'll start getting ready."

"That's what I'm going to do." I yawned. "See ya later."

I made my way to my room, taking off everything. Throwing my nude body across my bed, I slept like a newborn baby.

*****

Shay took a long pull of some weed she got from her boyfriend Moneaco called Madd Max. "This shit is fire!"

"Let me try it." Juicy stretched out her hand, taking the blunt from Shay, inhaling it. "Oh, it is fire. I didn't know they were getting it in like this over here."

Shay gave a goofy smile. "What did you say? I'm soooo fucked up right now." She giggled still wearing that silly ass look.

"See, I got to get the hell outta here." Why in the world did I say I would go with Shay to the Welcome Cruise? I must've lost all my good sense. I guess I felt bad because she said that I was ditching her. I don't know where that came from, but to keep the peace I agreed to hang out with her. "I can't be up in here with y'all, smelling like weed and shit. That ain't cute." I turned up my nose.

"It sure feels cute," Juicy said, falling back on the bed giggling. "I think I'm fucked up too." She laughed even harder, making funny faces at me. "I…think…I'm…fucked up," she said in slow motion and then giggled hysterically.

I couldn't take it. "Oh my goodness! Y'all tweaking."

Shay squinted at me with low eyes. "Bitch, you just a hater." They laughed like that was the funniest shit ever. "Check it though. Moneaco got a cousin he want to hook you up with."

I twisted my lips. "Naw, I'm good. I don't do hook ups. The niccas never look right. Something is always wrong with their asses. I'm straight."

"Girl, please. You don't know what you're missing. This dude is paid."

"AND?" She acted like I needed her help getting a paid nicca.

"And what? You sleeping on him. I'm telling you." Shay got really dramatic, waving her hands in the air along with other theatrics. "While you playing, his cousin owns the boat we getting on for the Welcome Cruise."

"That's nice. What does he look like?"

"Does it matter?"

"Fuck yeah, it matters. I don't like ugly men." Shay wouldn't know cute if it smacked her ass in the face. Ugly was cute to her.

"You'll see him for yourself when we get there. He's your type."

"Hold up. I know you didn't tell this man I was coming there to see him."

Shay grinned. "Why you tripping? I hooked you up."

I had the funniest feeling that she wasn't hooking me up. That it was going to be more like a set up. "Ok, let me get there and dude ain't right. I'm going to act a damn fool."

I knew Shay was high when she started cracking up laughing. "Why you trippin, though?"

Shay's laughter must've been contagious because Juicy had a laughing fit too.

"Oh, I can't do this shit no more. Come get me when y'all ready. I'm out."

"Where you going?" Shay asked as the room door slammed in her face. I didn't have time for two hyenas. They were on my last nerve.

I left Shay's room, which was on the same floor as ours, around the corner. As I approached my room, Stoney walked up, going to his room across the hall.

"What's up, Little Vanity," he said, smiling.

"Oh, you tried it." I smiled too. "You know my name. P. E. B. B. L.E.S." I put my hand on my hip, snapping my fingers at him. "Get it right, honey."

He laughed while opening the door. "Are you free?" he asked, standing in the doorway looking real delicious. "Earlier, you said you wanted to talk to me."

All of a sudden, I had a flash back of his sex tape. Images of his rock hard body, big dick, and sex moves replayed over and over in my head. I imagined myself making passionate love to him. Oh, how sweet it would be.

"Oh, yeah, that's right. I forgot all about that." I looked around the hallway suspiciously. "I don't know, Stoney. Me being in your room with you, alone, it's not a good idea. You know?"

He leaned back against the door so I could enter. "Yeah, I feel you, but we're just talking, right. Unless you had something else in mind?" His piercing eyes searched mine.

I hesitated, staring at him. I had a lot of things on mind and none of it involved talking. Pussy wet, nipples hard, and ready to open my legs for him. As much as I stayed in heat, I was afraid that I just might let him do it. I know me and I know how I get down. I didn't trust myself. Stoney is a very handsome, extremely attractive and charming man. Easily, I could fall for him. I could tell the he was a hypersexual being, just like me.

"Um," I said, moving a little closer standing in front of him in the tight doorway space. Just inches away, staring at the imprint of his dick.

He licked his lips. If I didn't know any better I would have thought he was flirting with me. This ain't a good look. Not at all. I tried to back up and walk away when I tripped over the carpet. I went tumbling down face first. My face would have been bruised if Stoney hadn't caught me.

"Are you ok?" He asked, trying to help me stand up.

I stepped down on my right foot and immediately felt pain. "No!" I yelled out, hopping on my left foot. "I hope I didn't twist my ankle." I took my heels off, trying to see if I could stand without them.

"Let me take a look," Stoney said, sweeping me off my feet. He carried me into his room, gently sitting me down on the bed. Kneeling in front of me, he took my shoes out of my hands, sitting them on the floor beside him. "Which foot hurts?"

I raised my right foot.

"You have really beautiful feet," he said, holding both of my feet in his hands.

"I take it you're a foot man."

He massaged my right foot while my left foot rested on his thigh. "I can be. Only pretty feet turn me on though."

Ah, this man is incredible with his hands. The more he caressed my foot, the wetter I got. "Is that right?"

"Yes, I like beautiful feet when they're attached to beautiful women," he replied, staring at me passionately.

"Really?" I asked, feeling like I was about to have an orgasm. "So I can safely assume you have a type too."

He continued to use his hands to make love to my foot. "I do. I have a craving for pretty petite women with pretty dainty feet."

Ok, now we're getting somewhere. "Why?"

"Because I like picking my woman up, especially in the bedroom." He winked at me, moving his hand up further, massaging my calf. "I'm sure you've been picked up before."

He was so close that I was sure he was able to see under my dress since my legs were gaped. I drew in a sharp breath when he switched to my left foot. My right foot landed on his groin.

"I gotta go," I said, jumping up, nearly stepping on him. I forgot all about the pain. My focus was on getting the hell away from him.

He looked bewildered. "Does your foot feel any better?"

"Yeah," I said, not caring if I was in pain or not. I slipped on my shoes, strutting towards the door.

"But we didn't get a chance to talk," he said, swiftly reaching the door before I did. Damn, he moved fast.

I gulped, looking at his sexy lips. I wanted to kiss him badly. "Some other time, ok?"

"Ok," he said nicely. That's what his mouth said, but his eyes said something else. And the huge lump in his pants did too.

He opened the door for me. I brushed past him, stepping back into the hallway. His eyes carefully watched me for a few seconds igniting the flame brewing inside of me even more.

"I'll see you later," he said, before closing the door.

I sighed when the door shut, standing in the hallway only left with my desires. I had no business feeling this way about Stoney. Sex tape or not, I needed to get rid of this attraction before I acted on it. I just wish my vagina understood that.

I heard the loud music coming from Shay's room as soon as I came around the corner. A big cloud of smoke smacked me in the face when she opened the door.

"Heffa, I knew you would be back. What? Vanity wouldn't let your ass in? That's what you get for leaving us. You'll think twice next time, won't you?"

I didn't even answer her. I just walked in and sat down, disgusted. "How long y'all gonna take. Cuz I'm ready."

"You not going nowhere with me looking like that."

I walked over to the mirror. "What's wrong with what I have on?"

"Nothing trick. Nothing trick. I said, nothing trick. You don't like it? You don't like it? You can suck my dick. Bow down to the king cuz you know I am the shit. That's right. I know you heard me. I said, I'm the shit. I'm the shit. I'm the shit. I'm the muthafuckin shit." Shay was jumping around rapping one of Cash's verses on Marcel's hit song, Bow Down.

"That song is bomb." Juicy joined in rapping the lyrics too.

"Bitch! Where you been? I ain't seen you in a minute." Joss had a drink in one hand and a blunt in the other. "I bet you been getting your freak on all over this damn island. Nothing but turn up."

I see that the only way I could stay in this room was to be fucked up too. "Pour me something," I asked, avoiding her accusation. I mean, I was getting it in, but it wasn't none of her damn business.

Shay mixed vodka and cranberry juice and handed it to me. "Damn, Cash's brother is fine as shit. What's his name again?"

"Stoney," Juicy said. I gave her a look like don't open your big ass mouth about what happened earlier. She caught the hint and didn't say another word.

"Yeah, that's his name. Oh my God! On everything, I would fuck every last drop of cum outta of him." Shay dropped down to the floor twerking, imitating as if she was on top of Stoney. "Shit, if I could get fifteen minutes with him. Boah! Y'all don't even know. He'd be ready to marry a bitch."

Joss looked her up and down. "Bitch! Fifteen minutes? That's all you want. You better get it in. I want an hour or better."

"I don't need an hour with him. I could nut three times in fifteen minutes with his fine ass. He's so fuckin sexy, though." She grunted. "I promise, I'd let him hit it anyway he wanted."

Joss sipped her drink. "Indeed, he is. And I bet he got a big fat dick too. You know I like it big."

I smacked my lips. "Can't we talk about something else? Like what we want to do after the Welcome Cruise."

Shay turned up her nose at me. "Why you got a stick up your ass?" She twisted her lips, staring at me. "What? You got a crush on him or something?"

They all laughed.

I took a big gulp of my drink, hoping I didn't exhibit how attracted I really was to Stoney. "Girl, please. It ain't got nothing to do with that. It's just that, you know, because of Cash and Marcel. My big brothers," I said with air quotes.

Shay struck a ghetto pose in the mirror. "Shit, they fine too. I would fuck them until my pussy was sore. And I would stay pregnant just like Natalia. Popping out baby after baby and collecting all them checks. Marcel wouldn't have to beg me to have his pretty babies."

"Lawd, don't let Natalia or Karen hear you say that," Juicy said. "They will go postal on all of us. They don't play that shit about their husbands."

Shay made the stank face. "Whatever. I'm not into married men anyway. But Stoney, oh, he could get it."

I shook my head. She was not his type. "Shay, that man isn't thinking about you."

"Then who is he thinking about. Cuz as fine as he is, I know he's thinking about some woman. He has to be."

"Or man," Joss added, turning around, bouncing her booty as if Stoney would be interested in her. "You never know these days."

"He don't swing that way, Joss," I said, laughing at her.

"He just might. You'd be surprised. I'd show him that I'm all woman too."

I was more than ready to get up out this damn room. "Are y'all even close to being ready?"

Joss rocked back and forth to the loud music. "Bitch! Stop rushing us. We trying to get this shit poppin early."

"What time is it?" Shay asked while putting on her clothes.

"Time to go," I said.

Juicy looked at her cell. "Almost seven."

Shay started dressing a little faster. "Ok, we do need to hurry up or we're going to miss our ride."

"Shit, I've been ready." And that shut everyone up because I was the only one who was.

After rushing my cousins for another thirty minutes, they were finally ready. Carl, the owner of the boat, sent car service to come and get us.

"Heffa, I told you he was paid," Shay bragged. "You better get with the program. Get some bills paid and put your bank account on swole."

"I'm not impressed," I said. "You act like I'm not used to nothing. I date men with money all the time."

"Yeah, but he don't live on no island like this though."

Shay was getting on my fuckin nerves being all on this nicca's nut sac. "What are you Carl's hype man or something? Get the hell outta here with all that hoopla. I'll be the judge of his ass when I see him."

Joss and Juicy started rolling.

Shay didn't find anything funny. "Heffa, you real ungrateful. I'm trying to put you on game."

"Whatever, Shay." I was glad we were finally here so I could get away from her ass.

The boat was gorgeous. I could honestly say Carl was paid. By the size of the boat, it was probably worth a million.

Shay, Joss, Juicy, and I were the first to arrive. As we stepped onto the boat, there was a man there to greet us, handing us a rose and a goody bag. Juicy dove right into hers so we knew that it was filled with expensive candies.

"This is so nice," Juicy said, munching on chocolates. "Mmmm. These melt right in my mouth."

Now, I was curious to see Carl. From the looks of things, he had to be old and ugly.

"Good evening, ladies." A young man with a thick Bahamian accent approached us. He was fine, sexy, and well dressed. "My name is Carl. Welcome to my boat."

My mouth hung open. I was stunned. Carl wasn't the old fart I thought he was going to be. He looked to be in his late twenties and very attractive.

"Pick your face up," Shay said, trying to close my mouth for me. "Hey, Carl." She leaned in giving him a hug. "Let me introduce you to my cousins. Joss, Juicy, and Pebbles."

Carl spoke to all of us, but his eyes lingered on me. "So, you're Pebbles." He took my hand into his, kissing it. "Simply beautiful. What a pleasure."

"Pleasure is all mine," I flirted back.

"Allow me to escort you beautiful ladies to the dining area." Carl held my hand, leading us to the upper deck.

Chapter 13

Vanity

The night was perfect. The view was incredible. We were sitting on the upper deck in the dining area of the boat. The room was absolutely gorgeous. It looked like it was fit for royalty. Crystal chandeliers hung from the ceiling. The tablecloths, chairs, napkins, and place holders were all white trimmed in gold. Everything else was glass or a plastic substitute that had a glass look to it. Surrounding the room were huge picture windows allowing us to view the ocean as we ate.

There were about sixty guests on deck. Even with that amount of people, there was still plenty of room for everyone.

Stoney took the gold covering off of his plate. "This food looks delicious."

Fresh lobster, fish, steak, veggies, baked potato, salad, and homemade rolls. In the middle of the table were large pitchers of rum punch and expensive champagne bottles.

I glanced at his plate and then removed my covering. The aroma hit my nose and made my stomach growl. "Smells good too."

Stoney was the only one from our group sitting with me. I watched him dip his lobster into the butter. Seductively, he wrapped his tongue around the tender piece of meat, giving me sexual innuendos.

I gave him a flirty stare, reading his lips. This is how good your pussy tastes. My clit throbbed as I thought about the tongue-lashing he put on my coochie. I looked away from his sensual gestures, lowering my eyes to my plate.

Meanwhile, the woman next to Stoney eyeballed him as he finished his plate. "I bet your lobster is succulent," the older woman said. "I would love to taste it." She looked down at his lap, making it very obvious that she wasn't talking about food.

She was bold as hell. I sipped on my champagne, trying to keep my cool. I wanted to see what Stoney was going to do. Because it was his job to check this old bitch. Not mine.

Stoney shifted his eyes to the woman on his right. "It is a big piece of hard meat that is very satisfying."

"Oh, really." She stared at Stoney as if she wanted to jump in his lap and ride him right at the dinner table. "You are simply gorgeous. I would love to have a piece of your meat."

"Thank you," he said, looking back across the table. "But my meat belongs to her," he said, pointing at me. "Have you met the woman of my dreams?"

The lady glanced at me and then Stoney, looking appalled. "No, I don't believe I have," she said dryly. I could tell that she was upset that Stoney acknowledged me.

"Well, let me introduce you." He stood up from his seat, tossing his napkin on the table, and walked around to where I was. "This is Vanity. And she gets my meat two or three times a day. Baby, would you say it was satisfying?"

The woman literally clutched her pearls around her neck. I couldn't help busting up laughing. I know she wasn't expecting to hear what came out of Stoney's mouth. Obviously upset, she jumped up from the table, disappearing into a swarm of guests across the room.

I giggled. "You know you were wrong for that?"

"No, she was wrong for being ill-mannered. I know she saw me flirting and talking to you. Rude ass lady."

"So that's my meat, huh?" I pointed at his groin. "That's what you told her."

Standing directly in front of me, he took my hand, and moved it down lower until I was cupping his dick through the linen shorts. "My whole body belongs to you. I want to be your man."

I laughed nervously. "I almost believed you. Stop kicking game."

"I'm not kicking game." He held my hand up to his soft lips, kissing it gently. "You know what I want? I want to go home with you instead of my fiancée. And you can send your husband home with her. They would probably make a good couple, just like me and you do."

I didn't laugh this time. Something told me he was for real. I was about to dig a little deeper when Carl announced that it was time for the entertainment. Everyone needed to head down to the lower deck.

Stoney stuck out his arm and I wrapped mine around his. He escorted me downstairs to a huge entertainment room. Plush seating wrapped around the sides of the boat. Then there was a dance floor with a DJ booth alongside a pool table.

Our group quickly filed in, taking a seat, joining us.

Cash wiped his mouth with a dinner napkin. "That food was spectacular. You think I can get a to go plate?"

Marcel laughed.

Stoney gave Cash the side eye.

Pebbles flopped down next to him. "You would think your ass was broke by that comment you just made. You getting paper. You're a producer and songwriter. You been all over the world so I know you had great food before. I saw your houses and cars and your name on some of those albums. So, why the hell you act like you broke all the damn time?"

"Because he's just cheap," Karen said, eyeballing her husband.

Natalia eyed him too. "And greedy."

Cash sat back, cheesing. "Ladies. Ladies. Ladies. Don't fight. I know I'm fine. Y'all ain't got to sweat me so hard. It's enough of me to go around."

"Whatever," Natalia and Karen said, waving Cash off.

"This nicca here." Pebbles picked up his napkin and through it on his head. "Have several seats."

Marcel snickered.

"I can't with you right now." Stoney sighed. "Way too much, bro. Way too much."

"May I have your attention, please," Carl said into the microphone. "I want to welcome you all to my boat. Are you having a good time so far?"

Everyone yelled, "YEEEEESSSS!"

I noticed Pebbles being extra flirty with Carl. I assumed Shay hooked her up. From what I could tell, he was handsome and rich. That's always a good combination. I'll get the scoop on him later.

"Good. Good. Good," Carl replied with a strong Bahamian accent. "Let the entertainment begin with the Limbo Kings."

Everyone clapped.

These two tiny guys came out, hyping up the crowd. I know they were grown men, but they looked like two little boys.

"They can't be the Limbo Kings," I whispered to Stoney.

"I know right. That's what I said when I first saw them. They look like somebody's children." We both laughed. "But wait until you see them. They're tight."

I found myself being amazed by them as they went lower and lower under the bar. It wasn't that high to begin with, starting at knee level. One would go and then the other would follow suit. I was really impressed when they did this one stunt. One climbed on top of the other, carrying them both under the pole.

I was awestruck. "Geez! They are flexible. Like they don't have any bones."

"I told you they were good."

The tallest of the little dudes replaced the pole with a wooden stick and set it on fire. The blaze shot out in my direction, making me jump into Stoney's lap to get away. "Hold on, now! Wait a damn minute."

Everyone laughed at me. I didn't see shit funny. I didn't want to jump in the ocean because I was on fire.

Stoney held me close. "That's a part of their act."

"Too late, I'm all shook up."

Stoney hugged me even tighter, kissing me on the cheek. "I got you, boo." His arms felt so comforting.

They raised the burning stick back to knee level, going underneath one at a time. Then they lowered it a little bit. The smaller one hopped on top of the bigger one and they went underneath together. Now the stick was at ankle level.

Everyone gasped when the taller one started going underneath.

"I can't watch." I buried my face in Stoney's chest.

Cash mushed me. "Stop being a big baby. They've done this a million times. Dramatic ass."

"Leave me alone," I said, pushing my face into Stoney's chest.

Stoney smacked Cash's hand. "Man, stop. You see she's scared."

Cash leaned over getting in my face, tickling me. "Well, look who's in love."

Stoney smacked his lips. "You're stupid." He removed my hand and made me sit up. "Look, baby, see he's ok."

I wasn't putting on an act. I was very afraid of fire acts. When I opened my eyes, I saw that his body already went under. He was bringing his head underneath. As soon as he finished, he stood up straight. The other little dude joined him. They took a few bows.

Everyone cheered as the next act set up.

"Let's give another round of applause to the Limbo Kings!" Carl shouted.

Everyone applauded again.

"Now, let's welcome the baddest magician in the Bahamas. Zulu!"

Claps and cheers were heard as Zulu moved towards the center. He pulled out a credit card and held it before us. The card was whole. Then, all of a sudden, it was broken in half. Within seconds, it was restored again.

Everyone clapped.

"Did you see that?" I asked Stoney.

He smiled, kissing me on the cheek again. "I saw it."

Zulu looked at a few people before he asked Cash for a dollar bill. Cash looked at him crazy until Karen nudged him with her elbow. That's when he reached in his pocket, giving it to Zulu.

I laughed. "A dollar? Really? You are so stingy."

Cash stuck his tongue out. "That's how you stay rich. Watching every dollar."

Zulu had the dollar in his hand. He showed it off, and just like that, it was gone. His hands were empty. After snapping his fingers, mysteriously, it reappeared. He showed everyone the dollar bill, waving it like so before folding it.

Zulu walked back over to Cash, asking him to hold out his hand. Nonchalantly, Cash held his palm out. Zulu put the dollar in his hand and told him to make a tight fist. Cash did it. Zulu tapped on his hand with a magic wand. He told Cash to open his hand, unfold the bill, and show everyone. The dollar was now a twenty.

"That was good," I said standing to my feet, clapping. I had no idea how the twenty switched places with the dollar.

Cash tried to keep the twenty in exchange for his dollar, but Karen snatched the twenty out of his hand and gave it back to Zulu.

"Dang, Karen, he's a magician. Tell him to make another twenty. This one's mine."

She just stared at him. "I don't know about you sometimes."

"But you love me, though."

"That's still to be determined."

Cash's face straightened up.

Now it was Karen's turn to laugh.

Two cages came out with white drapes opening before us. The first cage had a woman in it. The other one showcased a tiger. Zulu walked up to the cage with the woman in it. "Meet Daphne!"

We cheered for her as she opened the door, prancing out. She danced around her cage and then the tiger's cage before she got back inside. Zulu marched to the beat of a drumroll, spinning the cages around for us to see how transparent they were before the drapes closed. Holding his magic wand in the air, Zulu twirled it, zapping at both cages. The drumroll stopped. The drapes opened. Daphne and the tiger switched cages right before our eyes.

I clapped loudly. "Bravo! Bravo! Impressive."

"Sit down, clown." Cash said, yanking me in my seat.

I popped him. "Karen, get your husband."

Karen got up, switching seats with Cash.

Pebbles frowned. "I don't want his ass next to me either."

Cash rested his head on Pebbles shoulder. "I miss you so much."

She pushed his head off. "Keep messing with me, Cash. I'm going to hit you in the eye."

I shook my head, focusing on the magic act. Cash was so special.

Zulu closed the drapes again. The drums started playing. He waved his wand, making the cages turn around in circles. Everyone gasped when the drapes opened again. The tiger was gone but the woman was still there. The drumroll played again. He covered the woman's cage, turning it around. Waving his wand, he snapped his fingers three times, and the drapes opened once more. This time the woman was transposed from her cage to the empty cage that the tiger was in.

Everyone stood on their feet clapping and whistling as Zulu thanked us, taking a bow.

"How'd he do that?" I asked no one in particular.

"It's easier than you think," Marcel replied.

Stoney stroked my hair. "We went on tour with a magician once. And he showed us some of his tricks. Not this one but another disappearing act."

Carl stepped back into view. "Let's give Zulu another hand." Everyone clapped. Some whistled. "Now, it's time to spin the wheel. I need a guy and a girl. You and you," he said, pointing to Shay and Stoney.

Shay jumped up screaming like she won the lottery. "Yaaaassss! He knows beatness when he sees it."

Joss snaps her fingers in the air. "Bitch! You better work that shit."

Everyone couldn't help but laugh at their ghetto theatrics.

Stoney didn't budge. "Yo, what you want me to do? I'm not moving until I know what I have to do."

Carl pointed to the wheel. "You just need to spin the wheel. Whatever it lands on, that's what you will do." Stoney still looked hesitant. "C'mon, my brother, it's all in fun."

The crowd began to cheer so that Stoney would accept the challenge.

"Go on!" Cash yelled. "I know you're not scurred."

Stoney squinted his eyes at his brother, giving him a look that said, shut the hell up. He stood to his feet. He didn't look thrilled at all. "Ok, I guess."

The crowd cheered louder.

"If I pick something crazy, I'm spinning again."

"No problem, my brother." Carl moved out the way so Stoney could stand next to the wheel.

Shay stepped closer getting in front of Stoney. "I'm going first."

"Go ahead," Stoney said, gladly moving out of her way.

Shay spun the wheel. It landed on kiss a random man. She looked at Stoney, puckering up her lips.

"Don't even think about it," he replied, taking two steps back.

Shay rolled her eyes and smacked her lips. "Well, I'm spinning again. If you can spin again, so can I." She spun the wheel. This time it landed on twenty dollars. "Does that mean I won some money?"

Carl laughed. "Yes. He pulled out twenty dollars and handed it to her. There you go."

Shay jumped up and down with the twenty in her hand. She danced all the way back to her seat, flopping down next to her boyfriend, bragging.

"Your turn," Carl said to Stoney.

Stoney smacked his lips and then spun the wheel. It landed on dare. Everyone's eyes was glued to him as he removed the dare card, reading it aloud. "You must seductively dribble lemon juice on a woman's leg. Lick it off up to her thigh. Only using the tip of your tongue." Stoney glared at Carl. "Who the hell came up with this shit?"

Carl shrugged.

Stoney's eyes landed on Cash. He probably thought it was another one of his silly pranks. "Ha-Ha. Real funny, big bro, the jokes on me. I know you did this. I'm laughing. Seeeee." Stoney gave a fake laugh.

I looked over at Cash. He wasn't laughing. His expression said it all. "Not me this time, bro. I didn't do it."

"It's real?" Stoney questioned, looking back at Carl.

Carl smiled. "Yes, of course. Why wouldn't it be?"

The look on Stoney's face was priceless. He looked too outdone. "Aww, you got to be kidding me." He looked at the card once more. "Ok, then, fuck it. Where's the lemon at?"

The drunken crowd chanted, "Lemon! Lemon! Lemon! Lemon!" I'm sure everyone was tipsy by now. I know I was. The drinks never stopped coming. And I never stopped drinking.

"Aye," Stoney said, getting the DJ's attention. "Let me get some Isley Brothers."

"Yo, he about to be on one," Marcel said.

Cash nodded. "Yep, shit just got real."

The minute the beat dropped, Stoney put the lemon slice in his mouth. Seductively, he crawled across the floor towards me while Between The Sheets played. For a brief moment, he did this crossover stripper move, thrusting and grinding against the floor.

Some guests were singing along to the song. Others were screaming for Stoney as if he was performing just for them.

Cash glanced at Marcel. "This is all your fault. You know that, right? He's imitating you."

Marcel grinned with admiration, getting a kick out of watching his protégé. "He's doing a good job too. I couldn't have done this better myself."

"This nicca got all your moves down to a science. If you come up missing, we know what happened to your ass."

We all laughed.

I was enjoying the performance, not thinking anything more of it, until Stoney body rolled, kneeling between my legs.

"No! No! No!" I screamed in a panic. I was afraid everyone on the boat would see my goodies. I wasn't wearing any panties. They didn't go with my sexy dress so I decided to go commando. "Stoney, don't do this." My face turned red.

"Don't blush now," Pebbles said. "You were all into it a second ago."

Cookie yelled. "Girl, let him get a whiff of that na na."

Joss little butt was standing up on the expensive sofa seat. "Bitch! You better let him put his face in it."

Stoney winked at me, taking the lemon out of his mouth. "I got you, Commando." After slightly lifting my leg, he removed my slip-on heels and began to massage my foot. Resting on his knees, he leaned back bouncing, making my foot slowly slide down from his chest to his groin.

The crowd cheered, but all I heard was Joss and Shay's big mouths.

"Hot Damn!"

"YES GAWD HUNNY! Do me next."

Usually, I would be pissed off for being put on the spot like this, but the way Stoney stared at me had me on fire. His piercing eyes penetrated me like foreplay. And the way he snaked his body had me sweating bullets. He lifted his shirt with his teeth working his hips and rolling his stomach just like a stripper.

"Fuck it!" Joss screamed. "I'm done!" Dramatically, she fell back on the seat, fanning herself.

My heart was beating out of my chest by the time he squirted lemon juice on my thigh. It trickled down my leg. Holding my tiny foot in his hand, he stuck out his tongue, licking from the top of my foot to my inner thigh. I gasped when I felt his warm breath against my hairless cat.

"Now, that was a show people!" Carl yelled. "Let's hear it for him. Another applause for this young man right here." Stoney stood and took a bow.

"Good job, man," Marcel said, congratulating him. "I know who to call when I take a sick day. And you better not be busy either."

Stoney laughed.

"Show off," Cash said, slapping him on the back.

"Hater."

They laughed.

"We have one last activity," Carl announced. "Is Chicago in the house?" More than half the boat screamed. "Good. Because this last one is a Stepper's Competition."

"Awe, shit!" Cash jumped up, grabbing Karen's hand. "Baby, we got this shit. This is us right here."

Karen smiled like she already won.

I turned to face Stoney. "Can you step?"

"Yeah, but we can't beat Cash and Karen. Have you seen them step before? They live for this. I'm not even going to embarrass myself."

I looked at him disappointed. "But I want to do it. Besides, Karen's pregnant. I know I can beat her."

Stoney turned me around so I was facing them. They looked like professional steppers. Yes, even with her big ass belly. "You got to be kidding me?"

Stoney busted out laughing. "I told you so. Now, follow me."

I followed him away from everyone down a spiral staircase into what looked like a studio apartment.

He picked me up, lifting me high into the air with his face in my crotch. My heels fell to the floor as my legs swung over his shoulders. I was so hot and horny for him that I came in a matter of seconds. He just kept on licking my pussy like it was better than the lobster he had earlier, making me cum effortlessly again.

He put me down and laid back on the bed with his dick making a tent in his linen shorts. I pulled the mini dress over my head, climbing into the bed with him. He lifted his bottom while I pulled down his shorts and boxers, freeing his erection.

I leaned forward, putting my mouth on it.

"Wait—" Stoney reached for me and I scooted out of his reach with my lips still wrapped around his pole. "No, I like pleasing you."

While slobbing on his knob, I inched over on my knees, swinging my right leg over his chest, easing back onto his face. Greedily, he sucked on my pussy with his arms wrapped around my waist. I moaned making humming sounds, slurping on his dick until I tasted precum.

"Let me up," I said, letting his dick fall out of my mouth.

"No," Stoney mumbled while licking me.

"Yes." I tried to move off his face. I'm ready to cum.

"Cum on my face again."

I tapped on his forearm. "No. Let me sit on it."

Stoney finally unwrapped his arms. I got up, positioning myself over his erection. With my hand, I held the tip of his big dick toward my slick hole, sliding down on it.

"Ah!" I moaned, rolling my hips. "I needed this," I said, closing my eyes.

"Yeah?" Stoney asked, rolling his hips too. "It's like that?"

"Yes! Yes! Oh my God! Yes!" He held both my breasts in his hands while I bounced up and down. His deep thrusts felt incredible. "Oh my God! I'm almost there."

Stoney pulled me forward, ramming into me hard. He squeezed my ass tight, groaning loudly as he released his sperm. My pussy contracted, my mouth hung open, my eyes rolled into the back of my head, and my toes curled. Damn, this man is the best.

"Girl, I'm so addicted to you."

I was thinking the same thing. "Me too," I said, French kissing him.

Stoney held me close to his chest with his dick still up inside of me, semi-hard. "You know, I really got used to being with you. I don't know how I'm going to feel when we leave."

I caressed his face, loving his neatly trimmed facial hair. "I don't even want to think about that. Let's just enjoy our moments while they last."

Stoney flipped me onto my back. We kissed and made love once more. Then, dressed and quickly returned back upstairs just in time to see Cash and Karen win a trophy for stepping in the name of love.

"Let's get our party on," Carl said as the boat picked up speed.

The music cranked up.

Pebbles joined him dancing.

Stoney and I squeezed in next to them, getting our groove on too.

Chapter 14

Pebbles

Once the boat docked, I waited while Carl said goodbye to all his guests, including my family.

As soon as everyone left, Carl grabbed me, tongue kissing me. "I couldn't wait for them to leave."

"Me either." I wanted to be intimate with Carl. He was handsome, wealthy, and smooth. Just my type.

He picked me up, carrying me downstairs to his bedroom.

"This is nice," I said, walking around what appeared to be a studio apartment.

"Ugh!" Carl sighed. "The maid forgot to change the bed sheets again." I glanced at the messy bed. "Give me one moment. I'll be back with some clean sheets."

"Take your time," I said, going through his things, being nosey.

Carl left and came back with fresh bed linen. I undressed while he made the bed. "Mmmmmm," he expressed when he turned around and saw me nude.

I strutted my stuff over to him. Sprawled out across the bed, I held my thighs with my legs in the air. "Come and lick this cat."

Carl didn't even bother to undress. He jumped right on the bed, putting his face between my legs. He had me going crazy.

His oral skills were masterful. His tongue was like a mini vibrator. I held his face between my thighs using his tongue selfishly. I even flipped him on his back and rode his face until I leaked cum. He didn't seem to mind one bit. He gripped my ass as if he loved his face being all in my pudding. I busted three wonderful nuts and still wanted more.

"I'm ready for some dick," I said, pushing Carl's face away from my kitty.

Eagerly, he jumped off the bed and began taking off his clothes. His body was nice. Toned with muscles. So far, he was a winner. My mouth watered, anticipating how good his meat was going to be. He had me all the way turned up and ready to fuck.

Carl stepped out of his boxers and momentarily I stopped breathing. He stood proud in front of me sporting the littlest dick I'd ever seen in my life. I mean, it wasn't no bigger than my finger. If I had to guess, I would say it was about four inches. He had a lot of girth. But what the hell was I going to do with that?

My pussy dried up immediately. Not only did I not want to fuck him, I couldn't even look him in the face anymore. "I gotta go," I said, scooting towards the edge of the bed.

"B-but why? You just said you were ready for some dick." He stood proudly once again.

I didn't have the heart to tell him about his tiny manhood. If he didn't know by now that his penis looked like a baby carrot, then I wasn't going to be the one to bust his bubble.

"Um, I can't," I said, hoping I didn't show the disappointment on my face.

I snatched up my clothes, racing to his bathroom. While I was in the shower, Carl had the nerve to join me. I looked down at his little wee-wee and laughed. It had the nerve to be poked out, hard. I rushed out of the shower, drying off, and dressing in a hurry. If I didn't get off this boat soon, I was going to give him a piece of my mind.

Carl threw on his slacks nearly tripping over them as he jogged up the spiral staircase after me. "If you wait a moment, I'll go with you."

"Don't bother." I was walking so fast that I almost fell.

"What's the rush?" he asked me as I was about to step off the boat.

"This isn't going to work, Carl. It was nice meeting you," I smiled and waved at him the same way he did to the guest leaving the boat.

He stood there watching me depart with a foolish look on his face. I'll bet he didn't have no clue why I dissed his ass. His pee-pee popped in my mind again. I started laughing and couldn't stop. I was still laughing by the time I made it to the table where my family was.

"Bitch! What's so damn funny?" Joss asked, sipping on her drink. "Shit, we want to laugh too. And where the hell you been anyway? Mmmm-Hmmm. I see scandal written all over you."

Shay winked at me. "Probably laid up with Carl somewhere."

Just the mention of Carl's name started my laughing fit again.

"Awww, hell," Juicy said. "What the fuck is up? Cuz you laughing when she mentioned Carl's name. What's wrong with that nicca?"

Shay stopped grinning. "You laughing at Carl?" she asked, taking it personal.

"I need me a drink," I said, trying to weasel my way out of the conversation.

"I'll go get it if you tell me what happened," Juicy offered. "Cuz I know it's some shit by the way you're laughing."

I was glad that they had a separate table from everyone else because this conversation could get ratchet real quick. "Has anyone seen Gabriel?" I asked, still deflecting.

Joss got up out of her seat, standing before me. "Bitch! Who is Gabriel? And why are you ducking? Spill the muthafuckin tea. Don't nobody want to play riddles with your ass."

I didn't say a word. I just held out my pinky finger up and wiggled it.

"BITCH! SHUT THE FUCK UP!" Joss slapped my arm so hard, it felt like she left a bruise. "He's too damn fine to be working with a weeny."

"Shhhhhhh!" I looked around to see where Marcel, Cash, and Stoney were. "I don't want everyone in my damn business, Joss. That's why I didn't want to tell your ass."

"What y'all talking about?" Cookie asked. She walked up holding a nonalcoholic drink.

Joss laughed hearty, slapping her knee. "Carl's baby dick."

"SHUT THE FUCK UP!" Cookie yelled, spilling some of her drink. "I'm about to fuck up my outfit." She looked cute as always, wearing orange and gold. Her orange maternity halter with gold rhinestone accent went well with her short fitted orange shorts and gold sandals. Just like her tattooed makeup and glamorous hairstyles that people always thought were weave. Cookie stayed on point.

I sighed. "See, now y'all got her started too."

Cookie lowered her voice. "My bad. I'm sorry. Are you fuckin serious, though?"

"Dead ass."

"That's a crying shame. What a waste of a man. Fine and rich too. Damn. I knew something was wrong with his ass. I kept saying that he was too good to be true."

Shay stood there looking bewildered. "I can't believe it."

"Well believe it." I stared her right in the eye. "I saw that small fuckin penis my damn self. It looked more like four, maybe five inches max. And I'm not exaggerating either."

We all cracked up laughing.

Shay shook her head. "Hell the fuck naw."

"Now I know why he's single. And that's not even the sad part. He has no idea his dick is the size of a pea."

All four of them touched their chests and gasped. I laughed hysterically because it looked rehearsed. "Yes, he kept prancing around with it, like it was cute."

Juicy folded her lip over her nose as if she smelled something foul. "Ewww. I can only imagine what it looks like. You should have told his little dick ass off."

"Girl, I didn't have the heart. Besides, if he is proud of his bite-size penis, then who am I to kill his self-confidence. I don't care what he does as long as he leaves me the hell alone. The only way I'd tell him is if he don't get the hint. You know if he keeps trying to holler."

"I don't think he got the hint." Cookie pointed at Carl who just joined the party, sitting at the bar with Moneaco. He turned around looking at me, smiling. "I think you're going to have to bust his bubble. Something tells me he's not giving up that easy."

"He better stay the fuck away from me with his no dick ass, if he knows what's good for him. I was nice this time, but I don't know how many more times I can be nice before I spill the beans." I was getting heated. "This shit is all your fault, Shay. I told you I didn't want to be fixed up."

Shay looked at me bewildered. "Cuzzo, I'm sorry. That shit is ridiculous. He shouldn't have even undressed if that's what he was working with. In fact, he shouldn't have asked me for a hook up, period."

We all cracked up laughing again.

I went to the bar to get me a drink while my cousins continued to crack jokes at Carl's expense.

"Can I get a motherfucker?" I just happen to look to my left and saw Carl staring at me. I rolled my eyes. "Matter of fact, make that two with two shots of Tequila."

"Coming right up." The bartender began making my drinks.

"Do you want to dance?" Carl asked, approaching me.

I sighed loudly. "No! Go away."

As Carl walked back to the end of the bar, I looked over at my cousins who were pointing at me and laughing. I flipped them the bird.

The bartender came back, sitting both motherfuckers down with the shots. I was reaching in my purse to pay for them when she just walked away, servicing the next customer.

"Excuse me." I waved at her trying to get her attention. Nothing. Was she ignoring me?

"The gentleman at the end of the bar paid for it," she said, rapidly walking pass with two drinks in her hand. I looked over at Carl and he waved. Be stupid and keep spending money on me. I'm going to keep on ordering shit.

I was posted up at the bar, sipping on one of my drinks when someone covered my eyes. I nearly jumped out of my skin. I didn't play that shit. This is how folks get got.

"Guess who?" the smooth voice asked.

"Ummmm." I said, smiling. I wasn't sure, but the voice sounded familiar. "I can't."

I felt his body move closer, giving me a little poke. "I missed you."

I still didn't know who he was. "Tell me more."

I felt his lips on my cheek and then my neck. "I had fun with you earlier. I know you must've had fun too because you forgot your necklaces."

I shrieked with delight, turning around, hugging him. "Gabriel!"

He grinned, hugging me back. "Yes. The one and only."

I can't front. I was ecstatic to see him. "I didn't think you were going to show up."

"Of course I was going to come. I wanted to see you." He handed me the beautifully wrapped necklaces. "Can we go somewhere alone?"

"I thought you'd never ask."

I was sure that my cousins and Carl were watching me as I walked hand in hand away from the party with Gabriel. We strolled a few blocks away towards the beach. He sat down on a nearby bench, pulling me onto his lap. "Give me your phone."

I gave it to him and he programed his number and text himself from my phone. "I can't spend much time with you tonight, but I still wanted to come out and see you anyway."

I instantly got an attitude, cutting my eyes at him. "But you invited me to this party. And now, you're going to bail?"

"I know I did. And I'm sorry for that. I forgot about a prior commitment that I must keep."

I pouted. “That’s cool.” I put my phone away, easing off of his lap. “Take care.”

“Wait! Where are you going?”

“Back to the party to have some fun.” Gabriel wasn’t my man. This was just sex. I already knew this when we sexed the first time.

“Don’t go.” Gabriel caught up to me. “Let’s enjoy the little time we do have.”

I stopped walking, turning around towards him. “Don’t do me any favors.”

He pulled me into his arms. His hands were all over me as we kissed. I understood what type of time he wanted. And after being disappointed by Carl’s no dick having ass, I was ready to give him the time he needed. I hid how I really felt. Ready to bust a good nut.

While kissing, he backed me up into total darkness. I found myself behind a large building with his hands all over me. The passion between us was so intense. Reaching under my mini skirt, he slipped his fingers pass my thong. “Mmmm. So wet already.”

Yes I was. Soaked. I couldn’t help it. Gabriel turned me on like no other man could. I felt his manhood against my thigh and then the head was pushing between my pussy lips. Lifting my leg, Gabriel slid right inside of me.

“Aaaaaaaah! Fuck! Your dick feels good.” After that bullshit with Carl, I really appreciated being intimate with Gabriel.

I stood strong on one leg with my arms around his neck, bouncing as hard as I could. His hands were around my waist but they quickly moved to my bottom.

He squeezed my ass, releasing breathy moans in my ear. “I thought about you all day.” Kisses on my neck. “Did you think about me too?”

“Yessssss. Ah! Oh! I did. Ah! Oh!”

Gabriel lifted me up by my ass. My legs locked around his hips. We continue to kiss. I wanted to bounce harder but I couldn’t. He had such a hold on me, controlling the depth of my stroke. Slowly picking me up and slamming me down hard on his dick. The shit felt awesome.

I was near my orgasm. "Damn, you feel good as fuck."

He slapped my ass. "I could see myself spending the rest of my life with someone like you."

I held him, wondering why he was complicating our situation with sentimental shit. "Don't do that."

"Do what?"

"Don't worry about it. Put me down."

With an attitude, he dropped me to my feet. I almost lost my balance. "Really?" I smoothed my skirt out. He got me bent.

"We were just having a good time. What's the big deal?"

I wanted to punch him in the face. "You trying it right now."

"What are you talking about?" he asked with his face all twisted up.

We stared each other down. This man thinks I'm weak. And I was never, ever weak. I held my own. Boldly, I walked away. I didn't even go back to the bench to get my necklaces. Fuck them and him too.

I got back to the private outdoor party in need of a drink. Being so caught up in Gabriel, I only drank half of one motherfucker, and let the other one along with my two shots go to waste. At this moment, I needed every last drop to ease my damn nerves.

Sitting at the bar, I placed the same order with the same bartender and when I went to pay for it, she said the same thing. Carl took care of it. I looked around but I didn't see him anywhere. I held the glass in the air giving him a salute wherever he was, downing both shots.

I was feeling nice bobbing my head to the music. It was banging too. Standing along the side, I continue to sip on my second drink, rocking my hips. I stared at the huge outdoor dance floor and decided to join them, ready to get my party on. Dancing to the beat, I mingled with the crowd of partygoers.

I was in the middle of the jam-packed space twerking my ass off when some guy came up behind me, pulling me towards him. It didn't matter who he was. I wasted no time backing it up, moving my cheeks to the music. Grinding against the mystery man behind me, I popped back and forth rotating my hips, swinging my hair.

When the song said to drop it low, that's what I did. I worked my body down to the ground. Surprisingly, my dance partner hung in there with me. He dropped low and picked up the pace when the music sped up. Turning around, I was super shocked to see who I was throwing my butt against.

"Stoney!"

He grabbed at me, pulling me back to him. "Yeah, don't trip. We're just dancing."

I knew it was wrong, but I couldn't help it. I liked the attention. It felt good. Flash backs of him naked filled my thoughts again. Closing my eyes, I slid my hand down to his crotch.

"What if I don't want to just dance?"

When Stoney leaned down to answer me, I kissed him. He pulled away, but I was relentless. I squeezed his dick though his shorts with my tongue in his mouth. He resisted for a moment before he gave in. I knew he would. He was such a good kisser. I could only imagine how good his dick felt.

"Fuck me," I whispered, moving his hands to my ass.

He took in a handful before he backed away from me. "Damn, I can't."

"You can't? Or you don't want to?"

"I don't know."

I moved in close again, kissing his lips, grinding up on him. I know he wanted me. I'm sure if I wasn't liquored up I would have never been this bold. And I'm sure if he was more liquored up, he wouldn't be questioning the idea.

Turning back around, I threw my butt up against him, shaking what my Mama gave me. Taking his hands into mine, I put his arms around me, rubbing my backside all over him.

He gripped my hips, pumping all up on me. His thrusts were turning me on. I rolled my ass even more, loving the horny feeling I got. Between the scorching Bahamian heat, the sensual island music, the strong drinks, and his skillful dance moves, I was more than turned up. I wanted him to fuck me right where we stood.

I faced him again. "What are you waiting for? It's obvious that you want me."

I could tell he was considering it when Marcel walked up. "I've been looking everywhere for you. We're about to leave. Are you staying?" He glanced at me. I couldn't tell if he suspected something or not.

Stoney looked at me for a minute. "Give me a second."

Marcel eyed me again and then nodded his head at Stoney. "A second. That's it."

"So, what's up?" I asked Stoney when Marcel walked away. "We about to do this or what?"

He looked me up and down. I guess contemplating what I said. "Later."

What the fuck was that? I rolled my eyes at him as he left. All these men were getting on my damn nerves. Fuck him too. I went back to swaying to the music, enjoying myself. This bullshit wasn't about to cramp my style.

I moved out of the center, making my way to what looked like a stage. It was elevated a little higher than the main dance area. There were already some women up there dancing. I joined in with them popping to the music. They moved their bodies in a sexy manner. I did too. Booty popping and seductively eye-fucking anyone who watched. Showing off the Caribbean dance moves I just learned.

The music slowed down to a sensual tempo. This sexy chocolate brother came up behind me holding my waist, grinding behind me. He was a really good dancer. I tried to shake him a few times with my moves and he switched it up and rocked with me. I found that very sexy. A man who danced well, fucked well.

Out of nowhere, Juicy appeared next to me dutty wining. Shaking her body like her mother was Jamaican. She was dancing better than some of the island girls who were showing off their expert booty skills. Juicy turned around, sticking out her donk, shaking her cheeks real fast like the strippers do. We called it the tidal wave because that's what it looked like under her clothes. The rippling booty effect.

Between me and Juicy, we shut that whole fuckin stage down. Nothing against the girls that were up here getting it, but we stole the show. People came off the floor up where we were, joining us. After a while, it got so crowded that we could barely move.

"Fuck this," Juicy said, wiping sweat from her face with a napkin. "I feel like we've been bum-rushed."

I cracked up. "Why you stupid?"

She laughed too. "I'm thirsty as hell."

"Let's go to the bar. I got an open tab thanks to Carl."

"That's what the fuck is up. Let me go and get Joss and 'em."

We were chilling at the bar with drinks on Carl. I was shocked to see even pregnant Cookie was still out hanging too. She didn't look beat either.

"You been dancing too?"

"Don't no baby stop my show. I still gets it in." She turned around, popping her booty to the floor. She popped back up and then started twerking, swinging her hair from side to side to the beat of the music. "You better ask somebody."

Joss cracked up. "Bitch! She shut your ass the fuck up, didn't she?"

I smiled. "Sho'll the fuck did."

"And I bet you won't be talking out the side of your neck like that again, will you?"

I was rolling. "Hell naw. I ain't never seen no pregnant woman drop it like it's hot before." I high-fived Cookie. "My bad. You did that shit. I'll never doubt you again."

She giggled. "Cuz I'm a bad bitch."

Shay was sitting on a stool bobbing her head to the music. "We need to get together and have girl talk before we leave. You know, bond and shit."

"You just being nosey, bitch," Joss said.

"Just like your ass, Joss."

"Damn right. I want to know all the details. Spill that shit."

Cookie took a seat between Juicy and Shay, sipping on a virgin Daiquiri. "We can do it day after tomorrow. You know tomorrow is family day. We're all going to the beach to hang out together."

"That should be nice," Juicy said. "I haven't seen some people since we got here. This island ain't that damn big."

Cookie nodded her head. "Right. That's why Vanity said we were going to spend the day together as a family."

I stood, waving the bartender over. We needed another round. When she came over, I told her to keep the drinks flowing. She nodded and did just that. As soon as our glasses were empty, another round was on the way. I'm sure that tab was outrageous, but I didn't give a fuck. That was Carl's problem, not mine.

My cousins and I drank until the party was over. By the time we rolled out, everyone was super fucked up, except for Cookie, of course. If it wasn't for her, I'm sure we wouldn't have made it back to the hotel. She's the one that called the cab.

I was super tore up. Singing and staggering down the hall, mistakenly, I went to the wrong hotel room. I was standing there putting my key card in over and over, wondering why the shit wouldn't unlock. For the life of me, I couldn't figure out why. Finally, I focused on the room number and realized I was on the wrong damn floor. After going into a laughing fit, I made my way to my room.

I thought I saw someone. Even though, it was dark as shit. "Vanity!" I yelled. "Is your ass in here?"

When she didn't respond, I assumed she was getting some good dick across the hall from Stoney. Just to be sure, I shuffled across the hall, putting my ear to Stoney's door. Sure enough, I could hear her screaming with passion. He must've been beating it up too cuz she was wearing her lungs out.

"Must be nice," I mumbled, staggering back inside my room.

In need of a serious shower, I practically ripped my clothes off and jumped in. I washed quickly making sure I cleaned myself good before I hopped out. I was tired. Still horny but tired nonetheless. I didn't have the energy to go back out and find someone to fuck. If Marcel hadn't cock blocked, I would be across the hall getting my back blew out and Vanity would be over here sleeping.

After I lotion myself down, I climbed into bed wearing just my smooth skin. My head laid comfortably on the fluffy pillow. The satin sheet over my body. The air was still on so it was nice and chill. Closing my eyes, I drifted off into a drunken sleep.

I felt someone get in the bed with me, parting my legs wide, giving me slow, sensual licks. I couldn't tell if I was dreaming or not. The shit felt real if I was dreaming. And I had no intention of trying to wake up. I was going to nut even if it was in my sleep.

He palmed my ass, holding my vagina up like it was a platter, savoring the taste. I heard him moaning as he used his tongue and lips to give me sheer pleasure. His hands were no longer underneath me. They were touching me everywhere. I lost it, throwing my pussy at his face until I came. It felt like the best cum ever. I'm sure being inebriated put extra emphasis on this experience.

He kept licking as if he was addicted to my scent, alternating between sucking my clit and sticking his tongue inside of me. I was too out of it to move. Otherwise I would ride his face.

My body shivered. I knew I was about to cum again. He was skillfully licking the shit out of my pussy forcing me to climax. Sticking two fingers inside of me, he took my orgasm to the next level, pressing down on my g-spot. Cum leaked out like a running faucet while my body quaked against the bed.

Realizing that I wasn't dreaming, I wondered who was in my bed with me. It was pitch black. I couldn't see shit. He climbed on top of me, kissing me. This man was inches away from my face and I still couldn't see a damn thing. All I could do was use my other senses. Great kisser. Smelled delicious. Body rocked up. Firm ass. That's always a good thing. No loose booties over here.

Still, I had no idea who he was. Something tells me that I knew him. And the way he licked me, told me, that he was familiar with my treasure too. Enjoying the moment, I quit trying to analyze who this man was, delighting in the pleasure. He sucked my breast eagerly while poking his dick inside of me.

When he entered me, it was different. I could tell that he wasn't that big, but he was pretty thick, stretching my pussy wide, brushing against my spot. His thrusts weren't deep. They were shallow and deliberately slow, teasing the opening of my vagina.

Chip did something similar but his dick was so big, it didn't feel the same. This felt like his dick was taking short breaths on my coochie. He had my pussy panting. Each time he withdrew his penis, it automatically contracted, giving me involuntary spasms.

Whoever this was definitely had great control and a master level of dick control. Instead of fucking the shit out of me, he was teasing me to the point of a very powerful orgasm, making me live in the moment. I had no choice but to endure the buildup and wait for my reward later. Each stroke got me one step closer to the orgasmic hill we were climbing.

I was nearly begging for the dick when I came. My body stiffened like a board. The ripples started in my vagina and shot down to my toes back up to my vagina to my breasts back down to my vagina and then I felt enormous pleasure on my clit, my opening, and my anus. It felt like I had been pleasured in all three places at the same time.

My lover laid on top of me with his dick still inside of me, sucking my breasts. I laid still like a mummy paralyzed with pleasure. When my drawn-out orgasm was finished, he pulled his dick out, groaned, and shot sperm all over my stomach.

After wiping the cum off, he flipped me over on my stomach, ready for round two. I felt oil being rubbed on my back and ass as he massaged my body. His hands traveled from my shoulders, down my back, to the crack of my ass. His hands dipped between my cheeks, caressing the forbidden area. My pussy perked up immediately.

He was still kneading my ass when I passed out.

Chapter 15

Pebbles

Squinting my eyes, I blinked several times before I could open them. I lifted my head off the pillow and quickly regretted it. Strangely, I didn't have a hangover, but I was slightly dizzy. I would take that feeling any day over a splitting headache and vomiting. Been down that road several times.

Something was different about how I felt this time. If I didn't know any better, I'd say that I'd was drugged.

Stretching, I finally rolled over on my side to see the mystery man who sexed me last night. The dude was sound asleep with his back towards me. I couldn't wait to see who my lover was. Leaning over his body, I peeked at his face. I wheezed when I saw it was no dick having Carl. Truly, I wasn't expecting to see him. What was this nicca doing in my bed? In the back of my mind, I thought it was Gabriel, trying to get back in my good graces.

I guess Carl proved me wrong, making me cum with his baby dick. Just to be sure that was the same tiny appendage that I saw on the boat, I raised the covers, peeking at it. How did he do all that with such a small dick?

I can't even front, he handled his business. I wouldn't have believed it if I hadn't experienced it myself, but then again I was fucked up. Everything feels better when I'm drunk. There's a possibility that I might not have enjoyed him as much if I was sober.

Wait a minute. It just dawned on me that Carl must've been hiding in my damn room like a stalker. How did he get in though? I know I didn't let him in. And I know for damn sure Vanity didn't. Even if I wanted to change my mind and give him a chance, that bold ass move that he just pulled got me salty as fuck. The fact that he thought my coochie belonged to him really put me on swole. Creeping in this piece like a pussy burglar.

I shoved his ass, hard. "Get up, Carl. You gotta go."

He stretched, looking puzzled. I guess I must've startled him. Too damn bad. He had to go. He glared at me for a hot second and then closed his eyes going back to sleep.

Aww hell naw. I punched his ass even harder. "You gotta get the fuck up and get the hell out. I got shit to do."

He stretched again. "I was hoping you could spend the day with me."

I snaked my neck back, looking at him with the nastiest frown I could muster. I know he didn't just ask me that after what he did last night? "Um, ain't no damn way. I'm busy. And my sister will be here any minute. You need to roll out. Now!"

Finally, he got up and got dressed. "Call me later."

I was still looking at him sideways. Ain't no way in this lifetime I was calling his ass. He fucked that all up. I just wanted to see his ass go. I walked him to the door. He leaned in trying to kiss me. I turned my head. His kiss landed on my chin. I was hoping he didn't make contact at all.

"Later, my love."

I slammed the door right in his face. Delusional ass!

I kicked Carl out just in time. Literally, a few minutes later, Vanity was walking through the door. I was sitting on the floor trying to figure out what I was going to wear.

"Hey, Sissy Pooh. Where you been?" She had a glow about her. I guess that's what fucking Stoney will do.

She collapsed across her bed. "Hey, Sissy."

"You look drained." I giggled because she looked like she hadn't gotten a wink last night. "Stoney beat it up really good, huh?"

She was still sprawled out on the bed. "Girl! You don't even know. He stays all over me, like he can't get enough." She stared off, smiling.

I'll bet. I'm dying to find out.

She broke out of her trance. "I swear he got that Zulu dick."

"Zulu dick? I don't follow."

"Yeah, like the magician. His dick works magic."

We both laughed.

I was still digging through my clothes trying to figure out what to wear. "He got you sprung."

"Naw, I'm not sprung." I gave her a knowing look. "Ok, maybe I am sprung. Just a little though. It's hard not to be. That man is truly blessed in the bedroom."

"Oh, yeah, you're definitely sprung."

We laughed again.

"So what are you going to do about Stoney when we leave?"

Vanity sighed. "Nothing. We're done once this vacation is over."

"I mean you're not going to see him at all?"

"I don't have any plans to. Besides, he has a fiancée. And I love Ivan. I still want my marriage to work."

"So, Stoney is just something to do right now? I thought you were feeling him."

"I am, but he's still vacation booty. That's it."

"You're lying."

"I'm not."

"I hear what you're saying, but he's all over you and you're all over him. It looks like something more. Y'all act like a couple. "

"Let me make it clear for you. He's not my man. We're just fucking. That's all." Vanity rolled over on her back, looking at me. "I mean there does seem to be this crazy chemistry between us. But I have no intentions of leaving Ivan."

"So would you be mad if he fucked someone else, like a family member? Let's be real. Stoney is mad fine. Women are going to want a piece of that sexy dick. You can't keep him all to yourself if you're not claiming him." I was just curious to see what she was going to say since I nearly fucked him last night.

She laughed. "Now, you sound like Stoney." My ears really perked up when she said that. "He asked me the same thing. And I told him it's his business. I don't care who he fucks with. Just make time for me. I don't need to know nothing else."

"Was this before he fucked you delirious? Or afterwards?"

She threw her decorative pillow at me. "Before, but I meant what I said."

"Are you sure? Cuz if he's putting it down like that, it's going to be hard not to catch feelings."

She smiled. "Girl, I'm good."

"So, if you found out that Stoney was fucking someone else on this trip, let's say it was Shay, you wouldn't trip?"

"You asked me that already. Plus, Shay is not his type."

"I know. I just want to be sure that you're sure. That you're really hearing what you're saying."

"Listen, the only way I would even think about being with Stoney on that level is if Ivan didn't want me no more. That man is my heart. If for some reason I lost Ivan, I would definitely want to be with Stoney. No doubt about that."

I finally found something to wear. "Yeah, I know you love Ivan."

"Just like I know how much you love Chip."

"Don't go there. Chip is an asshole."

Vanity got up off the bed, sitting in the chair by me, opening her suitcase. "Ok, I won't. But we both know the truth. You love that man with all of your heart. I think that's why you settle for just getting dick instead of a relationship. You're still hurt because of what Chip did. People make mistakes, Peb. You need to give him another chance."

Fuck what she's talking about. "What you wearing?" I asked changing the subject.

"I don't know." She shifted some things around in the suitcase. "Well, I know I need my swimsuit. I have three of them and I can't find neither one of the damn things."

I laughed. “I was thinking the same thing. I’m just going to wear my bikini and a cover-up. Hell, we going to the beach.”

“I think I’m going to bite your idea. I don’t have the brain power to think of anything else.”

By the time we got ourselves together, it was time to go.

Walking out of our room, we saw Stoney. He made his way between us, putting his arm around both of us. He kissed Vanity on the cheek and then me. “My two favorite women.”

“Is that right?” I asked. Wow, he smelled good.

“Oh, I don’t make mistakes.”

We all laughed.

“Ok, Suave.” I said.

He kept his arm around both of us as we walked through the hotel lobby towards the waiting vans.

“We should do a threesome.” He gave me a seductive look, moving his hand down to my butt.

Vanity sucked her teeth. “That’s all y’all men think about. Sexing more than one woman. That’s so lame.”

“A man can dream, right?”

“Ugh, I’m so sick of hearing that shit though.” She moved his arm off of her, but I stayed, loving his attention.

“C’mere, you don’t think I can hang?” He chuckled. I could tell he like pushing Vanity’s buttons.

“It ain’t even about that. I know you can.”

“What’s up, then?”

She rolled her eyes, looking at her phone.

“Forget you then,” he said, turning towards me, putting both arms around me.

I wanted to push him off of me, but I liked it. I was so weak for this man. He had me yearning to be intimate with him. Just being under him had my pussy on ten.

“I’m going to replace your sister with you.” His hands dropped back to my ass, squeezing both cheeks. “Sexy ass.”

Vanity wasn’t paying either one of us any mind. Her face was glued to her phone, texting.

Stoney refused to be ignored. He drug me over to where she was with his arm still around me. "What's up? Why you looking like that? What's wrong?"

"Nothing," she said, pretty much fanning him away as she texted.

"Something's up. I can tell by your face."

She ignored him continuing to text.

"Ok, be like that then. C'mon, Pebbles. We don't have to take this," he said with his arm still around me.

"Hold on." I approached Vanity. She might have shunned him, but she surely wouldn't shun me, her sister. "What's going on?"

She sucked her teeth. "Nothing you would understand."

See here we go with the funky attitude. This is the Vanity that I know. "Don't get brand new, trick."

She jumped bad. "Who you calling brand new, trick?"

"You!" I said, holding my own. "You always got a shitty attitude."

"Whoa! Ladies!" Stoney got in the middle of us again. "I can't have my two favorite women, fighting."

"Shut up, Stoney," we said together.

"Get her out of my face," Vanity said to Stoney, talking about me. "I'm not in the mood."

"He don't have to get me. I'll gladly walk away and leave your petty ass in misery. Whatever is bothering you, I hope it bites you in the ass. C'mon, Stoney," I said, putting his arm back around me. "For the rest of this trip, you stay out of my way and I'll say out of yours."

"Fine!"

"Fine!"

For a hot minute, we were getting along like sisters should. Whenever I get too close, she always pushed me away. That's why I'm going to fuck Stoney. For all those times she talked crazy to me and I hadn't done nothing to her.

But this is how Vanity was. One minute she was the best sister ever. And the next minute she was a bitch from hell. It's like she kept PMS all month long. Growing up, we didn't get along. We always fought. I never understood why. I loved my sister, but for some reason she kept a wall up with me. She was cool with everyone else.

Stoney and I boarded the bus, sitting way in the back with the live crew, Juicy and 'em. Originally, this was Vanity's seat, but it was mine now. And I dared her ass to come and take it from me. We would be thumping. Right there on the bus in front of everyone.

I stared Vanity down when she got on. She never even looked my way. I was hoping she would so I could crack her in the head. Avoiding me all together, she sat up front next to Piper. I didn't care because I got what I wanted—Stoney. I placed my hand on his thigh, smiling all in his face. He moved closer, putting his arm around me.

The fleet of buses pulled up at the Hawaiian themed beach. We all filed out to a delightful spread. Four picnic tables worth of food—tossed salad, barbeque, baked beans, potato salad, macaroni salad, Teriyaki beef and chicken, island fried rice, all different types of rolls, pineapple upside down cake, mango cookies, chips and salsa, and a lot more. Single serving containers of wine. Pineapples soaked in rum. Watermelon soaked vodka. Large barrels of pop and water. And my favorite, snow cones.

While we ate, there was a live show performed by the Hula Girls. Juicy and I jumped at the opportunity to show off our hip action when they asked for volunteers. As usual, we nailed it.

After getting our grub on, many of us hit the sand to partake in the activities set up. All the pregnant women with the exception of Cookie were laid out on the beach soaking up sun. Cookie was up and ready to move around, trying to get in where she fit. In true bitch fashion, Vanity had totally distanced herself from everyone, not participating at all, still texting on her phone.

We had a good time running around acting like big kids playing games like Gigantic Twister, building sand castles with mini pails and shovels, ring toss, flying kites, and water dodge ball. Cash got me really good. He lit me up with three balloons back to back, soaking me from head to toe.

After hours of fun, we were all beat.

Some were even sun burned.

I was standing near the shore looking at the seashells when Stoney walked up, asking me to take a stroll with him. We walked much further down away from the family. I guess to be out of eyesight and earshot.

"What's up?" he asked me.

"What's up with what? You asked me to come all the way over here. Evidently, you had something you wanted to say to me."

I gave him major attitude to block how I was really feeling. I was delirious with desire for him. He was looking real appealing. All he had on was a pair of aqua swim trunks, revealing his perfect body. I wanted to tell him meet me somewhere even further away so we could get our freak on.

His piercing eyes stayed on me watching me carefully before he spoke again. "Were you serious about last night?" His eyes slowly scanned my half-naked body. "You asked me to fuck you. Was that you asking? Or was it the liquor?"

I giggled. Wow, he just came right out with it. "What if I said it was both?"

"Both what?" he asked, his eyes searching for clarification.

Really Stoney? What does it matter? "You're not making this easy are you?"

"I thought you liked it hard." He smiled.

"You playing." I needed to get in his head like he got in mine. "You were all up on me last night. I didn't go looking for you. You came looking for me. I was dancing by myself."

He grabbed my hand, dragging me towards the water. "Walk with me."

What's on his mind now? I slowly walked with Stoney deeper into the water. I started to get nervous when the water came up to my shoulders. "Hold up, I can't go any further. You know I'm short. I'm not trying to drown."

"You won't drown. I'm a certified lifeguard. I'll save you."

Damn, what can't this man do? "See, you're trying to distract me."

"No, I'm not. I think you're hot with a cute little attitude to match. I bet you're wild in bed too."

"And? I know there's more. I can see the wheels churning in your head."

"I think we have a lot in common. I think you love to have sex as much as I do. And I think that you are curious to know what I feel like. Am I right?"

"Right on point. Now, here's what I think. I think you are just as curious about me. And I think you've been secretly thinking about sleeping with me too."

"You're right. I have."

"So what do you want from me?"

"I want to sex you like crazy."

Oh! I was ready to give it up right in the water in front of everyone. "What about my sister?"

"What about her? She said that she didn't care who I messed with, including family. That's her exact words. I even posed the scenario if I got with a family member. And she told me that she didn't care. I didn't belong to her. For me to do me. So, that's what I'm doing—me."

"She told me the exact same thing because I asked her too."

"Then, we're all good, beautiful. Nothing to worry about." He reached out for me. "Come a little closer."

I was keeping my distance for a reason. I know what Vanity said, but I got a feeling that's not what she meant. But at the same time, I can only go by her words. We both asked her. She pretty much gave us consent to fuck around. So, she couldn't be mad when she found out I sampled his dick. I just hoped that fooling around with Stoney wasn't going to come back and bite me in the ass.

Floating in the water, I made my way over to him, standing right in front of him. He barely touched me and my bikini top came undone. Gently, he caressed my breasts. "You like kissing?"

"Yes. I'm the one who kissed you last night, remember?"

"True. So, what do you want after this? I'm asking because I want things to be clear."

"I don't know what you're going to do, but I'm moving on to the next nicca. I mean, don't get things twisted. I think you're very handsome, sexy, and I know you can fuck, but I'm not interested in nothing more with you. All I want is some good dick. Is that clear enough for you?"

He grinned and then he chuckled. "Blunt, direct, and to the point. I love it. So, you're using me for my manhood?"

"No more than you're using me for my cookie. Hey, let me ask you something. Why do you want to be with me when it's clear that you are really into my sister?"

"Why wouldn't I want you? You look just like her. Now, I get to find out how much."

"Funny you said that because I've always had a crush on Emerald. I guess we both get to pretend."

"I guess we do. We can be each other's fantasy. Let's go in a little deeper."

"How deep do you plan to go? Cuz I'm in pretty deep. You must want the water over my head."

"Actually, I do. I need the water up to my chin." He thought for a minute. "I'll have to carry you."

If this had been any other dude, I would have been on my way back to the other side of the beach. Since it was sexy ass Stoney, I gave him a pass. Straight up, if shit went wrong, and for some odd reason I was up to my eyeballs with water, I was going to kill him when I made it back to shore.

He picked me up carrying me further into the water like Hercules. I held on tight with my legs locked around his waist and my arms around his neck as the ocean blue water surrounded us. We were far enough away. Nobody was going to see what was going on. But even if they did, his back was facing them. I'm quite sure they couldn't even see me.

"Ok, now what?" I asked.

"Leave the rest up to me."

His swollen dick pressed in between my legs. I could feel it throbbing through my bikini bottoms as I welcomed his tongue in my mouth.

"You're shivering. Are you scared?"

I was about to lie, but I was shaking so bad that I couldn't. "Yes. As bad as I want you, and trust me I want you in the worst way, I can't help but feel like I shouldn't. Like this isn't the right time or something. Plus, this water thing got me feeling some kinda way too."

He held me tighter. "We don't have to do this. I respect your decision if you want to say no. We can go back and join the others like nothing ever happened." He kissed me again. "Ok, pretty?"

How could I be afraid while in the arms of this sexy, strong man? What the hell was wrong with me? I've been longing for this moment. I stared into his eyes. "I want to. I just—" I happen to look to my left and saw Marcel walking in our direction. "Fuck! Here comes Marcel. I knew this shit was a bad idea."

Stoney casually turned around and looked. "Don't trip. It's cool. If he asks what we were doing, just say I was teaching you how to swim, and you got scared. You're already shivering. Sounds believable."

I fixed my bikini top. "I don't know whether to be impressed with how quick you thought of that lie or to be disgusted."

None of this shit felt right. I didn't like lying. Not if I didn't have to. Stoney carried me back into shallow water. He put me down as soon as I could walk and we met Marcel half way in his journey toward us.

Marcel gave that same inquisitive look from the night before, eyeing Stoney and then me again. "What y'all doing all the way out here, alone?"

Stoney looked Marcel right in the face and lied. "Swimming."

Marcel stared at Stoney as if he knew he was telling a lie. "Swimming?"

"Yeah," Stoney said coolly.

"Ok," Marcel said, finally buying the lie. I think. "Everyone's ready to leave."

"Alright. We're ready too."

Stoney began walking back to shore. As I was about to follow behind him, Marcel yanked me back. He waited until Stoney walked far away from us before he spoke to me. “So, what were you really doing all the way out there?”

All of a sudden, the Bahama heat seemed a lot hotter since I was being grilled by Marcel. “Swimming. Just like he said.”

“I heard what he said, but I know what I saw. That didn’t look like swimming to me. Did you have sex with him?”

“No.” I kept a straight face, trying to keep it cool like Stoney did. However, I was getting the bubble guts standing here under Marcel’s watchful eye.

“I’m not sold on that story, Pebbles. But if that’s the lie that you and Stoney agreed to, then so be it. But let me warn you, stay away from him.”

“I thought he was like a brother to you. Why wouldn’t you want me to spend time with him?”

“Stoney is like my brother. And that means I know him a lot better than you do. He has enough bullshit in his life.”

“Are you calling me bullshit?”

Marcel chuckled. “Nah, never that. Just saying, temptation can be a bitch. One lustful situation can change your life forever. I’m speaking from experience.”

“I hear you, Marcel. There’s nothing for you to be concerned about. I can handle myself.”

“You know you’re like my baby sister. And just like I know him, I know you. Stoney isn’t your type.”

“I don’t want him as my man.” Marcel hugged me, kissing my cheeks just like when I was younger. “Why do you and Cash always do that?”

“Because we love you.”

“Well, y’all need to find another way to show it.”

He pinched my cheeks. “You owe me when we get back. I didn’t forget about you babysitting.”

“Oh, yeah, I forgot about that.” No I didn’t. His kids were bad as fuck. Well, not so much bad. They were really spoiled. Cutest kids ever but their looks could be deceiving. “I’ll hit you up about that later.”

"I won't let you forget. They've been asking about you. And you know I don't let anyone disappoint my kids."

Everyone was packed up and ready to roll out by the time Marcel and I made it back. Just to avoid the controversy, I didn't even ride on the same bus as Stoney. That didn't stop him from whispering in my ear as he walked pass. "Come to my room as soon as we get back."

I looked at him over my shoulder. He looked back at me, winking before getting on bus two.

Once we arrived back at the hotel, I lagged behind cracking jokes with Juicy and Joss while Stoney walked ahead. I heard everything Marcel said. However, the yearning to fuck spoke louder. No matter how far I kept my distance, I'd made up my mind that I was going straight to Stoney's room.

Before I went across the hall, I decided to shower the sand off and change. I expected to see Vanity. She wasn't there. That's good because I didn't feel like dealing with her no way. Pulling off my cover-up and bikini, I hopped in the shower, thinking about Stoney. I would have loved to get busy with him in the ocean. I regret being scared. That would have been a luscious experience.

Racing over to my bed, I put on scented lotion, dried my hair and twisted it up with a hairpin. Then, I reached in my suitcase and pulled out a spandex mini dress. I didn't even bother with bra and panties. They would just get in the way. Opening the hotel door, I peeked out, cautiously looking both ways, before I dashed across the hall, tapping on Stoney's door.

"What took you so long?" he asked, opening the door wearing just a towel. I could tell he was fresh out of the shower too.

I walked in. "Don't you look in the mood?"

"And this is coming from a woman who has nothing on under a dress that looks like a stocking."

I cracked up. "You're a goof."

"Takes one to know one."

I walked up to him, snatching the towel off his rock hard body. "I'm not shaking now." I took his thick tool in my hand, stroking it.

He grinned. "Aggressive. I like that."

Removing my hand, he pulled down the straps of my slinky dress, sliding it down my body to the floor so I would be nude too. Grabbing my ass, he elevated my body and I locked my legs around his waist, sealing his lips with a kiss. He laid back on the bed with me on top of him. I arched my back and spread my legs wide, hoping that he would slide right in.

"Fuck me," I begged.

"Slow down, hot ass. There's no rush."

That's what he thought. I had a strange feeling that someone was about to be on his door any minute. If we didn't get it on ASAP it wasn't going to happen.

I moaned when his hand glided between my legs, grazing my clit. I humped against it. "Give it to me, Stoney, damn."

Lying underneath me, he smiled. "I like to hear you beg. You sound so sexy. It really turns me on."

This man was driving me crazy. "If you don't give me your dick, I'm going to take it."

He chuckled like it was the funniest thing in the world before flipping me onto my back, crawling between my legs. "You're going to take what?" Kissing me, his dick rested in my fleshy folds. Every time he moved, his hard tool slid up and down my wet pussy, teasing me even more.

"Put it in," I moaned. "Please."

Taking his dick in his right hand, he positioned the head at the opening of my vagina about to put it in when there was a knock at the door. Stoney dropped his dick, looking back at the door.

"Ignore whoever that is. Just put it in," I panted, lifting my pelvis towards him.

Stoney resumed the position when his phone started buzzing, singing a loud tune. And whoever it was, they were still on the door knocking.

"Stoney! I need to talk to you," Vanity said. "I know you're in there. Open up. Please."

We both froze. He looked at me. I looked at him. We both looked at the door.

My gut said it wasn't going to happen if we didn't hurry up. Sure enough, I was right. "Well, I'm not in the mood anymore."

"Me either," he said, even though his dick was hard as steel.

My sister was adamant about getting in his room. "Please Stoney! Just open the door. I need to talk to you."

"So, what are we going to do?" I asked him.

Stoney climbed off of me, handing me my dress. "Put it back on and get behind the door. When I let her in, I'll distract her and you can leave unnoticed."

"Ok," I said, agreeing to this dumb ass plan.

This was the stupidest shit I ever heard. We're about to get caught. I don't even know why I was tripping. Vanity said she didn't care. This is clearly a damn lie because she was on the other side of his door. Getting in the way of me getting my fuck on.

I was totally shocked when his plan worked like a charm. He opened the door. Vanity came in. She was visibly upset. I didn't know what her problem was. I didn't care. I tried to talk to her earlier. She dissed me. Fuck her. He swiftly turned her back to me and I slipped out the door just like he said, unseen.

Chapter 16

Pebbles

Juicy and I stepped towards the pool in our fuck me pumps and designer bikinis. Our strut left the onlookers of men and women wondering who we were. A few of them even tried to holler. Neither one of us bothered lifting our expensive oversized shades. None of them were worth our time. And just so they knew, we walked around the pool the long way passing by them as if they were beneath us.

"If y'all don't stop that Hollywood shit," Shay said, splashing water on us. We always became Hollywood whenever Shay thought we were acting brand new.

Juicy and I struck a super-model pose while laughing.

"Hating ain't never cute," Juicy said, finally taking off her shades and pumps. She put a swim cap on and jumped in the pool. "This water feels good. It's hotter than a bitch out here."

I copped a squat in a lawn chair, stretching out poolside.

"Um, diva, are you going to join us?"

I didn't even bother budging. "In a bit, Shay. I want to soak up some sun for a minute."

She waved me off. "Hollywood ass."

I was in deep thought as the sun beat down on me. The heat felt good on my skin, like the sun was making love to me. Laying here with such a sweet burn resonated with my libido causing my sex drive to kick into high gear. Being in the sun always made me horny. Behind my shades, my eyes were closed as my hands slowly travel down to my vagina ready to rub my clit. I guess it's time to get in the pool and cool off before I embarrass myself.

"Glad you could join us, bitch," Joss said, sitting lovely on a float with curly hair flowing down her back. She was glamourous as all ways, wearing a new bikini and matching cover-up with sexy beach heels that one of her new boo's bought her.

"I just needed a moment in the sun. Y'all know how much I love it."

Cookie floated over to me. "Wasn't nobody trying to disturb your groove."

"Yes, we were too," Shay said, cutting Cookie off. "Heffa, I need to know all about that sexy man you were at the bar with the other night. What's his name?"

"Who?" I said, trying to remember who the hell she was talking about. I barely remember yesterday and she's talking about the day before.

Shay snapped her fingers at me. "What's his name? Damn. Um, um, you said what his name was when we were talking about Carl's no dick having ass."

I sucked my teeth when she said Carl's name. "Ugh! Just thinking about him gave me a headache. If I never saw him again, it would be too soon."

I replayed that night with Carl over and over again in my mind. I couldn't get over the fact that he was waiting in my room like a maniac. Then to make matters worse, I'm not sure what he did to me after I passed out. I felt a little funny when I woke up. And I still think I was drugged. I just can't prove it.

Juicy twisted her face. "Man, ain't nobody talking about that little dick nicca. Don't even bring his ass up again."

I nodded. "Thank you, Juicy." I thought for a moment, trying to remember who Shay was talking about. Then it hit me. She was talking about Gabriel. Another fuckin sore spot. "Oh, you want to know about Gabriel. There's nothing to tell."

"So, you haven't gotten up on that yet? Cuz that man was fione I would have fucked him all over this island if I was you."

I wasn't ready to talk about Gabriel. I was kinda digging his vibe so I just lied. "Not yet, Shay. Why don't you tell us what's up with you? You the one with island booty on hand. Cuz last I heard before we got here, you were ready to crack Moneaco's skull."

Cookie clipped up her long hair. "Yeah, I want to know too. Cuz y'all looked mighty cozy over these last few days."

We all giggled as Shay grinned. "Well…" She sucked her teeth. "If y'all must know. My boo has definitely made it up to me. Romantic walks on the beach. Candle light dinners. Massages. Buying me things."

"What about the sex?" Juicy asked impatiently. "That's what the fuck we wanna know. Did he eat your coochie good? Did you bust three or four nuts back to back? Tell us the good shit."

Everyone cracked up laughing.

I just looked at Juicy and laughed some more. "You don't have no tact."

"I just don't give a shit." She shrugged her shoulders. "Y'all know that's what y'all wanted to know too. Stop playing."

We laughed again.

"True," I cosigned. "So did he, Shay?"

Shay smiled, covering her mouth with her hand in a dramatic way, like she was acting on stage somewhere. "Ok, ok, since you heffas are twisting my arm." She gave an overly dramatic sigh. "I have to say, that um, the dick was BOMB DIGGITY BITCHES!"

Joss clapped her hands. "Bravo, bitch, bravo. And the award for most dramatic actress while on vacation goes to—drum roll please." Everyone patted themselves making a drum beat. "Shayla!"

Shay stood straight up in the water, giving us a Beauty Queen wave as if she was accepting an award. "Thank you, everyone. Thank you so much. I couldn't have done any of this without you. I didn't prepare a speech—"

"Sit your ass down," Cookie said, making us all laugh.

"What's up with you?" I asked Cookie. "You and that young boy really got it in. You couldn't even make it to breakfast with us the next day. And your pregnant ass don't miss no meals."

Cookie cheesed. "Umph. That little boy knows how to work the shit out of his dick. I mean my Travis is the best hands down. But, Scott, oh my God!" Cookie started pumping in the water, demonstrating how well things went with Scott. "And he don't live that far from me. I'm going to talk to Travis and see if we can bring him into our bedroom. I need a new boy toy."

Huh? Ain't no way. "You got that. That's even too freaky for me. I'm not sharing my husband with nobody."

Juicy snaked her neck. "Shoooot. I could."

"Whaaaaat? You got your freak on too?" Shay asked Cookie with her mouth hanging open.

"Bitch! Close your mouth," Joss said to Shay then she spoke to Cookie. "Now, who is this nicca? And why is this the first time I'm hearing about this. I been talking to your ass every day."

Shay agreed." That's what I'm saying."

"Well, me and Juicy already knew cuz she was with us when she met him. We all got some good dick that night." Me and Juicy slapped hands.

"Oh, man," Juicy said, reminiscing. "Dude was right. I'm definitely gonna call him when I get back. I need that type of dick in my life on a regular."

"Y'all heffas always holding out the good shit." Shay stood up, pulling her swimsuit out of her ass.

"Can you be a little more discreet about that? I mean you're digging for gold. All in your ass in front of strangers."

"So! Fuck them. Don't look, shit."

Cookie leaned over to me. "You know she ain't got no damn class. I don't know why you're acting surprised."

I dunked my head underwater and came back up. "You're right. For a second, I forgot. What's up with you, Joss? How you making out?"

"I got me two ballers, hunny." She snapped her fingers at me. "And they doing everything right. I'm going to miss them when we leave. Big spenders with good dick is hard to find."

We all saluted to that.

I got out of the water and grabbed one of the rafts on the side. I wanted to sit pretty too. "Joss, you are going to have to stop saying bitch all the time. Ladies don't talk like that. And Shay, you just need some class. I don't know how you're going to get it. Buy it if you have too, but that's why you can't keep a good man. They think you're crazy."

Joss rolled her eyes. "And bitch…I mean, girl, what do you need? Don't make it seem like everything is wrong with us."

"Yeah, cuz I have class." Shay was obviously offended by what I said. "I just forget to use it sometimes."

I pondered the question. I loved my cousins but I wasn't about to tell them my issues. I'd never hear the end of them talking about it. "I know I'm not perfect. I got plenty of issues, but I'm working on them. Can y'all say the same?"

Juicy squeezed her little butt up on my raft. "I know my issues, but I'm not trying to change right now. I like being flawed."

I just looked at her ass like she was retarded.

Cookie chimed in. "Well, my baby married me knowing I like to fuck other men. And he's cool with that cuz I let him fuck other women," Cookie gloated. "We have the perfect marriage. It's ok for us to cheat and I love it."

Shay sucked her teeth. "And I'm fucked up, right? Sheeeeeit." We rolled laughing. "That shit right there that Cookie just said, now that's fucked up."

I laughed so hard at Shay going in on Cookie and her open marriage that my side hurt.

Lying in the sun chit chatting with my cousins was a nice way to kick off my morning. Now, I was ready to be under a man. I needed a nut badly. Since I couldn't get any dick at the moment, I decided to excuse myself and go handle the itch.

As soon as I got out the pool and grabbed my stuff, three dudes approached me, trying to holler. I sized them up. None of them were my type. I liked to fuck but I didn't fuck just anybody. I liked handsome, sexy men. Preferably with money. I politely turned them all down and raced towards my room. I'm sure I looked like I had to pee by the way I was jogging. As I was about to go inside, Stoney yanked me by the arm across the hall, pulling me inside of his room instead.

He sat on the bed with my wet body in his lap. "Where are you coming from?"

I know he's not trying to check me like he's my man. "Why?" I asked, giving him major attitude.

His hand rested on my thigh. "Because I asked you nicely." He flashed me a winning smile that was contagious.

I found myself smiling too. "What do you want, Stoney? I'm trying my best to avoid you."

His eyes dropped to my breasts. "Yeah, see, that's the thing. I don't want you avoiding me."

I tried to ease off his lap, but he held me in place. "Why won't you let me go?"

His finger traced my lips. "You're even sexier when you get upset."

I wasn't really upset. I was just sexually frustrated. There's a difference. "Look, I'm not upset, ok? Actually, I like you—"

He kissed my neck with his hand moving up my thigh towards my vagina. "I like you too, sexy. You really turn me on."

Aaaaah, that feels good. Before I knew it, I opened my legs wider. "Naw, I can't go there with you. I can't do the sneaking around thing. That's never been my style."

Doing a wrestling move, he flipped me onto my back, crawling between my legs. He had me in a compromising position. His kisses were succulent.

"Stoney, stop," I said in a weak voice. I was way too horny to keep protesting.

"Shhhhh." He kissed me, shutting me up. His fingers rubbed between my legs. I nearly came. "I can tell you're in heat."

My heart was beating fast. How'd he know that? This is the horniest I'd ever been. It felt like someone injected me with a super aphrodisiac. The pinned up desire had me feeling like I had the stamina to fuck for days.

He tapped my box. "I'm going to put that fire out for you. Give it to you like you've never had it before."

"I heard that a million times. Don't hype yourself up." I closed my eyes, loving how he touched me. "Mmmmmm. If you don't show and prove, I'm going to clown your ass." I was steadily talking shit knowing Stoney could back up everything in bed and then some.

"That's never been a problem for me. I always show up and show out. When I'm done, you'll be kissing my ass."

I was sold. That shit sound so damn good. As bad as I needed to nut, I couldn't wait for him to prove me wrong.

Pulling the string to my bikini, he exposed my B cups. After taking my top off, he tossed it across the room. I guess so I couldn't get it so easily. His hands squeezed my boobs intensifying the burn between my legs. The tip of his tongue traced my nipples. Then he gently sucked my perky breasts while undoing my bikini bottoms.

He snatched my bikini bottoms off before he got off me standing on the side of the bed, undressing. After stripping out of his clothes, he came to the edge of the bed, flexing his dick. I always loved it when men did that. It made me think the dick was talking directly to me.

I bit my bottom lip, staring deep into his sex-filled eyes. Nonverbally he was speaking volumes. I got the impression he was just as horny for me as I was for him.

Taking my hand, he wrapped it around his dick, making me stroke it. Sliding my hand up and down his shaft gave me fever. I stood up, ready to feel his big dick inside of me. "Lay down."

"So, you want me to be the bitch, huh?"

"Yes," I said pushing him back on the bed. "Let me fuck this cat."

He scooted back on the bed, lying on his back getting comfortable. His hands were behind his head and his dick pointing at the ceiling. "Come and get it."

I snatched off my bikini bottoms and crawled into the bed ready to attack my prey. Swinging my leg over his pelvis, I positioned my vagina just right, sliding down on his rigid pole.

"Aaaaah! Fuck!" I yelled, holding my tits in my hands, bouncing quick and fast.

I closed my eyes concentrating on how unbelievable his dick felt. He did know magic. I was only humping for about a minute before I came. I fell forward onto Stoney's chest, enjoying my orgasm.

Quickly recovering, I was ready for more. Moving my knees apart, I planted my hands on his stomach ready to tackle his monster again. I closed my eyes again loving how deep he was, bouncing once again. I couldn't believe his dick was this good. I lasted approximately two minutes before I was falling forward trembling again.

I got back up for a third round. I was determined to ride his dick and not cum so fast. Changing positions, I turned around reverse cowgirl, hopping on like it was a bull. Working my ass in the air, I bounced until I came three minutes later.

I planted my feet on his thighs and stretched my hands behind me on his chest, sliding up and down. After five minutes, Stoney touched my clit and my body shook. I fell back on him skeeting cum in the air.

"Now, let me fuck this cat," he said, still inside of me. Stoney flipped me onto my stomach, ramming into me from behind, making me a slave to his dick.

My body stayed in an orgasmic state. With each stroke I had another mini orgasm.

"You still doubting my skills?" he asked grabbing a fist full of my wild hair.

"No! Oh my God! No!" I gripped the bed sheet as another big O came.

"Say my name!" He reached under me, rubbing my clit. "Say it!"

"Stoney! Stoney! Stoney! Stoooooooney!" I cried out, cumming for the umpteenth time.

"Whose pussy is this?"

"Yours!" I screamed still hypnotized by his dick. "It's yours. All yours. Just don't stop. Oh my God, don't stop." The shit was so fuckin good if he asked me to swallow my own tongue I probably would have tried.

Slowing down his thrusts, he locked his hands with mine, tongue kissing me with shallow thrusts, giving me back-to-back orgasms.

"Damn, you got some good, tight pussy." I felt Stoney's body vibrate on top of me. Then he pulled out and shot sperm all over my ass. "Don't move."

He got out of the bed and came back with a wet towel, wiping the cum off. I was so out of it that I would have laid right here with a cum-stained ass.

He climbed back in bed, lying on his side. Reaching over him, I puckered my lips and literally kissed his bare ass like he said I would. "Mwah! You did that shit. Your dick is bomb."

We looked at each other and laughed.

"C'mere, sexy." He pulled me under the sheet with him, snuggling me tight. "I enjoyed you too."

I smiled running my fingernails lightly up and down his arm that was around me. "I'm speechless. I don't even know what to call what you did to me. I think you invented sex."

He started singing the song, sounding better than the original track. Wow, his voice was beautiful.

"Listen, your energy is very addictive." He pulled away from me. "I'm not going to lie, I could sex you on a regular, but I'm crazy about your sister. She's the one I'm truly feeling. Things might have been different if I was with you first. I don't know. I just don't want things to be awkward between us."

"Boy, bye. I'm not checking for you either. I got my eye on someone else." Fuck he thought.

"As long as you know what we're doing."

"Stop feeling yourself. You ain't the only dick around. I wouldn't dare catch feelings for your ass. You're not my type."

"Good. Cuz I plan on hitting it again."

I didn't disagree when Stoney rolled me onto my stomach, pounding me hard and fast from behind once again.

Chapter 17

Vanity

I was having a really bad day. It started yesterday with a text war with Ivan's insecure ass. The longer I stay in the Bahamas the crazier he seemed to get. At this point, I don't know if our relationship is repairable. I'm willing to try and salvage things, but it takes two. I shouldn't have to run to Stoney for comfort because Ivan was being a dick head. If Ivan kept on being an ass, I might reconsider Stoney's offer. Just pack my shit and run off with him.

As I headed out of the hotel room to apologize to Stoney for my erratic behavior, I see Pebbles coming out of his room, fixing her bikini top. I'm no fool I know what just went down. Stoney's sexually charged all day long and so is she. I let it slide when they were all in each other's faces before now, like at the beach. Flirting. That shit was disrespectful as hell. I wasn't going to let this roll off my back. My sister was about to feel my wrath. I was about to show her who's the boss.

Pebbles was smiling and grinning all in Stoney's face. She didn't even see me coming. Without warning, I punched her in the head as soon as she turned around. Before she could recover, I yanked her ass up by her hair, swung her little ass around, tossing her body into the wall. Still enraged, I yoked her man-stealing ass up again, dragging her into the hotel room, kicking and screaming.

Stoney tried to pull me off of her, which infuriated me even more. In my mind, he was taking up for her when he should have been taking up for me. No matter how hard Stoney tried to stop me, I had a dead-lock grip on Pebbles, beating her ass.

"You're always trying to prove that you're better than me," I said, punching her in the face. "You gon learn today.

"Let me go, bitch, and see how many licks you get in. Stop being a sucka and fight fair."

I had Pebbles hemmed up to the point where she couldn't get to me no matter how much she tried. All of her swings caught air.

I'm sure we looked crazy. In the mist of us tussling, Pebbles' bikini came off. She was totally nude and my clothes were tattered, hanging on by threads. At any minute I was going to be naked too.

Butt ass naked and all, Pebbles was still going for hers. And I knew she would. That's why I didn't feel sorry for her and let up. As soon as I did, she was going to make me regret it. The only reason why I was winning was because I caught her off guard. I knew exactly what I was doing. Pebbles was like a boxer when it came to her blows.

Cash, Marcel, Natalia, and Karen appeared out of nowhere, parading into our hotel room.

"Daaaaamn," Cash said, entering our room. "Ass and tits everywhere. I don't know whether to break it up or break out the baby oil. This is a real live chick flick. I mean, fight."

"Shut up man," Stoney said, still trying to get me off of Pebbles. He took a few blows in the process. "Stop watching and help."

Karen and Natalia moved out the way.

Marcel grabbed Pebbles. Cash separated my hands from her hair and throat. Natalia went out in the hall and got her bikini top. She handed it to Marcel. Karen already handed him her bottoms.

Pebbles kept her eyes on me while slipping her bikini back on. Standing right by her suitcase, she reached in and pulled out a fitted romper. Then, she pulled her hair back, braiding it.

Marcel exhaled loudly like we got on his very last nerve. "What is this all about?"

Pebbles acted like she was about to answer him, but faked him out, charging at me instead. She looked like a running back, spinning pass Marcel and moving much faster than Stoney, just to get at me. Diving across the room, she landed on my bed, right on top of me. This time, she caught me off guard. I just knew Marcel had her. I caught two punches in the head. I was pissed because I couldn't even defend myself. She was sitting on my chest like a banshee with my arms pinned under her, using my face as a punching bag.

"I told you, I was going to fuck you up, bitch." She punched me two more times in the face. "Get your fuckin facts straight, I am better than you. Recognize that shit."

Karen and Natalia scattered like two roaches.

Stoney was the first one over to us. He yanked Pebbles off of me. Marcel came running right behind him. It took both of them to contain Pebbles. Cash was in the bathroom. He came out when he heard the commotion. Everything was happening so fast. He just got out of the way, standing off to the side with Karen and Natalia.

Pebbles was wearing them out. She broke free, coming for me once again, knocking us both off the bed onto the floor. That was the break that I needed. I pushed her off of me and started swinging. I missed twice before I connected. It was on and poppin now. We were both out for blood. Going toe to toe. Punch for punch. It was so ridiculous that everyone moved out of the way, letting us duke it out.

We went from tussling on the floor on one side of the room to fighting back to the other side. Finally, we ended up in the bathroom where I was getting the drop on Pebbles because she slipped. I had on shoes. She didn't. Quickly, I kicked her in the ass, stomach, and chest before Marcel snatched me up, like a dude, putting me in a headlock.

"Stop!" he said, hindering me. "I'm sick of this shit."

I was still resisting.

Marcel squeezed tighter. "I suggest you calm your ass down."

I was furious when Stoney came to Pebbles defense, again. Helping her up and then carrying her over to her bed, making sure she was ok. The loving way he touched her really hurt me. All the anger in me towards Pebbles left. Now, I wanted to pluck Stoney's eyes out.

Marcel loosened his grip on me and I slipped out of his embrace. Leaping at Stoney, I was ready to do some major damage. I thought I was going to kick his ass like I did Pebbles. Not the case at all. Stoney caught me in mid-stride. Before I could even touch him, he threw the cover over me. I got all twisted up in it to the point where I almost fell.

"Will you stop it?" Stoney said, holding me tight with the cover still over my head. "All this is uncalled for. Acting like a damn lunatic. You need to chill out. And you—" I assumed he was talking to Pebbles. "Don't bring your ass over here. Marcel get her. Make her sit in that chair over there."

Things were finally quiet.

I couldn't see a thing. Stoney had a strong grip on me. He didn't budge no matter how much I wrestled.

I fought under the cover. "Let me go!"

Stoney held onto me a little too easy. "Slow down, girl, before you choke yourself out." He took the cover off my head, but my body was still wrapped up in it. "You gonna act right?"

My hair was wild as hell. All in my face. I couldn't even see. "Yeah."

"Sit here and think about it for a minute."

I glanced around the room. Pebbles was in a chair diagonal from me, across the room. Marcel was sitting on the arm of the chair, detaining her. Natalia was to my right sitting in a chair by the door. Cash was across Pebbles' bed, chilling. Karen was sitting down by Cash, directly across from me and Stoney.

Marcel looked thoroughly pissed the fuck off. "We have to fix this. I can't have all this negative energy in my space." He stood to his feet and then looked back at Pebbles. "Don't get your ass up. I'm not playing with you." He took his belt off. "I'ma give you a good old fashion ass whooping"

Pebbles smacked her lips, picking up her phone. "I ain't going to try you."

He waved the belt in her face. "You better not. Cuz I'm done being a stuntman. I'm ready to inflict some pain, nah mean?" He cracked the belt right in front of her.

"Ok, Marcel, I heard you. I'm staying in my seat. Dang. Always trying to scare somebody."

I smirked which caused Marcel to look my way. "And you should be ashamed of yourself. Being the oldest, you have a responsibility. Your younger sister is always going to want to be like you and do what you do. It's just how it is. Suck it up and deal with it."

I nodded my head, indicating that I heard Marcel loud and clear.

"Did you hear that, Stoney? You need to take notes. It's natural for you to be like me."

Stoney waved Cash off. "Nicca, I ain't gotta take notes on shit. Being like you never even crossed my mind."

"Wow. That was disrespectful."

"Really? And this is coming from the same dude who thought it was cute to record us having sex. Petty ass muthafucka. You can dish it but you can't take it. Get the fuck on."

"Petty on these muthafuckin nuts, nicca."

"What nuts? Holla at me when you grow some. Shooting blanks ass."

Cash climbed over the bed. He just missed stepping on Karen. He jumped off the bed, standing in front of Stoney. "Say that shit to my face, homie."

Stoney was laying back on the bed, still holding me down, but he rose up when Cash stepped to him, looking him over twice before speaking. "I'll break your ass in half, put you back together, and break your ass all over again. Don't fuck with me, Cash. This ain't what you want."

They stood eye to eye, breathing heavy, seconds from clawing each other apart. Both of them had their fists balled up, about to swing at any minute.

Marcel got in between them, looking from one to the other. “Come on, y’all supposed to be bruvas,” he said, overly dramatic with the facial expressions and all.

We all busted up laughing, including Cash and Stoney. Everyone except for Marcel. He stood there with the same no nonsense expression.

“Damn, Marcel, you had to go all the way back to 1992 on us?” Cash bent over holding his stomach, laughing. “You couldn’t think of nothing current to say. I mean like, nothing. Really? A million other sayings came out since then.”

Stoney laughed too, putting his hand on Marcel’s shoulder. “Dude, I think you need a break from those acting classes. You’re killing me with these old school lines. I can’t right now.”

Marcel smirked. “Ha. Ha. Ha I see how things go. Turn the joke around on me. That’s cool. I’m getting both of y’all back,” he said, waving the belt at them.

Cash and Stoney stopped laughing at the exact same time like someone hit the pause button on them.

Marcel faked a laugh. “It’s so funny. I cracked myself up. Who’s laughing now? Hug it out.”

Cash and Stoney stood face to face again. Cash reached out first hugging Stoney. “I’m sorry, little bro. I really am trying to do better. It’s hard though. Forgive me?”

“I forgive you. I know you’re trying. I’m trying too.”

“Yeah, I know, man. This whole situation still has me all fucked up. Every time I think I’m over it, a new set of emotions rise up.”

“Me too. But if you’re really sorry, let me hold something at the casino.”

“I got you.” Cash kissed Stoney on the cheek.

“Awwwwww, c’mon, dawg.” He wiped his face with his hand. “Don’t do that shit. It’s nasty.” Cash wore a devilish grin, trying to kiss Stoney again. “Quit playing, man. That’s real fruity.”

"How is it fruity when we're brothers? I'm just showing you some love."

"Don't!" Stoney looked grossed out on his way to the bathroom to wash his face. "You always playing too damn much. Punk ass."

Cash smiled, knowing he got the last laugh. He looked like he took pleasure in irritating Stoney. "Hey, Stone, you need to be asking Marcel for money. This nicca has an island named after him."

Stoney peeked out of the bathroom with soap on his face. "Whaaaat? When did that happen?"

"We got lost," Natalia said, answering for Marcel. "And it was awful too. I don't care if we did stumble upon an unclaimed island. We had all the kids with us. I just found out I was pregnant with this baby. I was sick as hell. The kids were crying and hungry. All because Marcel decided to be on some ego trip and charter a boat for us with no guide."

"Yeah, but you won't be complaining when Marcel Island becomes a tourist attraction." Natalia sat back with tight lips, refusing to speak. "That's what I thought. Loose lips, sink ships."

Cash shook his head. "There you go again with those old sayings, bro."

Marcel chuckled and then straightened up, looking at me and Pebbles. "Now, back to you two. Let's get to it. How'd all this shenanigans start?"

Pebbles looked up from her phone, blurting out. "She mad because I fucked Stoney."

Before I could pipe up and put her ass in her place, Stoney spoke up first. I guess he saw the look on my face. "Vanity, you can't get mad. You said that you didn't care who I slept with. Even family members. Your exact words. Not mine."

Pebbles put her two cents in again. "And you told me the same thing. You should have never said it if you didn't mean it. That's your problem. You always trying to front like everything is all good. You should have just kept it real and told the truth."

I wanted to rip Pebbles' face off, but she was right. I should have told Stoney the truth. Instead, I told him what I thought he wanted to hear and it backfired on me.

Stoney spoke again. "Right. So if you want to be mad at someone, be mad at yourself. You should have just kept it one hundred. I asked you multiple times. How was I supposed to know how you really feel? You told me to do me, so I did it. Then, you got the nerve to get jealous. Shit's crazy."

Karen shook her head, sighing "Uggh! I'm getting a headache. This is a hot damn mess."

Marcel looked heated. He stared at Pebbles. His nostrils flaring. "I knew this bullshit was going to happen. That's why I tried to talk to you. I'm so hot with you right now. Because I asked you." Pebbles held her head down. "And you looked me in the face and lied."

"I didn't lie," Pebbles said trying to defend herself. "Nothing happened."

Holding both arms of the chair, Marcel got all in her face. "Look me in my eye and tell me that nothing happened."

Pebbles wouldn't look at him.

He shook the chair making her eyes blink. "So, you're still lying?" He let the chair go. "I'll deal with you later. And you," Marcel said looking at Stoney. "You better learn that when a woman says it's ok to fuck someone else that it's NEVER OK! Look at her." Stoney glanced at me and then looked back at Marcel. "Does she look like she would be ok with you smashing her sister? What the fuck is wrong with you? You need to think sometimes. Stop using your dick in place of your brain.

Marcel pointed around the room. "All this mess could have been avoided. It's bad enough you're already creeping with a married woman. I'm not comfortable with that either. It's grimey. Being married myself, I can't cosign on no shit like that. That's like saying that I agree with cheating. But we're brothers so I'm going to ride with you, but you need to clean your shit up. ASAP. I'm not feeling none of this triflin activity. None of it!"

"I know. You're right," Stoney said calmly. "I'm working on it."

"Yo, you need to hurry up. You got me looking at you sideways. How do I know you won't be after my wife next?"

Cash piped up. "Or mine."

Stoney nodded his head agreeing with Marcel. "I hear y'all, but I don't want Karen or Natalia. At. All. Believe that."

I saw the look on Karen and Natalia's face. "What's that supposed to mean?" Karen said, pursing her lips. "You said at all, like we ain't shit."

"Right," Natalia said, grimacing. "What you on?"

Stoney continued. "I'm not trying to hit neither one of y'all with all those damn kids." Stoney twisted his face. "Ugh. Plus, I don't even think y'all cute like that."

Karen snaked her neck. "Pssssst. I know you must've fell and bumped your damn head. You can't possibly be talking about me. Humph. I'm gorg."

"Whaaaaat?" Natalia said, getting amped. "Oh, you really got me fucked up now. Ain't shit about me ugly. You must be blind. Do you wear glasses? If you don't you should be. Cuz something must be wrong with your damn vision. Crazy as hell."

"Don't go into labor," Stoney said looking over at Natalia. "I didn't mean it like that. What I'm saying is I don't see either of you that way. That's all I meant. Besides, I'm not trying to hit no pregnant chick, especially if the baby ain't mine. That shit is gross." Stoney frowned. "And y'all stay pregnant."

"Don't knock it until you try it. Pregnant pussy is the best, man." Cash kissed Karen's belly. "Why you think Marcel got so many damn kids."

Marcel grinned, punching Cash in the thigh. "That's not why, asshole."

Cash laughed, holding his thigh. "That little pussy ass hit didn't hurt."

"Then, why are you holding your leg then?"

Marcel tried to hit Cash again. "Well, let me do it again."

Cash put his hands up, surrendering. "I lied. The shit hurt like hell. Now, get away from me with your little sissy hits." Cash laughed.

Marcel laughed. "You're stupid."

Stoney grimaced. "Whatever. Y'all can have that. I'm so straight. Miss me completely. Give me non-pregnant pussy, please."

Natalia was still heated. "That's some foul shit, Stoney. We all should whoop your ass."

Stoney sighed. "Natalia, chill, I'm not dissing you. You taking it the wrong way. I'm just saying—"

Marcel walked over to Stoney, putting both hands on his shoulders, looking him square in the eye. "Shut up, man. You're digging a big ass hole that you're about to fall in. Be quiet. You can't argue with no woman. What's wrong with you? See, you're not ready for marriage."

Stoney sighed again. "I don't know how this conversation went left, but you get what I meant, right? I don't want either of them. I don't find them attractive. That's all I meant. Nothing against pregnant women or pregnancy." Stoney sighed. "Women." He sighed again. "I need a drink."

Marcel nodded at Stoney. "I get it. But if you keep running your mouth, I'm going to get cussed the fuck out. Just shut the hell up, please. I don't want to have to get a separate hotel room cause of you."

Stoney snickered. "Aight. I hear you. I'm sorry Natalia and Karen for saying what I said. I'll be quiet now."

"Thank you." Marcel exhaled.

Cash laughed at Stoney. "Wait until you're on lockdown. I mean, married."

Karen gave Cash the evil eye. "I'ma show your ass lockdown. You won't get no more of this."

Cash laid his head in Karen's lap. "I was talking about Marcel and Natalia. Not you, baby." He looked up at her, cheesing with his arms around her big belly.

Lawd, I don't know how the hell she dealt with Cash on a daily basis. He would drive me completely insane.

"Now, back to the subject at hand," Marcel said. "Are they right, Vanity?" He looked me directly in the eye. I looked away. "Is that what you said? Because they are both stating that you said that. If that's true, you really don't have a right to be mad.

You're going to have to charge this one to the game. You played yourself."

I felt like I was being attacked. Pebbles and Stoney already hurt my feelings. Marcel agreeing with them was the final straw. Usually, I would swing on somebody. This time I just put my face in my hands, balling. I couldn't take anymore.

Stoney put his arm around me, pulling me close to him. "Why are you crying?"

"Everyone is mad at me." I cried even louder. "Ivan was already mad at me for coming on this trip. He wanted to come. I told him no. And when he found out that you guys came, he went off on me about that. He said I planned it because I didn't want him to come. But I didn't. We've been arguing back and forth since I got here. That's why I cheated in the first place. And now with the picture Pebbles put up, I'll be lucky if I have a husband to go home to. He's talking real reckless now that he's seen Stoney."

"How reckless?" Stoney asked, glaring at me.

"What picture?" Pebbles asked, taking a break from her phone.

I didn't answer Stoney. "The picture you posted of me and Stoney when he was licking lemon juice off me on the boat."

"Oh, yeah. I did post that. But how did Ivan see it? I'm not friends with him. And he's not friends with none of my friends either."

"No, but you're friends with Chip. He must've shown it to him."

"Damn, I forgot all about Chip. I just accepted his friend request. My bad"

"But why would you post something like that? Are you trying to ruin my life?"

Pebbles got up and came over by me. "I only posted the picture because you looked so happy." She pulled the picture up on her phone and showed me. "Look."

I stared at her phone. She's right. This was a nice picture. I looked very happy. Like I was having the time of my life.

"You just been so moody lately. I was just glad to see you having a good time. Did you read the caption?"

I looked at her phone again. It said, my sister having much needed fun. She works so hard. Haven't seen her smile like this since forever. She needed this vacation. I like it when she's happy.

I hugged my sister, tight. "I'm so sorry. This is all my fault." I really felt bad. More tears came to my eyes. I was so emotional until it was almost pathetic. "I've just been going through so much lately. It just feels like my whole life is crumbling."

Pebbles' eyes filled with tears too. She quickly wiped them away. It started a chain reaction because Karen and Natalia were wiping their eyes as well.

"Why didn't you tell us?" Karen asked.

Natalia handed me some tissue. "Yeah, why didn't you? You know you can always talk to us."

"I know. It's just been hard. None of this is easy to talk about. It hurts too bad."

Pebbles hugged me again.

"Y'all women need to man-up. Check them tears from flowing." Cash got up off the bed, stretching, putting his shoes back on. "Cuz I can't deal with the cry baby shit no more. Way too much for the kid. Straight up."

All of the women said, "Shut up, Cash!"

"See," Cash said, walking by us. "That's why I'm leaving y'all crybabies. I don't want to drown."

"Is everybody good?" Marcel asked, still concerned.

"We're good," me and Pebbles said together, still hugging.

"I want to talk to you two," Marcel said, looking at us.

"Ok, but I want a moment alone with my sister first," I said to him.

"That's cool. I'm going to get Natalia settled in. I'll be back in a minute."

I glanced at Stoney. "Wait for me. I want to talk to you in private."

Stoney nodded and left.

It was just me and Pebbles, alone. I looked at her teary eyes. "I want to be honest with you." I started crying again, but I was determined to get this out. "I shut you out all the time because I'm jealous of you."

"But why? We look just alike." She smoothed down my wild hair. "You're beautiful."

I sniffled and cleared my throat so that I could get my words out. "Look at you. Men adore you. Women want to be you. You walk around like you own the world. And me, I'm stuck in my shell. I try to be like you but I can't do it. I'm such a loser."

"That's because you need to stop trying to be like me and just be yourself. There is nothing wrong with being you. I look up to you."

This was news to me. "You do?"

"Yes. That's why I don't want you to keep shutting me out. I wish I could talk to you about certain things. When I have problems, I have to go to Joss or someone else because you won't talk to me. And speak up. Don't be afraid of what others think. Let people know what's on your mind. And if Ivan is getting on your nerves that bad, let his ass go."

Pebbles held my hands looking me square in the eye. "Be with Stoney if he makes you happy." I was about to ask about her and him but she hushed me up. "There is nothing special between us. Now, you know me. If I was feeling him like that, I would tell you. I'm serious. I know you don't want to hear this, but I'm keeping it real. It was just sex. I saw the tape and I wanted what you had, but he's not mine to have. Be with him, Vee. He cares deeply for you. He told me."

"I don't know. I already feel bad for cheating on Ivan."

Pebbles smacked her lips. "Girl, please. Do you think if this was Ivan that he would stop to consider you? No. If the shoe was on the other foot, Ivan would be slanging his dick all over this island. Trust and believe."

I laughed. "Maybe you're right.'

"I am. Now go see Stoney and work things out with him. I'm about to find out what my crew is doing."

I grinned. "Thanks, Pebbles."

"That's what little, big sisters are for." She winked at me and left the room.

I didn't feel one hundred percent with her and Stoney having sex, but I know my sister. She is selfish about what she wants. The fact that she is offering up Stoney means that she is telling me the truth.

Marcel came in as Pebbles was going out. He paused for a minute, telling her something before be entered the room, wearing workout gear. "Where you going?" I asked.

"I'm going on tour soon." He flexed his muscles. "Gotta keep it right, you know?" He raised his shirt, holding it by his teeth, doing his famous body roll.

Marcel was as beautiful as they come. Inside and out. He was extremely handsome. I speak about Stoney being sexy but Cash and Marcel were both in that category too. They've just toned it down a little because they were husbands and fathers.

"I didn't know they had a gym."

"Yep. You good, though?" Marcel took a seat next to me on my bed.

"I'm still a little shocked, but I'm ready to move on from all this. I love my sister. And I won't be fighting her over Stoney no matter what happens in the future."

"I hope you mean that. Because now that the door has been opened, it might not be so easy for them to close it. Lust is powerful."

"I know," I said still upset blaming myself for this fiasco. "I'll just have to deal with it."

"Also, I wanted to get at you about Ivan. What you said about him rubbed me the wrong way. No husband should ever make you feel the way Ivan does. I know every married couple has their issues, but I've never seen you this unhappy before. Maybe you married the wrong man."

"I love my husband, Marcel."

"I didn't say you didn't. What I'm saying is, sometimes we pick our mates instead of God picking them for us. I'm sure that God lined me and Natalia up. I would have liked for it to have been smoother. Lord knows it was rocky for a hot minute. I'm sure that God lined up Cash and Karen. Look at how they met. It was wild too. Nothing about their encounter made any sense. But before we all met the right one, we were all in failed relationships. Similar to what you're experiencing."

"I hear you, but I'm not leaving my husband."

"And I wouldn't tell you to. I'm just saying put you first. If you can work things out with Ivan, then do so. But if you're only staying because you're afraid to get a divorce, afraid of being alone, then you're making a huge mistake. I think Ivan's a cool dude. At the same time, I can't help but notice that you and Stoney have amazing chemistry. Maybe you met for a reason. And maybe that's why you really fought your sister. Because deep down inside, you're feeling exactly what I'm saying."

Marcel stood up. "Think about it."

Chapter 18

Pebbles

I walked out of the hotel looking like a boss, surrounded by money. Marcel was to my right and Cash was to my left. Slightly ahead by a couple steps, it looked like they were with me instead of me tagging along with them. My gyms were fresh. Exercise gear on point, showing off my flat stomach and navel piercing. At that moment, nobody couldn't tell me I wasn't the shit.

"I'm going to stop in here right quick." Marcel disappeared into the store to get bottled water.

Some girl came out of nowhere talking to me. "I'm too jealous. You don't have one fine man, you have two. What I would pay to be you right now." She stopped right in front of Cash, looking him up and down. "Hey, sexy."

Cash played it a lot cooler than I expected, giving a casual nod. "What's up?"

"I'm sorry if this is your man, but he's so damn fine. I just had to stop and say something."

"He's not my man. He's my brother, but he's MARRIED to my COUSIN."

"Damn, that's too bad cuz he could get it, for real." She smiled at me and winked at Cash. "Take care, handsome."

The cheesy grin on his face told me he liked the compliment a lot more than he showed.

I wanted to pop him. "You nasty. I seen you look at her booty. "

"Really? I'm nasty? I didn't just get busy with Stoney."

I rolled my eyes. "Whatever."

"So what's really up with that? Cuz I know Stoney very well. And he has chicks strung out like crack. You on drugs now?""

I shrugged it off. "Let's be clear, I'm never going to be strung out. I was curious. I wanted to know. Now, I do."

"Do you still want to know?"

"Nope," I said, sticking out my tongue. "But I bet he still wants to know. Look at all this right here." I started juking.

"All what? You're nothing but feet and hair. You ain't got no ass or tits."

"Stop hating. And I'll have you know, I puts it down. Niccas get strung out on me too."

"I don't see how. You don't have enough to string out no damn body."

"Kiss my ass, Cash."

He laughed. "What ass?"

"Leave me alone," I said, jogging away from him over to Marcel when he came out of the store.

"Why you running away?" Cash asked, chasing after me.

Cash continue to bother me like he always does as we walked over to the gym. It wasn't that far, but the hot sun made it seem like we were walking across the desert. I was so glad when we got inside the air-conditioned facility.

"Whew! Hand me my water now."

Cash laughed. "You need this workout. You're weak."

"We don't have time for water breaks." Marcel took the water out of my hand, sitting it on the side. "We need to stretch."

I think I was invited along to be tortured. They were taking turns beating up on me. I plopped down on the comfy mat opening my legs wide so I could really stretch. Marcel sat down next to me, dictating what I was supposed to do. Now, I was limber, but he was pushing and pulling my body every which way but loose.

"Hold on, now. I can't do all that."

"No excuses. Make it happen."

I was tired already and we haven't even begun. I looked around the room and saw Cash jogging like a maniac on the treadmill. What have I gotten myself into?

Marcel jumped up off the floor. "Drop and give me twenty."

"Twenty what?" He got me twisted.

"Push-ups, sit ups, and ten minutes on the treadmill. Then, we're going to do crunches, squats, leg lifts, lunges, and the bike. Then it will be planks. Five sets and the elliptical. Last, we'll hit the weights."

Sounds like a lot of shit to do.

I was doing good on first set. By the second set, I was dragging. Cash jumped off the treadmill and joined us. They ran around like they had all the energy in the world. Meanwhile, I was barely able to walk by the time we finished. I crashed on the floor while Cash and Marcel pumped iron.

I was almost asleep when Marcel tapped me. "We about to leave, but I want to chat with you for a hot second."

"What's up?" I asked not even bothering to open my eyes.

"You know what happen to my sister, right?"

I knew bits and pieces but I didn't want to speak on it since I didn't know all the details. "Not really. I just know that she was killed."

"Brooklynn got involved with the wrong dude. She lost her life because of it. Running around New York like she owned it. Not worrying about tomorrow or consequences to her actions. Just like you."

"Me?" I asked, opening my eyes. Did he say like me?

"Yes, you. And I see you headed in the same direction. I refuse to let that happen. That crazy ass nicca she got involved with robbed me of my whole family. My mother, my sister, and my nieces. All gone because of one stupid fuckin nicca's insecure ass."

"I'm sorry, Marcel. I can't even imagine how you feel."

"I'm angry, sad, pissed off, and ready to kill everything moving, but that won't bring any of them back." He showed me a picture of his sister. We did favor a lot. "You have your sister. You need to cherish her now and think before you do something you will regret."

All this lecturing was getting on my damn nerves. "That's what I plan to do."

"I'm glad you said that because I'm going to be on your ass like white on rice." Our eyes met. Not only was Marcel serious, he had a look that I'd never seen before. I assumed this was his other side that people talked about. I knew Marcel could get street when need be. "You need to be checked. If your brother wasn't your sister, he could help you. And your dad can't do it because he spoils you. Nice man but he's more like your friend. So, I'm going to do it. No back talk. No resistance. Just shut up and do what I say, nah mean?"

"Ok," I said. I appreciated his gesture, but I didn't want him hounding me. I liked my life. Carefree and in the wind as I please.

"Did you hear me? Because it looked like your mind was somewhere else."

"Yeah, yeah, I heard you."

Marcel was as nice as they come. I didn't want to piss him off though. He had a very, very, very bad temper when provoked. Knowing that I look like his sister means that he took this big brother role with me very seriously. I would hate for me to be the first chick he snaps out on and beat my ass. Millions or not, he was still from the hood. I wouldn't put it past him.

"I'm dead ass, Pebbles." He gave me a look that said try me if you want to.

"I said, ok, Big Brother All On My Back Marcel. I'm not going to give you no problems. At least I'm not going to try to."

Hearing me say big brother put a huge smile on his face. His demeanor changed from scaring the shit out of me to caring and loving again. Reaching his hand out to me, he said, "Let's go, baby sis."

Why the hell did I have to remind him of his deceased sister? Lucky ass me. I gripped his hand, standing to my feet, getting up off the floor.

Heading back to my room, I felt like I got hit by an eighteen-wheeler. Everything on my body hurt. I threw myself across the bed going to sleep, instantly.

*****

It was dark by the time I woke up. My phone was lit up. I retrieved it seeing that I had a few messages. I was outraged the moment I heard the first one. It was from Carl. Ugh! He must be kidding if he thinks I'm spending any more time with him. Delete! I know I made the right decision to drop his ass. This dude had mental issues. He left me three more messages, saying the same shit. I ought to kill Shay's ass.

I was about to delete the fifth message. I thought it was Carl again. I'm glad I didn't. It was from Gabriel. His voice was so smooth and silky. I forgot why I was mad at him. He said he was going to meet me in the lobby of the hotel to apologize. I had fifteen minutes. I needed to get cute real quick.

I snatched off my workout clothes and hit the shower. I was funky after being with Marcel doing that deadly workout routine. Scrubbing frantically, I cleaned my body, washed my hair, and put it into a cute twist-knot. I put on a little bit of makeup and dug through my bag to see what I had left that was clean. I found my last clean bikini and put on a short tight booty dress on top of it. This dress really left nothing for the imagination. My tits and ass were all hanging out.

Gabriel was standing in the lobby looking hopeless as if I wasn't going to show up. He checked his watch twice before I reached him. At ten after, I was just glad that he was still waiting for me.

"Hey there, stranger," I said walking up behind him, putting my arms around his waist, taking a whiff of his masculine scent.

He turned around facing me, enjoying our embrace. His smile met mine. “Hello, beautiful. I didn’t think you were going to show up. I was such a jerk last time. I wouldn’t blame you if you didn’t.”

I let go of all those ill feelings. “Oh, Gabriel, it was going to take more than that to stop me from seeing you.”

He squeezed me tighter. “I really want to apologize for my behavior. There was no excuse for me to act the way I did. I’m so sorry. Do you accept my apology?”

“I accept.” I could have stayed mad at him, but what’s the point. Right now, I wanted to enjoy his company and hopefully get some good dick in the process.

I gazed into his pretty brown eyes. “I don’t want to fight with you no more.”

“I’m so glad to hear that. I thought you were never going to talk to me again. I could have kicked myself for making you so angry.”

I giggled. “Yeah, I was pretty pissed. All I wanted was to spend time with you. That’s it. You hurt my feelings when you rejected me.”

Gabriel sighed. “I like you a lot. More than you’ll ever know. From the moment I saw you, I wanted you to be mine. I didn’t tell you that because I didn’t want you to laugh at me. ”

I heard him. This time I checked my own feelings, concentrating on my future nut. I needed his dick in my life. I wasn’t going to mess it up. “Well good. I’m glad we’re on the same page.”

His eyes were low, giving me nothing but sexiness. “Me too. So, you want to pick up where we left off?”

Ah, this man was so smooth. He had my juices flowing already. I stood on my tippy toes, kissing him. My hands palmed his ass as he tongued me down.

“Mmmmm. I’ve been hard for two days thinking about you.”

I reached down, squeezing his dick. It was brick. Felt like I had steel in my hand. “You want this pussy?” I asked, pulling my dress over my head. “Come and get it.”

Being in his presence did something to me. All of a sudden, I had an extreme sexual appetite. Similar to the intense sexual desire that I felt earlier when I was with Stoney. The urge was so strong I could barely breathe. This type of desire had to be next level.

Literally, I felt like if Gabriel didn't fuck me, right here, right now, I was going to stop breathing or something. I needed his dick like lungs needed air. My pussy continuously throbbed. My boobs felt like tiny rocks. My clit was so swollen and sensitive that it felt like if anything brushed against it, I was going to leak cum everywhere.

I switched my ass over to the hot tub, dropping my mini dress on the side. I needed Gabriel to fuck me in this water to replace the memories of Stoney's sex tape. Whenever I thought of the hot tub, I would see Gabriel instead. Removing my bikini, I got in totally nude.

Gabriel followed suit, dropping his clothes next to mine, getting in bare. He moved in the water closer to me, taking me back into his strong arms, dominating our kiss. I pressed my body against his, holding his dick in my hand.

"Your body is so nice." He sucked one tit while squeezing my ass. "You have just enough of what I like." His fingers dipped between my legs. "And the sweetest pussy. Let me taste it again."

I stood up on the bench. Gabriel leaned down, licking my pussy lips and then sticking his tongue between them before scooping me up into the air with my crotch covering his face. I held his head as he slurped on my juices.

A couple, I guess coming to get in the hot tub, suddenly stopped when they saw me and Gabriel getting it on. The man ogled us when he saw the excitement I got from Gabriel pleasuring me. His tongue felt too good for me to worry about the onlookers.

Instead of walking away, the man pulled out his hard dick and began stroking himself while the lady remained frozen. The man's eyes were glued to me as he pulled on his dick. Being watched turned me on even more. I found myself moaning louder and moving more seductive, putting on quite a show. Gabriel didn't seem fazed at all, like he was used to fucking in public. I found that super-hot too.

Gabriel gripped my thighs when I came, licking, sucking, and slurping until I exploded in his mouth. Still not satisfied, I grinded against his face until I got off a second one.

Skillfully, Gabriel lowered my body down until his dick was deep inside of me. I wrapped my legs around his waist, enjoying his deep thrusts. "Damn, you're fucking me right."

"That's because you got the best pussy ever," he moaned in between kisses.

"Is that right?" My eyes landed on the couple again. The woman was now on her knees with the man's dick in her mouth. The live sex act really brought out the lust in me. I began to roll my hips while in Gabriel's embrace. "Yeah, get this pussy. Get all in it. Shiiiiit!"

Gabriel lifted me up and down, pounding me hard as I came. I held his neck while my body jerked like crazy. He kept fucking me hard and I kept on cumming. It's like once my orgasm turned on, I couldn't turn it off. Nut after nut after nut after nut. I bet watching me cum consecutively pumped Gabriel's ego all the way up.

I kept making high-pitched incoherent rants while Gabriel continued to put in work. My body shook frantically as Gabriel kept on giving me dick action. I have had some awesome nuts in my sexual memoirs but hands down, Gabriel was rocking my world.

Still going hard, Gabriel pounded me until he approached the bench. He sat on it and I gladly took my position on top. This was one of my favorite positions anyway. I loved controlling the dick. It made me feel like it belonged only to me. I showed off my skills, riding him like a subway train.

I knew it was good when Gabriel held on to me for dear life. "Damn, girl, you make me want to spend the rest of my life with you."

I giggled, knowing that it was my pudding making him talk so foolishly. Had him saying dumb shit that he probably wouldn't say if he wasn't knee-deep in it.

Being the type of chick that I was, I was going to roll with the moment. "Yeah, my pussy is that good?" I kissed his lips, sucking on his bottom lip. "Makes you want to lock it down and wife it, huh?"

"Hell yeah. Grade A, premium, platinum, miracle pussy."

Did he say miracle? "You really know how to blow a girl's head up," I said, working him slow. "You ain't felt nothing yet."

I tightened my vaginal walls, putting his dick in a pussy vise grip.

"Shiiiiiiiiiiiit!" he groaned.

I held his hand to my face, taking his index finger into my mouth, sucking it like it was his manhood. I licked it, worked it in my mouth, and then sucked the tip.

"You're about to make me stalk your ass," he said through clenched teeth.

"Stalk me, baby," I said seductively sticking my tongue out, licking my lips. "Next time, you can watch me play in it and make myself cum."

"Fuuuuuuuck!"

My hands rested on Gabriel's broad shoulders as I flexed my coochie muscles. "You ready to get rid of this two day back up?"

"Oh gawd, yes!" he groaned, grinding inside of me, clawing at my ass.

Chills traveled from my core to my toes.

"Aaaaaaaaaaaaaah!" we yelled together as the most magnificent feeling hit us at the same time.

We held each other moaning simultaneously in each other's ear. Our tongues danced as our bodies collided making the perfect melody.

Gabriel stared at me as we basked in the afterglow. His pretty brown eyes studied my face, brushing a strand of loose hair that had fallen.

"I like everything about you."

"But you don't even know me." He wasn't about to get me caught in his international player moves. I was already feeling him way too much.

"I know enough to like what I see."

"Ok, player," I said standing up. "Let's get dressed and finish this conversation back in my room."

I knew we would be alone because Vanity had making up to do with Stoney.

I stretched out on my bed. "I'm starving."

Gabriel pulled out his phone. "I can call my man. He owns a restaurant here on the island. He'll bring us something."

"Thanks, baby," I said, rolling from my stomach to my back, giving him nothing but seduction.

"He said give him an hour." Gabriel put the phone down, climbing into the bed with me, resting between my legs. "I can't get enough of you." He slipped his tool back inside of me, hitting my spot. "I need you in my life."

I looked up at him, staring into his handsome face on the verge of cumming again. "You're just saying that because my sex got you feeling some kinda way."

"No, baby, I'm not whipped." I wrapped my legs around his back, thrusting harder than him. He moaned loudly. "Ok, maybe a little."

I laughed then I got serious. "I can't get enough of you either."

"Good. I plan on being in your life in a major way."

"Good. Because I want you too."

"I'm leaving tomorrow evening, but I want you to call me when you get back home so we can link up."

"Sounds whipped to me."

He lifted my legs on his shoulders plunging into me, making me cum immediately. "Aaaaaaah! Yes! So fucking goooooood!" I held his firm body close, savoring my wonderful orgasm.

"Who's whipped now?"

Chapter 19

Vanity

My mind was all over the place when Marcel left my hotel room. I was already torn. Ivan was the love of my life, my other half. Then there was Stoney. He meant something to me too. Not just because of the great sex. Every time I looked into his eyes, I felt a deeper connection. We just vibed.

Stoney opened the door after the first knock. "C'mere."

I stepped inside trying to be strong. The moment Stoney put his arms around me, I broke down. My head and my body hurt. I expected him to ask more questions or even worse tell me to leave.

He didn't do either. Stoney held me close, walking me toward the bathroom where he ran bath water. Treating me like a delicate flower, he undressed me, then himself. He got in first and then helped me in, washing both of our bodies before taking a seat, holding me in a loving embrace.

I laid my wet hair against his chest, sobbing. All of my problems came crashing down. I just couldn't take it anymore.

Stoney held me as I cried my eyes out. No words. Just our hearts beating together. Then, he stood, got out of the tub and helped me out too. Drying us both off, he carried me to the bed, cradling me like an infant.

At this point, I was all cried out. No more tears would fall. My tear ducts must've been tired too. After dry heaving for a moment, I was finally quiet.

"You need to speak your mind. Holding it in will make you sick."

I looked at him with standstill tears that refused to fall. "I don't want to put my problems off on you."

"Bae, I can take it. I have strong shoulders. Tell me."

I just stared at him.

"See this is what people mean when they say you shut down. How can I even begin to understand you if you won't talk to me."

I was still staring into his green eyes. My mind began to wonder. What would things be like if I was married to Stoney? I sighed. "It's not right discussing my issues about Ivan with you. It's disrespectful."

"I want to hear your concerns. You being in pain is hurting me too."

I looked deep into Stoney's eyes. Pain looked me back in the face. He was hurting because I was hurting. "I've been trying to relax. Not let things bother me. My mind just won't let shit go." I paused, trying my best not to have a crying fit again.

Stoney rubbed my back. "Take your time."

I took a deep breath before continuing. "Ivan is really tripping, hard."

"Did that nicca threaten you?" Stoney asked, balling up his fists.

"No—"

"I swear, if he did—"

"No, he didn't," I replied, cutting him off. Ivan said some threatening things but I wasn't about to tell Stoney that. I knew Ivan was speaking in anger. There was no need to have Stoney all worked up. I was sure we would work things out, like we usually did.

"Well, let me know if he does. I got something for his ass."

"Ivan's anger towards me is all my fault though. I'm the one who's cheating."

"Does he really know? Because you make it seem like he knows you're cheating. Or does he just suspect it? There's a difference."

"It doesn't matter. Either way, I'm wrong."

"I don't think he knows. He's playing you. Testing to see if you are. Trying to get you to offer up information so you'll hang yourself." Stoney frowned like mentioning Ivan's name hurt his tongue. "Why was he mad at you before?"

"Because I've spent most of our savings trying to get pregnant. I'm infertile."

Stoney looked confused. "So you want a baby?"

Tears came to my eyes again. "That's why I didn't want to tell you. You wouldn't understand."

"Listen," he said, stroking my cheek. "I don't have to understand. If it's important to you, it's important to me." Stoney sighed. Not a sigh of frustration, but more like a sigh of concern. "So, let me get this straight. You want a baby and Ivan doesn't?"

I nodded my head yes.

Stoney wiped away my tears. "And he's pissed about spending money on you trying to get pregnant?"

I nodded again.

"You're with the wrong man, babe."

Now it was my turn to sigh. This was the second time today that I'd heard this.

"Hear me out," he said, noticing my attitude. "Your husband should want babies by you. Look at all that," he said, raising the sheet looking at my nude body. I blushed. "It should be natural for the man that you married to want to share that experience with you. God said be fruitful and multiply."

I lowered my eyes thinking about what Stoney just said. What was wrong with me that my own husband didn't want kids with me? "You're right. I guess our love isn't as strong as I thought it was."

"If you ask me, Ivan sounds like he has some issues. When we get back, I want you to call me if you need me. Doesn't matter what it is or what time. I got you. Car, food, a place to stay, it's whatever. And if Ivan does know about you cheating, hit me up on that too. I'm in this with you one-hundred percent."

"I don't know, Stoney. Ivan gets crazy sometimes."

"I'm not scared of your punk ass husband. I will fuck his ass up."

"I don't want you to hurt him."

"I won't unless I have to," Stoney flipped me onto my back, moving in between my legs. "Now, let's make that baby you want." He gently entered me.

"No," I said, trying to push him off of me. "You were just with my sister. I didn't forget."

Stoney held my wrists above my head. "That's because you keep dumping me. One minute, you want me the next minute you don't. Since you can't make up your mind, I'm doing it for you." He let go of my hands, grinding inside of me, sucking on my left breasts, teasing my harden nipple. "You still want me to stop?" He gave me eye contact while sucking my breast, rocking back and forth on top of me.

I laid there speechless, enjoying every bit of it. My hands had a mind of their own, squeezing his firm ass.

"Your pussy feels perfect." He planted tiny kisses all over my face before kissing my lips. "You want my baby?" His strokes were deliberately deep.

Hearing him speak to me about what I desired most really had me aroused. "Yeeeessss!"

The power of good dick. Something about the way he put it on me. I found myself agreeing out of lust. In this moment, I did want to have his baby.

"You want me to cum in you?"

"Oooooh! Ah! Oooooh! Ah! "

"Tell me then. Tell me how bad you want this cum."

"Yes! I want it. Cum in me. Oh! Yes!"

I found myself lost in each stroke. Blown away when he hit my spot. No more tears. All the stress was gone. The only thing that mattered was his dick and my pussy.

Stoney got more aggressive, stretching my arms back over my head. He continued to pump inside of me at a steady pace. Not too fast. Not too slow. Just right.

Lifting my ass off the mattress, I held on tight riding our sexual wave. Hitting my sexual peak, I screamed as my body vibrated. I held him tighter as my body convulsed. "Fuck me! Fuck me! Fuck me! Aaaaaaaaah!"

Still inside of me, he managed to turn me around so that I was on my stomach face down. He jerked my hips back, pulling me to my knees with my ass high in the air, ramming into me super hard. Continuously hitting my spot, Stoney sent me into an orgasm tailspin. Just like before, once I started cumming, I couldn't stop.

"You still want to have my baby?"

"Yes! Yes! Yes!"

"Shit! I'm about to nut in this wet pussy and get you pregnant."

"Yes! Yes! Fuck me! Yes!"

He reached under me rubbing my clit. I came super hard. Crying out as if I were a dog in heat.

"Shiiiiiiiiiiiiiiiiit!" Stoney yelled, filling me up with semen. He kept thrusting inside of me for what seemed like forever as he came. When he finished unloading, I felt thick globs of semen inside of me.

"Now, carefully, turn around and lay on your back." I flipped over and he handed me a pillow. "Put this underneath you. Lay with your knees to your chest for about twenty minutes."

*****

"Wake up, sleepy head." Stoney tapped my shoulder. "It's almost noon."

I woke up to breakfast in bed. The tray was on top of my body. Stoney was sitting on my side. I opened my eyes and smiled. "Good morning, handsome."

He kissed my cheek. "Good morning, gorgeous."

I stretched, yawned, and sat up to see what was hiding under the food tray. "How long have you been up?"

Stoney was standing up now undressing out of his workout clothes. "I got up early and went to work out with Marcel and Cash. Gotta make sure my dick stays working. Don't want to be fat and shit with a limp dick."

I giggled. "I don't think you'll have that problem. Not the way you put it down. How long have you been going to the gym?"

"Since we got here. And your sister was there too." He cracked up. "You should have seen her. She looked completely miserable. Marcel was on her ass the whole time."

"That's cuz she's lazy. She needs to work out. But y'all can have that. I'm on vacation. Ain't no way. I'll work out when I get back home."

"We have no choice. Being in the industry, we have to stay fit, especially Marcel." Stoney made the noise of the cheering fans. "We love you Urbane! I want to drink your bath water. I want to have your baby. Make me your mistress. Women would go crazy if he lost his physique."

"Do women really say that stuff? Like they want to drink his bath water? Ugh! So nasty."

"They say more than that. You'd be surprise. I've seen and heard some pretty nasty shit, especially on the road. Women would do anything to get at him."

"What about you? They come at you like that too?" I was starting to feel some kinda way thinking about all the women who might be trying to get at him too.

Stoney climbed in the bed wearing nothing but his skin. Resting his head in my lap, he pulled the sheet over his naked body. "I won't lie to you and say that I ain't never fucked a groupie. I have. But my heart ain't into that no more. Been there done that. I want something permanent. Something real. A beautiful chick that can hold me down. We can ride for each other. Making a bunch of babies and living a wonderful life. Big house. Lots of cars. Just me and her. Paid."

I was really feeling him when he said that. "That's the same thing that I want."

"That's all I ever wanted," we both said in harmony.

The synchronicity. It's been there with us since the day we first met.

"Let me ask you." He turned his head, looking up at me, straight in the eye. "What if you met me first?" I frowned. "Hear me out. What if there was no Ivan. Just me and you. What would you say?"

I sat back and thought for a moment. "In what way? I mean, does that mean just sexually? Back in the day or right now? Boyfriend and girlfriend? Marriage? What are we talking about here?"

"Let's go there. All of it. Would that change your perception about us?"

He had me thinking now. "Maybe."

"Would you feel like maybe, just maybe, that if you knew me first, you might not have dated someone like Ivan?"

I was trying to see where he was going with this. "You're stretching this thing all the way out, aren't you?"

He stared at me for a minute. "Never mind. Just a thought. Finish up. I have a nice day planned for you."

"What?" I asked, getting all excited and forgetting about the what ifs Stoney just sprung on me.

"Now, it wouldn't be a surprise if I told you. Now would it?"

I smiled. He reached up and kissed my lips. Then he pulled the sheet back and kissed my belly, rubbing it. "We made our baby girl last night."

I laughed, hard. "I'm not pregnant. I only went along with your charades last night because I was dickmitized."

"We'll see in nine months. It might be twins though. You know twins run deep in my family. Both of my grandparents on my father's side are twins. And every other person in my family is a twin."

I giggled. "You're just so sure that I'm pregnant. How do you know?"

"Because a man knows. You'll be calling me in about six weeks. After you take a pregnancy test, crying." He yelled out a fake cry and then cracked up like it was the funniest thing ever.

"You're wildin right now."

He kissed my belly again. "Vanna, you hear your daddy? Your mama is tripping. You need to hurry up and get here. I can't deal with her by myself. She's a handful." He chuckled.

I laughed. "Now, you're really tripping."

He winked at me and got up with his dick swinging. "You better be done eating when I finish in here. Or I'm leaving you."

I twisted my lips. "How are you leaving me when it's my surprise?"

He laughed loudly. "You better hurry up then."

After Stoney got out of the shower, I got in and dressed. We walked out of the hotel, looking like a couple even though we weren't. Every time I was with him, people always assumed we were together. Mistakenly, everyone thought he was my husband. The strange part about it was neither one of us denied it. We just smiled and kept it moving.

As soon as I got into the taxi, Stoney covered my eyes with a blindfold. "Is this necessary?"

"Yes. I want you to truly be surprised."

When the taxi stopped, Stoney helped me out and led me to my surprise, removing the blindfold. "All for you."

I looked around at the romantic set up on the beach. A huge heart shape blanket with rose petals surrounding it. Outlined by candles in the sand. A very large tent covering that shaded us from the sun. On the table were two bottles of champagne chilled on ice with glass flutes along with a huge picnic basket.

I hugged and kissed him, jumping up and down, clapping my hands. "This is wonderful. I love it."

Stoney helped me sit down in the pillow seat. Then, he sat on the pillow across from me, filling both of our glasses with champagne. "I want to propose a toast. To our future."

I was feeling him so much right now. I raised my glass to his. "Our future."

We both took a sip.

"I really wanted to bring you here to get to know you a little better. It just occurred to me that as much time as we've spent together, we've never talked that much. We spent most of our time getting our freak on."

He was right. "Ok. What do you want to know?"

He fed me a chocolate strawberry dipped in whipped cream. "What are you mixed with?"

"Who says I'm mixed?"

"Don't even try it. You're mixed with something."

I grinned. "To me, I'm just like any another black woman even though my father is white." I drank my champagne. "What are you mixed with?

He snickered. "What makes you think that I'm mixed?"

"Are you serious? Your eyes, your hair, your complexion. Everything about you screams mixed. Even your name."

"I feel the same as you. I don't view myself as mixed. I'm just a black man. That's how I was raised. That's how it will always be. Well, let me see. My mixture is a little more complicated than yours. My father is black and Italian. I get my eyes from him. And my mother is Puerto Rican and Dominican. I get my hot nature from her."

I nearly spit out my champagne. "Your mother is what? I thought she was Black. She looks Black. Sounds like it too. And she cooks some fire soul food. I can't believe it. As many times as I've talked to her. I never noticed."

He smiled. "She considers herself a Black Hispanic. Same difference to me. Black is Black."

I nodded my head. "So, what was your family like growing up?"

"Complicated. The people who I thought were my parents, Keno and Karen, died when I was sixteen. I grew up being the baby of my family with two older brothers, Dash and Dan. Then, I found out the truth. That my Aunt Emilia was really my mother. She cheated with her husband's twin brother, Keno, and conceived me. And to cover up her indiscretion, she gave me to them to raise."

"OH WOW!" That's all I could say. That's some talk show shit right there.

"Yeah. That's why Cash and I have issues. I thought he was my cousin up until then. To this day, I'm still messed up over all of that. Not to mention there are other things that happened. Bad things. And I have a lot of unanswered questions too."

"I'm sorry," I said, squeezing his hand to show my affection.

"Don't be sorry. It's not your fault. What about you?"

"Most people would consider me lucky. I grew up with two of the best parents in the world. My home life was amazing. My parents were supportive. Always will be. I guess the only issue my family has is Joss. Of course, we don't see it that way. We all love her, but the world is so cruel sometimes. As you probably figured out, she was born a boy. Her birth name was Joel. But as early as two, she would always try and wear girl clothes. She wouldn't respond to Joel either. As soon as she could talk, she renamed herself Joss. So, she's always been a girl in my eyes."

"That's what's up. You have to love your family. Maybe not like them, or approve of what they do, but love them nonetheless. Nice to know that your brother, I mean, sister can be comfortable at home. Parents should love their children regardless. What about work? What do you do?"

"I work in sales. One of the perks is this trip. I get it at a discounted rate."

"You know my cousin Quay got me a job where he works. Well, I'm not really employed. More like a contractor. I'll find out my start date when I get back. What I like about this company is, they are flexible with my schedule so that I can still go on tour with Marcel."

I giggled. "Isn't that something? My cousin Chica helped me get my job too."

"It sounds like your family is full of women. And from what I can tell, you all look alike."

I smiled. "Yeah, we are over populated with women. Maybe that's another reason why Joel decided to become Joss."

Stoney fed me another chocolate dipped strawberry. "Oddly enough, my family is over populated with men. I have female cousins too, but not as many. Between my mother's side and my father's side, I think I'm kin to half of Chicago. For real."

I can only imagine what his family reunions are like. "Seriously? That's a big family."

"My family is enormous. I have so many cousins that it's ridiculous. I meet new cousins all the time."

I was just curious. "Do they look just like you too?"

"Sort of. A variation between me and Cash. Most of them are very handsome. If that's what you're getting at." He raised his eyebrows and grinned. "What you want to see pictures or something?

I smacked his arm. "Conceit is not cute."

"Oh, I'm fly and you know it," he said, tackling me, resting in between my legs, dry humping me. "You love it when I work the middle. Don't you?"

I wasn't about to blow his head up any more and tell him yes. I loved when he worked the middle. "Since you being such a smart ass. Yeah. Whip them out. Show me everybody."

Stoney pulled out his phone, showing me pictures. His brothers, Dash and Dan. They looked like another version of Cash and Marcel. A lot of cousins. I couldn't keep up with all of their names. Amante. Rico. Angel. Ecko. "Here's my cousin Aquarius aka Quay."

"Oh, I see the resemblance," I said coolly. Humph. Quay was fine. I regrouped while Stoney rolled off of me, putting his phone away. "I want to know more about you being on tour. What's that like?"

"Freaky. Crazy. Madness. Mayhem. Pretty much anything goes."

There was silence for a moment.

"I have been dying to ask you this question. How do you feel about me?"

I stared away from his gaze. "I can't lie. I like you. A lot."

He took another sip of champagne. "Like how?"

I looked back at him. "Like if the grass is really greener. You're so perfect right now. Romantic picnics. Great sex. Showering me with attention. Understanding. Concerned. In this moment, I couldn't ask for a better man."

I had a flashback. "Ivan used to be like this too, you know. How do I know that if I left him and got with you, that you wouldn't turn out the same way? How do I know you won't leave me for the next chick? Or worse cheat on me."

Taking my hand to his mouth, he kissed it. "I would never treat you like that. You're really special to me."

I snatched my hand back. "I'm special until you find out I can't give you a bunch of babies? Then what?"

"I said I want a bunch of babies, but that isn't a deal breaker. We would cross that road when we got there. Together. Like couples do."

I heard him but it was hard believing him. "That sounds like bullshit." I struggled to stand in the sand. It was making it hard for me to dramatically walk away like I saw in my head. The sand had me looking clumsy and stupid. Still, I managed to get pretty far before Stoney caught up to me.

"Don't go," he said sincerely.

"Why? Tell me one good reason why?"

"Because I want to be with you."

I couldn't believe he was going there. "That's not even possible. I'm married."

"So what. Leave him. Be with me. Besides, it's clear that you love me more than you love him."

"What are you talking about?"

He locked my hand with his. "I have proof. Come back and sit with me so I can explain."

I had to hear this shit. Sitting back down on the fluffy pillow, I filled my flute, drank the whole glass, poured me another one, and drank that too. "Ok, now I'm ready for you to explain this shit. Cuz I need to know." The scowl on my face must've told Stoney I wasn't playing with his ass.

"Slow down on the champagne. That's one of the reasons why you don't remember."

"What the hell are you talking about? Spit this shit out. I don't have time for the riddles." He was starting to piss me off. "You got one minute to make me understand what the hell you talking about. Otherwise, I'm going back to my hotel room alone. And I don't care how good your dick is, I'll be using my hand for the rest of this trip."

"Ok, don't get your panties in a bunch." He exhaled. "You told me at Cash and Karen's wedding reception."

What the fuck is he talking about? See, he's about to make me act a fool. "I thought you said you weren't there."

"No, I said I wasn't in the wedding. I was there, sitting with the rest of the family. There's more."

I folded my arms across my chest. "Like what? I seduced you?" I laughed hearty, but quickly stopped when Stoney didn't laugh with me. "Aww, you can't expect me to believe that I came on to you. I'ma need you to get your lies straight."

He gave me a look that said I was going to eat my words real soon. "Not only did you come on to me, you practically raped me." I chuckled. "You got pretty wild that night."

I was through, for real, now. "Ain't no fuckin way on earth that I did some crazy shit like that!"

"Way," he said pulling out his phone again, scrolling through. He sat it down in front of me, playing a video.

I looked at the recording. It had the date of Cash and Karen's wedding. In the video, my face was all in the camera just like a drunk woman. I heard Stoney's voice in the background. "Say hi, Vanity."

I moved in closer to the lens making my face look distorted. "I l-love yooooou," I said, slurring. "Why can't we just be together?"

Now, Stoney's face was in the camera. He had on a suit. I could see me in my bride's maid gown in the background. "If you're watching this, I only recorded it to show you what happened. I knew you wouldn't believe me so I wanted proof. When our paths crossed again. I didn't want you to think I was lying. Besides, I love you too."

"I know you love me too," I said in the video, kissing Stoney's face.

I looked up from the recording. "Keep watching," he told me. "There's much, much more."

The phone must've been sitting down somewhere now, because in the video, I was sitting on the bed in my gown and Stoney was sitting next to me. He told me I was drunk. I screamed at him saying I didn't care.

"Are you going to fuck me or not?" I asked boldly.

Stoney sighed. "But you're married."

"The hell with Ivan. I don't want to be with him anymore. I want to be with you. I've always wanted you." I gasped when I heard myself say that. What was I saying?

Thc video showed me stripping out of my gown while Stoney tried to dress me back in it. "You don't mean that. It's just the liquor talking."

"I'm not that drunk, Stoney. I know what I'm saying. This might come as a surprise, but I've always wanted you. Always."

I gasped again.

"Yes, you are. I just wanted to get you to your room safely. I'm leaving."

I assumed Stoney must've picked up the phone because the video shifted around the room out of focus before it showed me again.

"That's it. Run out on me like you did before. Deny us the chance at happiness. You ain't shit. You talk all this and that about us but you never mean it." I started stripping out of my undergarments. "If all you want is some pussy, I'll give you what you want. Come fuck me then."

"I don't want just your body. I want you. All of you. But I can't have all of you. You belong to someone else."

"Not tonight, I don't. I'm all yours, baby."

Standing before him nude, I dropped to my knees, hugging him around the waste, begging him to sleep with me. When he tried to help me up, I snatched away from him and quickly unfastened his pants. He was trying to fight me off. We wrestled for a moment and before long, I had his pants and boxers down with his thickness in my mouth.

I can't believe I said and did those things. I rocked back and forth, holding myself tight as I continued to watch the video. He was right. I did practically rape him. Tears came to my eyes. After watching the whole video, I realize that Stoney was telling the truth.

Seeing this has confused me even more. What if I really did love Stoney more than Ivan? Oh my God! That would mean I'm married to the wrong man.

"I'm sorry," I said, feeling so mortified. "I don't remember any of that. The girl in the video didn't represent me. I would never do something like that."

"See, that's the thing. I kinda think the girl in that video represented you a lot more than what you think."

"A whore. That's what I saw. And you think that's a good representation of me."

"That's not what I saw. I saw a woman who was finally free to speak her mind and do as she pleased."

Wiping my tears, I stood again. "I better go."

"No, don't leave. I didn't show you the video to make you upset. I just wanted you to know what I know. That's all. I was hoping it would bring us closer. That it would help you let your guard down even more."

"Well, it didn't. It made things worse. I realized that I'm a worse wife than what I thought. I got drunk and threw my vows away before now. And the sad part is, I had no idea until today."

"That's because you married the wrong man."

I cut my eyes at him. "No, it's because I keep cheating with you."

He stood too. "Please, don't leave. You and I both know that you meant everything that you said in that video."

He reached out for me and I pulled away. "I need some space."

"That's the problem. You're always leaving."

"That's right. I'm leaving you the same way you left me all those years ago. Alone."

"What are you talking about all those years ago?"

"Don't fuckin worry about it!" I screamed, walking away. "And don't fuckin follow me. I need a serious break from your ass."

I left him on the beach romancing himself while I caught a cab back to the hotel.

Chapter 20

Vanity

Crying in my room, I lost track of time. All this with Stoney felt like déjà vu. Once again, I was in another situation with him. Seeing that video bothered me badly. Deep down, I knew it was true. Yes, I loved him.

When he said he loved me in the video. I already knew that. Stoney has always been clear about his feelings for me. From day one. He's never hid how he felt. I was the one hiding. That's why I was constantly pushing him away. I didn't want to throw away the life that I've built just because Stoney resurfaced. Things just didn't work that way. I couldn't get rid of Ivan, the man who's been by my side when Stoney wasn't.

Thinking back over my life, I realized that I've always been torn between these two men. I wished that I could split myself in half. One part of me would always belong to Ivan no matter what. The other part of me wanted to run off into the sunset with Stoney. Build that wonderful life that we both desired.

Ivan was the man that I knew most of my life. We did a lot together. When people saw him, they usually saw me too. Inseparable. Quite naturally, it would make sense for us to get married, have kids, and live happily ever after. Oddly enough, that just never happened.

As much as I loved Ivan, it seemed like our marriage had out grown our childhood love. Lately, we seemed stuck together more out of convenience than love. Desperately fighting to stay together. Living in sheer misery to ease the pain of being alone. Since Ivan's always been there, I don't know how things would be without him in my life.

Stoney was the wild card. The one that made me question everything. This man lit a fire inside of me that only he could put out. The way he cared for me. Held me. Touched me. Looked at me. How he spoke to me. Just being in his presence made everything alright. When I was with him, time seemed to stand still. Nothing existed but him and I. Not a care in the world. This man genuinely made me happy. If someone asked me if God made this man just for me, I'd quickly answer YES!

I never questioned Stoney's love or loyalty. I questioned me. How did I truly feel? What was it that I loved about him? I had no idea. Was this an extension of pure lust? Or was it really love? If he wasn't sexing me like crazy, would things still be the same? I don't know. He's always fucked me good so I really can't say.

After this incident with my sister, I also questioned Stoney's faithfulness. He didn't seem like the type to be with one woman. Sex takes priority in his life. Almost more than me. Then, there's his finances. Ivan is a great provider. Is Stoney? Would he take care of me if I was his wife? I know he made decent money working for Marcel, but something tells me he's broke. He was waiting on a job offer as we speak. That doesn't sound too stable. So far, all he has to offer is incredible sex. I might be wrong. However, at this point, I can't see him replacing Ivan. I just can't.

Burying my face in my pillow, I cried even harder thinking about the back-alley abortion I had in high school. By the time I found out I was pregnant, Stoney was long gone. Scared, I told Ivan the baby was his. Immediately, he started rambling about his football career, preparation for college and his scholarship. How a baby would do nothing but slow us down. How we're too young to be parents. Pretty much the same bullshit he was feeding me now about not having a baby, ten years later.

I agreed to an abortion. Not for the reasons Ivan suggested. I had no idea how I was going to explain a baby that looked nothing like him or me. Aborting my baby was my last alternative. I wanted to keep her. That's why I went by Stoney's house several times, hoping that I could talk to him. Maybe he could help me figure this dilemma out. Each time I went by, it appeared to be vacant. Like no one had occupied it for quite some time. As usual his street was quiet. No one was in sight for me to ask questions of his whereabouts. So, I did what I had to do.

With all the sneaking around that we did, I never got to know any of his family members. I blamed myself for that. He had plenty of cousins, but it was my idea to keep our relationship a secret. Which means I never really existed in his life. Even to this day. My family is under the impression that I just started cheating with Stoney. They have no idea that this is an extension of what we started in high school and never got to finish.

Skipping class, Ivan took me to this weird woman around the way. Everyone thought she was a witch doctor. I was desperate so I didn't care what she was. She stopped Ivan dead in his tracks, making him wait outside.

Sitting in her home office, she asked me where the father of the baby was. I pretended like I didn't know what she was talking about. When I stuck to my guns saying that Ivan was the father, she shocked me by telling me all about Stoney.

Scared the living shit out of me. I had no idea how she knew about him. She described Stoney, my relationship with him, and my hazel-eyed baby. It messed me up when she insisted that I was making a huge mistake by getting rid of my daughter. From the moment I found out I was pregnant I knew it was a baby girl. What I always wanted. The doctor said I would regret terminating this pregnancy because Stoney was coming back into my life. Having an abortion would not solve my problems. It would only complicate them. Start a war in my life that would result in hurt, anguish, pain, and death. By the end of my journey, I would look back on this moment and connect the dots.

At the time, I didn't care what she was talking about. I just wanted to get rid of my love child. Laying in her makeshift doctor's office with nothing but a gown on, I expected for her to stick something inside of me like I saw in the movies. Instead, after she examined me confirming my pregnancy, she gave me two pills to take, and sent me on my way.

I left out of there feeling like nothing had happened. Clearly, Ivan didn't realize the severity of it either. He dropped me off and went straight to practice.

Five hours later, I started cramping. Nothing too bad at first. I excused myself from dinner and went to my room to call Ivan. As usual, he was unavailable. Out with his football buddies. As soon as I laid down on the bed, I got a fever. Then, my stomach started hurting really bad. The doctor said it would feel like a bad period. This felt nothing like that. It felt more like I was going to die. A mixture between the stomach flu and being in a head-on collision. Doubling over, I reached for the garbage can, puking my insides out.

Hiding in my room, only going to bathroom when necessary, I endured my miscarriage in silence. All by myself. In that moment, I longed for Stoney. Not Ivan. It wasn't his baby so I didn't fault him for skipping out on me. I blamed this all on Stoney. Being young and stupid, believing his lies and empty promises. And what did it get me? Knocked up.

Three weeks later, I was still having symptoms of nausea, cramping, and heavy bleeding. I think I lost ten pounds during that time because I could hardly eat. It wasn't until I passed out at the dinner table, that my parents were alerted about my condition. I was rushed to the hospital by ambulance. That's when they found about my pregnancy. I'm not sure what went wrong but I was still miscarrying three weeks later, hemorrhaging. I'd lost so much blood I had to be hospitalized. Pebbles had to donate blood since we have the exact same blood type.

I had dreams of my baby girl for years after that. I guess that's why I want a baby so bad. Stoney saying he wanted to get me pregnant again resonated with me because only he could right my wrong. Only he could replace the baby that I killed.

I tried to put the whole abortion thing behind me and move on with my life. I would be lying if I said it was that easy. This whole incident was a memory until I started trying to conceive with Ivan. That's when it haunted me all over again. My current doctor told me I was infertile. I suffered a bad infection due to the botched miscarriage, making it almost unlikely for me to conceive now. Knowing that I was the cause of my own infertility made me cry a sea of tears.

There was a knock at the door. If it was Stoney, I swear I was going to act a damn fool. He was the last person I wanted to see right now. Looking out the peephole, I saw Lyric. Opening the door, immediately, I felt some kinda way, staring at her big round belly.

"What do you want, Lyric?" I asked, standing in the doorway. I had no intentions of letting her pregnant ass in.

She avoided my fiery gaze. "Um, Karen sent me over here to see if you were ready to go to the, um, casino. Did I come at a bad time? You look angry."

I really felt bad now. I was taking my frustrations out on her. She hadn't done anything to me. Lyric was the sweetest person I knew. Besides, she'd been through enough shit to last a lifetime. And here I was about to cause her more grief.

"I'm sorry, Lyric," I said, unable to hold my emotions in. Tears streamed down my face. "I'm just having a really, really awful day. With so much on my mind, I forgot all about going to the casino." I moved aside so she could come in while I got myself together.

"I know I'm the last person you probably want to talk to after all the relationship mess ups I've had. But I'm here if you need me."

I might as well. What did I have to lose at this point? "I can't get pregnant because I got an abortion back in high school. Now, I'm infertile." I cried some more. I left out the other details. That was just way too much for me to handle right now.

Lyric looked at me with sad blue eyes. "You can have my baby," she said so lovingly. "The last thing I need is another child. I can't take care of the three I got."

I wiped my tears. “No, Lyric. I wasn’t suggesting that. I was just upset at myself for being so stupid. I should have had my baby instead of worrying about what other people thought. Then I wouldn’t be in the mess I’m in today.”

“You know,” Lyric said looking down at the floor. “I fault myself for being stupid too. I never told anyone this, Vanity, but all my kids are the product of rape. Well, except for this little bundle of joy. His father was shot and killed trying to protect me.” She stared at me, waiting for me to process the information.

“Lyric, I would have never guessed that. I’m so sorry. Here I am being miserable about my situation and yours is much, much worse.” Now, I really felt bad for acting the way I did towards her.

“Not to mention, I just got out of jail. My life is so crazy right now. Although, I am glad I didn’t have to do my whole sentence. I thank God for that. Still, I’m on probation and I have no money to take care of the kids that I got. I don’t know what I’m going to do about this baby. There’s just no room in my life for one more mouth.”

I didn’t know Lyric’s full story. I just know that her mother ended up in jail. She went into the foster care system. We had no way of finding out where she was because her mother was estranged from the family at the time. She suffered abuse in foster care. Then she was lured into prostitution by her pimp boyfriend. She ended up doing time after snapping and committing murder.

Coming out of my funk, I decided to stop feeling sorry for myself. I got up from the bed and hugged her, kissing her cheek. “You got me. Anything you need, you just call. I want a list of what your kids need. I’m going to make sure they get it.” I hugged her tighter. “Your family loves you. You hear me?”

She nodded her head still looking numb.

“I know Karen and Natalia don’t have a clue about what’s going on. Or they would have helped you a long time ago. Make sure you talk to them. Tell them what happened to you. They would want to know.”

She finally smiled. "Thanks Vanity. It feels good to know that you got my back. For the longest, all I had was myself."

"Girl, please. We're family. I know you're not used to reaching out to us, but you need to start." It's a shame that we just met Lyric not that long ago. She'd gone her whole life alone when she could have used our support. I would blame her mother, but she suffered the same fate. Rape, babies, and jail.

"I feel like I'm cursed, Vee. I'm not wife material like you are. Men only see me as an object of their desire. They use me and abuse me. That's all I'm good for."

"Lyric, you are one of the prettiest women walking this earth. Just stunning." I looked into her gloomy eyes. "Your worth is not defined by a man. With everything that you've been through, you should be dead or half-crazy by now. Yet, your spirit is still beautiful and pure. Not to mention, you pop them babies out and bounce right back. Your body is amazing. You don't even have stretch marks. Who does that? I bet Natalia is super jealous of you right now." I laughed, making her smile again. I was just kidding. Natalia popped those kids out too and bounced right back. Just not effortlessly like Lyric did.

"Thanks again, Vanity. When I look in the mirror, I don't see beauty. I see prostitute. Jailbird. Whore. Bad mother. Loser." Big teardrops formed in her eyes. "Worthless."

She was about to make me cry again. I held back my tears, trying to be strong for her. "I'm going to help you find a man. A real man who loves you and your kids. There's someone for everyone."

"There is?" she said with crocodile tears.

"Yes. I truly believe that. And I'm claiming it for you."

She wiped her tears. "Hey, if you and Ivan ever decide you want to go with a surrogate, I'd be glad to help you out. As you know, I'm super fertile. I can carry as many babies as you guys want."

I hugged her again. She just made my day. "Thanks, Lyric. That means so much to me. I never even thought about that. I guess I was tripping for nothing."

"No. We all have our weaknesses. Just in different forms."

"I love you, Lyric."

"Love you too, Vanity."

"You know what? I got a feeling something good is going to happen to you tonight. That will be the beginning of your good luck."

A glow came over her when I said that. Lyric didn't talk a lot, especially, if she didn't know you. I made a mental note to spend more time with her, get her a serious make over, and find her a man. Stoney said he had a ton of cousins. I'd ask him first. Well, once we worked through our issues.

She patiently waited for me as I showered and dressed.

Walking out of the hotel room, I bumped into Stoney. He looked at me and kept it moving. I didn't know what his attitude was about. I'm the one that was humiliated. I decided to keep it moving too.

Just the girls went to the casino. They guys were going to a party. I didn't care. That meant I didn't have to see Stoney. Marcel was nice enough to leave Natalia with a credit card that had a fifty-thousand dollar limit. We were about to gamble for real.

I was up two-hundred dollars when Karen sat next to me, messing my concentration up. I could tell that she wanted to chat so I stopped in the middle of my game. "What's goodie?"

"Ugh! I don't like your attitude." She pretended to roll her eyes at me. "No, but seriously, I just wanted to make sure you were ok. I hadn't seen much of you since everything happened."

"I'm straight. Me and Pebbles, we're good. Blood is thicker than water. And it was my fault. I did say that I didn't care when I really did. My situation with Stoney runs a lot deeper than you all know."

I was about to go back to playing my game when Karen started talking. "I know you two have history. Not sure what the details are. He didn't tell me. Since Stoney and I are so close, I know how he feels about you too. And I see the way you look at him. There's something there."

"I'm not leaving Ivan, Karen," I said, cutting her off. "Nice try."

"No, I wouldn't ask you to do that. I was just going to say, I hope your using protection. If not condoms, some kind of birth control. Stoney is super fertile."

I twisted my face. "How would you know?" I started getting defensive because it seemed like the secrets were coming at me left and right. "Have you fucked him too?"

She giggled as if that comment tickled her pink. "No. No. Nothing like that. I'm just saying that he comes from a very fertile family. Emerald and Cash are both potent. Their fathers and uncles are too. Making babies is hereditary for them. I can't imagine Stoney being any different. As soon as I got off the pill and Cash stopped using condoms, I conceived right away. I had a miscarriage and within two months I was pregnant again with Bash. Then I made the mistake of giving Cash some before my six-week checkup and boom, here I am. Pregnant again."

"Wow. I didn't know that. You never told me."

"I know. I had my doubts about fertility issues so I kinda kept it to myself. I'm only saying something now because I know you're having fun with Stoney. However, if you plan on working things out with Ivan, you might want to double up on the contraceptives. Just in case. If anyone can get you pregnant, it would definitely be Stoney."

"I appreciate your concern, but I don't have that problem. I'm infertile. That's another reason why Ivan and I have been arguing. Over the last two years I've been trying to get pregnant. I've almost blown all of our savings on fertility treatments."

Karen hugged me. "Oh, honey, I'm so sorry. I wouldn't have brought this up if I knew."

"It's ok, really. I'm taking it one day at a time." For once, I wasn't down about not being pregnant. Talking to Lyric made me realize that things weren't as bad as I thought. I had other options too.

"Good. I'm glad to hear that. Natalia got enough babies for the both of us. She got so many, she can keep some, and still give away a few." Karen laughed.

I laughed too. "You would think that Marcel was a part of their family too. Making babies the way he does."

"He might as well be. They claim him like he's family. Mrs. Emilia loves her some Marcel. And the babies call her grandma."

"Now, that's cute. I can only imagine how it would be to lose my whole family. Marcel is so strong."

"He is. Such a great soul too. For someone who is almost a billionaire, he has truly stayed humble."

"Now, ain't that the truth."

While Karen and I were talking, Stoney walked up.

"Oh, that's my cue to bounce." Karen hopped out of her seat going on about her business.

"Hey." He flopped down in Karen's seat.

I turned back around playing the slots again. "Hey. I thought you were at the party?"

"We're on our way. Marcel needed to speak to Natalia first." He scooted a little closer, whispering. I guess so nobody would hear. "Listen, I didn't mean to make you upset earlier. That wasn't my intention. I just—" He sighed.

"I believe you." I sighed too. "It's just that nothing between us is cut and dry. I thought it would be sex and that's it. That I could leave all this with you behind in the Bahamas. I'm seeing that's not the case." I shrugged as if I didn't care.

He kept a cool demeanor, but I felt his sadness. "Just let me know what you decide," he said looking at the floor instead of me. "I just—"

Ching. Ching. Ching.

The ringing of my slot machine interrupted Stoney.

I glanced at it excited that I just won more money. "Another twenty dollars." I danced in my seat for a moment. I'm really getting the hang of this gambling thing. After my mini celebration, I looked back in Stoney's direction. He was gone. Whatever. He was messing up my flow anyway.

Ding. Ding. Ding. Ding. Ding.

Another machine was going off, sounding a loud red alarm.

I jumped up to see who just hit the jackpot. Lyric smiled from ear to ear as Piper danced around her. Piper looked cute with her sexy lime and gold short outfit and matching heels.

The machine was ringing off the hook.

I went over there to see how much Lyric won. My mouth hung open when I saw that she just won twenty-thousand dollars.

"I won. I won," Lyric said, doing old school dances with Piper.

Honestly, if any one needed it, it was her. "I told you I had a good feeling."

She stood by her machine smiling bright.

Well, I guess we were calling it a night. Nobody else was going to hit anything in this place. I'm sure this small casino had reached its limit with Lyric's winnings. This payout probably broke their little bank.

Chapter 21

Pebbles

Flawless. That's all I can say when we entered the club. We shut that bitch down with fashion. All of us were wearing liquid gear in different styles and colors with stilettos. Me, Juicy, and Joss had the same booty shorts. Joss wore red and her top was strapless. Juicy had on silver and her top went up around her neck. I had on gold and my top looked more like a bra, except it came down a little bit more. Shay had on a liquid purple mini dress. Cookie had on a pink liquid shirt that only covered one arm and a mini skirt.

Scott met Cookie at the door, whisking her away. Joss sat at the bar ordering her a drink. Juicy hit the dance floor partnering up with this handsome guy.

That left me and Shay. I followed her over to the table where Moneaco was waiting. He politely stood, greeting me with a hug and a kiss on the cheek, before excusing himself to get our drinks.

I was hyped. I had been waiting to hit the club since we got here.

"This is nice," Shay said, dancing in her chair.

"Ok!" I exclaimed, dancing in mine. "I'm going to join Juicy in a minute. Girl, ain't nothing going to kill my vibe tonight."

"I think you spoke too soon."

As soon as I looked up, Moneaco was walking up with Shay's drink and his lame ass cousin Carl had mine. "Hello, beautiful. So nice to see you again."

"Hi." I think I gave the driest greetings in the history of greetings. That's how much I wasn't feeling this nicca.

He pulled up a seat like I asked him to join me. I cut my eyes at Shay. She pleaded with me to act right. His wack ass wasn't about to ruin my fun. I downed my drink and held the empty glass in his face so that he could see I needed another one. That's all he was good for, buying me drinks.

He came back toting three more drinks for me. And I drank all three. Now, that I was feeling nice, I didn't need him anymore. "Toodles."

I was about to stand up and leave when Carl spoke to me. "I've been calling you. Did you get my messages?"

"Um, yeah," I said as if he should have known.

"I wanted to spend more time with you before you left."

"Why do you have my cousin begging?" Moneaco asked me.

Shay jumped to my defense right away. "You need to stay your ass out of it. That's between them."

Moneaco was hell bent on hyping up his wack ass cousin. "Let me just say that he's a good catch. He has plenty of money to spend on you. Buy you nice things. Take you around the world. Every woman wants to be treated like a queen. Why don't you give him a try?"

"First off, can't no man buy me. I'm not for sale. So he could be making crazy bank and I'd still diss his ass. Secondly, your cousin is lacking something that I need. I'm going to keep it classy and not go into detail about that. Third, you need to stay out my damn business before I get 26th and California on that ass."

Moneaco was puzzled. "What is 26th and California?"

Shay's arm was wrapped around his. "Baby, it's where the jail is. Around the way, that's what we say when we're about to whoop someone's ass and catch a case."

"Oh," Moneaco said, shutting his ass up, real quick, sipping his drink.

Muthafucka better ask somebody. Everyone from Chicago knew that's where Cook County jail was. Moneaco might not have known, but he was about to quickly find out if he kept on fucking with me.

Carl put his arm around me as if we were together. "Let's spend time together tonight." He leaned over whispering in my ear. "I want to repeat the other night."

"Hold that thought," I told Carl, making my way to the dance floor. He got me too fucked up, if he thought for one second, I was going to spend my last night in the Bahamas babysitting his little dick ass.

The Deejay was murdering the turntables. As soon as I hit the floor a guy asked me to dance. The Reggaeton was bumping and I began to show off my skills. The guy dancing with me could hardly keep up. He tried his best to hang in there though.

After nearly an hour of nonstop movement, I needed to use the restroom. Dude said he'd order me a drink while I went to relieve myself. I walked inside thinking I never did get his name. Still moving to the music, I squatted over the toilet, did my business, flushed, and washed my hands. Checking myself out in the mirror, I turned around to see how fat my booty looked. The liquid outfit was stunning on me. That's why I had hating ass bitches looking in my direction and men drooling. I smiled at myself, walking out.

The moment I came out of the bathroom someone grabbed me, putting his hand over my mouth. I kicked and screamed as he drug me out the back exit. I was hauled into the pitchblack grassy area behind the club.

"Get off of me," I said, although it came out muffled.

I continued to kick and scream until he pushed me down in the grass face first. His body landed on top of mine with his hand still over my mouth and my arms pinned underneath me.

"You got my dick so hard wearing such tight clothes."

"Carl?" I mumbled. This pussy ass nicca.

"I just have to have you."

He tugged at my fitted bottoms, pulling them down to my thighs. His fingers slipped through the crack of my ass, caressing the tender flesh of my anus.

"Ah! So soft."

I cringed when he stuck his finger inside of me.

"I'm going to have you the same way I did the other night while you were sleep."

What a sicko!

"I wish I could suck on your sweet pussy too."

He moaned in my ear grinding that little pecker against me with his finger still deep inside of me. I was sick to my stomach with anger. When he finally turned me loose I was going to fuck his ass up.

"Get your nasty ass off of her," I heard someone say."

I couldn't see shit. But there was nothing wrong with my hearing. Carl received a hit to his mid-section and I heard him howl in pain. He rolled off of me and my savior helped me up.

In true Chicago fashion, I went animal on his ass, landing a few body blows and a final kick to his face. "Muthafucka! You got me fucked up. For real."

I would have done more if my savior didn't jerk me in the opposite direction.

"Pull your shorts up."

I forgot they were still down. That's how livid I was. Being in beast mode, I would have gone at him wearing nothing. As soon as I pulled up my shorts, I tried to charge back in that direction. The mystery man picked me up off my feet, carrying me back towards the front of the club. When we got into the light, I was finally able to see this guy's face.

"Jayson!" I hugged him real tight. I've never been so happy to see Jayson's bug-a-boo ass in all my life.

I had to admit he really impressed me by stepping up the way he did. Honestly, I didn't think he had the balls. Then again, Carl wasn't much of a man anyway. I could have handled him if he didn't pull a sneak attack. On the other hand, Jayson can step up all he wants to, handling things for me. I didn't feel like breaking my heels or my nails whooping nobody's ass.

"Are you ok?" He looked at me with concern. His eyes fell to my crotch. "Did he hurt you?"

I let out a crazy laugh. "I don't think he's capable of hurting me with the package he's carrying." I laughed a little longer before sighing.

"Are you sure you're ok?"

"I'm fine." I looked down at my gold outfit. I had a couple of grass stains. Nothing too noticeable though.

"I can take you home if you want me to. My car is right over there." He pointed to it. "That's how I saw you. I circled the club trying to find a parking spot. Are you sure you're ok?"

"Other than wanting to smash his face in, I'm good." I sighed, thinking of payback for Carl. "I haven't seen you the whole trip. Where have you been hiding?"

"I've been out and about. I saw you at the Welcome Party." He grinned. "I can't lie, you're a bad chick."

I smirked and did a cute little dance. "You know, I do what I do."

We both cracked up.

Entering the club, Carl came out of nowhere with a knife aimed at Jayson. Pushing me out the way, Jayson moved to the side and Carl ended up slicing the big bulky dude in front of us instead. Bulky dude turned around with the look of death on his face. Reacting immediately, he punched Carl in the face, knocking him back a few feet.

"Bitch! Move out my damn way," I heard Joss yell over the loud music. I couldn't see her but I heard her big ass mouth. "I'm about to go HAM in this muthafucka if I can't find my sister."

Bulky dude saw the blood on his arm and lost it. He dived at Carl, head-butting him, throwing bows. Carl was in a daze. I used it to my advantage sneaking a few more blows too. He didn't know who had hit him. Assuming it was the bulky dude, he went at him in full force only to get his ass tore up.

All my cousins showed up out of now where, ready to put in work. Even pregnant Cookie. She had a broken beer bottle in her hand.

I looked at her and laughed. "What are you going to do?"

"Shit, a bitch can whoop some ass if she need to. This baby don't stop shit. You know that. They fuck with you, they fuck with us," she said, waving the broken glass in the air. "Chi-town, baby. All day."

I was still cracking up. "I already know how you get down."

"What happened?" Shay asked with Moneaco in tow. "Why is Carl fighting that guy? And where the hell have you been?"

I looked directly at Moneaco. "Your trifling cousin snatched me up when I came out of the bathroom and tried to rape me out back. Jayson," I said, pointing over at him. "Saw me on the ground and pulled Carl's low life piece of shit ass off of me. That's why I didn't give your cousin any play. The nicca's a muthafuckin creep."

"I can't believe it!" Moneaco yelled, rushing over to Carl who just got knocked the fuck out.

Club security was late than a muthafucka. I guess it took them so long because they were cops too. They questioned the bulky dude and then talked to Moneaco. What they did next blew me away. I was thinking about back home when some shit broke out. Niccas went to jail. Not in the Bahamas though. They picked Carl's ass up and tossed him smooth the fuck out of the club into the street.

We all said at the same time, "Daaaaaaaayum!"

Then they came over to me and asked me what happened. I told them exactly how he attacked me. They told me to come and file charges at the police station in the morning. I explained to them that I would be back home by then. My flight leaves in the morning. Then I suggested that if I could get two more licks off his ass, I'd call it even. They said go right ahead. That shit bugged me out too. However, it didn't stop me from kicking the dog piss out of Carl's perverted ass. I tried to stomp a hole in his little stubby dick.

Joss carefully ran in her heels and arched her back, using the ball of her wrist, socking him twice. "BIIIITCH!"

Moneaco rushed outside where Carl was making a phone call. I guess he was calling someone to come and get his trifling ass cousin. Fuck him. Now, I'm ready to turn up. What he did was a thing of the past.

"C'mon, Jayson. Buy me a drink."

Jayson smiled at me. "Lead the way, beautiful."

After ordering our drinks, he asked me to join him out on the patio and I agreed. Shit after Carl, I'd better stick close. I settled in a cozy spot with him while the waitress brought over our cocktails. The ambiance was really romantic. A few other couples were out there with us, enjoying the gorgeous night.

"I need to be upfront with you. I'm married."

"You're whaaaaat?" Aw, hell naw. I nearly spit out my drink. "I don't fuck with married men."

Jayson saw the look on my face. "Let me explain. My wife was cheating on me for over a year before I found out. Now, I'm not sure if my six-week-old son is mine. At the moment, we're not speaking."

"Whoa! That's a lot to take in. You got major bullshit going on in your life. I don't do drama. You got that."

He sighed. "I understand where you're coming from. I just didn't want to lie to you. You know, just in case."

"Well, had you lied, you would have gotten what Carl's lame ass got. A beat down."

Jayson chuckled. "I can't believe they just threw homie out on the curb like that. Like he was yesterday's trash. The Bahamas is wild. That's why I love this place."

I gave him a suspicious eye. "Why aren't you wearing your wedding ring?"

"I took my ring off when we separated." I looked at him like what he said was some bullshit. "Thinking about divorce is the last thing I wanted when I got married. I'm thirty and I have enough money to retire right now. I own ten restaurants. Four were passed down to me by my grandfather. I acquired the other six myself. So, you see, I work hard."

I looked down at the platinum pinky ring he had on his finger. It showed how paid he was. "I deserve a woman who treats me right. I gave her everything. All I asked is for her to love me in return."

I had to speak up before he got all mushy on me. "Look, let me be real with you, you seem cool and all, but I'm not looking for nothing serious right now. Just a friend."

"Never?"

"I didn't say never. I don't know what the future might hold. I might get struck by cupid's arrow and fall in love tomorrow. All I can do is speak for today. I'll chill with you, but after this, I don't know." I looked at him waiting for him to say something slick. I was ready for his ass too.

"That's fair. Well, let's make the best of it then." He looked behind me over at the game room. "You play pool?"

"Not really," I said, twisting up my face. That didn't sound like fun. I wanted to get my party on.

He sipped the last of his drink. "Don't knock it until you try it."

I shrugged my shoulders and finished my drink off. "Let's do it then." I wasn't sure if I was going to like it.

We played three games. I can officially say that I sucked at pool. He tried to show me how to hold the stick. I kept dropping it. The stick stayed more on the floor than in my damn hand. Then, when I finally held it right, I couldn't shoot the damn ball. If I wasn't knocking the ball on the floor, I was hitting his balls in instead of mine. I was beyond frustrated. Jayson cracked up laughing. It tickled the hell out of him to see me so perplexed.

"I'm tired of this shit," I said throwing the stick down on the pool table. At this point I didn't care where it landed. "I need another drink."

"I got you. Let's sit at the bar."

We grabbed two available seats. Jayson ordered for us. I got another Bahama Mama. That's what I started drinking so I just stuck with it. I wasn't trying to be puking everywhere, looking like a lush.

"C'mon," Jayson said, pulling me to my feet. "Let's dance."

I nearly spilled my drink. "Wait. Let me sit my drink down first."

We danced to a Reggae mix over Hip-Hop beats. Jayson pushed his hardness up against me. He felt kinda big too. I enjoyed the music, backing my ass up on him until the club closed.

By the time we left, I had nine drinks. I wasn't drunk but I was way pass tipsy. All those Bahama Mamas had me horny as hell. My panties were super wet. I wanted to cum so bad, but I didn't want to fuck. Something about Jayson just turned me off. But I could sure use a good lick.

"Take me back to my hotel room," I instructed Jayson as soon as I got in the car.

Disappointment was all over his face. "But I wanted you to stay the night with me."

"I'm not in the mood for all that. I just want to go back to the hotel, take care of myself, get a good nut, and go to sleep."

Jayson watched me for a moment. "You don't have to take care of yourself. I can do it for you." He stared between my legs. "That's if you want me too."

"Straight up, I just want to be licked. If you can't do that for me, then I can go home and make it happen for myself."

Jayson smiled with desire. "Are you wet right now?"

Seeing the big lump in his shorts made me want to reconsider getting stuck too. "Yeah, why?"

"Let me touch it," he asked, licking his lips

I opened my legs wider inviting him to feel. He slipped his hand down my shorts causing me to moan. His touch was like silk. It made me wonder what his meat was like too. He leaned over kissing my lips. A romantic kiss that made me want to have sex with him.

"Mmmm. Nice. How about you stay the night with me? I'll lick you and make you cum as many times as you want. And when I'm done, if you don't want me inside of you, I'll please myself. Is that cool?"

"Ok," I moaned. He would ask me that while his hand was still inside of my shorts, knowing I would agree.

He kissed me again. "I don't want to do anything you don't want me to, beautiful. So, let me know if I go too far. We can stop at any time. I promise."

"You don't have to handle me with kid's gloves. I'm not fragile."

"I know, but I want to make sure you know that I'm nothing like Carl."

I believed him. "Ugh! Don't even mention that loser's name."

He chuckled. "My bad."

Jayson took me back to his spot. He actually had a timeshare there in the Bahamas. I was glad he didn't live that far because my feet were killing me from dancing in these high ass heels.

I started to strip out of my clothes when Jayson stopped me. He wanted to undress me. We kissed the whole time. When I was completely naked, Jayson took his time kissing all over my body before he sucked my breasts and then my pussy. I stood as he kneeled before me holding one of my legs in the air. His tongue snaked between my lower lips. Before long, I was cumming.

I pinched my nipples trying to keep my balance as my juices flowed out. Jayson tongued between my legs as if he couldn't get enough and then locked his lips around my clit once again making me cum instantly.

Hands down, I knew for sure he enjoyed eating pussy. I watched as he paid attention to me while unzipping his shorts, releasing his penis. It was a nice eight inches of thickness. Staring at his tool forced me into a violent orgasm. I would have fell on the floor if Jayson didn't catch me.

"Let's take it to bed before you kill yourself."

Leaping into the bed, I rested on my back.

Jayson took off his clothes and joined me with his dick leading the way. "Naw, not like that. Sit on my face."

He didn't have to ask me twice. I got up so that Jayson could take my place. My eyes stared at his hard-on pointed in the air as he laid down. Jayson motioned for me to ride his face. I had another thought in mind. Straddling my legs over his chest, I decided to face his penis so I could look at it while he pleased me. Hungry for it, Jayson jerked my hips back onto his face as if he couldn't live without it.

"Mmmmm," he moaned. "You taste so good. Makes me want to cum all over myself."

His dick was inches from my face while I rocked back and forth on his face. Suddenly, I yearned to have his sexy dick in my mouth. That was crazy to me. I didn't find him sexy at all. Kinda cute but no appeal whatsoever. But I was very much attracted to his tool. I kept looking at. I could have sworn it called my name, making my mouth water.

"I want you to nut in my mouth again," he mumbled with his lips still buried in my treasure.

Drunk in lust, I grabbed his meat, loving the way his flesh felt in my hand. At first, I jerked slow and sensual, enjoying the smoothness. As my orgasm came near, I began to jerk him faster and faster. Before long, he was eating me out at hyper-speed and I was jacking his dick at the same tempo.

Playing with his meat had me so worked up that when I finally did cum, I ended up gushing out. He must've felt the same way because globs of cum squirted out of his dick at the same time.

Jayson smacked me on the ass. "Shower with me, beautiful."

I got off of him. He got up and walked in the direction of the shower. When I entered, I thought it was another bedroom. I was in awe when I saw his astonishing bathroom fit for a king.

"I love your bathroom," I said, turning in a complete circle looking around at everything.

He grinned. "Thank you, sweetness."

Taking his time, he admired my body, washing me from head to toe. The way the sponge moved over my body felt more erotic than cleansing. Surely, I wasn't going to admit that to him. All the touching lit the fire burning between my legs once again. By the stiffness of his erection, I guess he was feeling the same way.

"I need another release," he said to me, closing his eyes.

I watched as he aggressively stroked himself with his eyes closed, concentrating. At least that's what it looked like to me.

"What are you thinking about?"

His eyes popped open. "You, beautiful," he said in a sexy low voice.

"What is it about me that you like?" I asked, moving closer to him. Watching him handle his meat had me completely fired up.

"Everything," he said with his eyes still closed.

"Tell me," I asked, slipping my fingers between my lower lips. "Tell me."

He jerked harder. "Your pretty feet. Your pouty lips."

"Mmmm-Hmmm."

"Your bouncy ass. Your juicy pussy. AH!" He yelled. His body stiffened, releasing cum down the drain.

"YEEEESSSS!" I hollered, cumming right along with him. He wasn't about to leave me out. I wanted another one too.

After washing again, we both dived in the bed, falling asleep right away.

Chapter 22

Pebbles

Stretching my arms, I accidently hit Jayson in the head. He must've really enjoyed himself last night because he didn't even budge. He was out cold, lying on his back. I guess he wasn't that bad. I actually had fun with him. And he kept his word. He didn't try anything in the middle of the night. Just to be sure there were pillows dividing us.

My eyes traveled down the length of his body, which was really defined with muscles. As I kept my eyes glued on him, his penis grew into an erection forming a tent under the sheet. I leaned over looking at him closely. He was still sleep. I tried to ignore his erection but I couldn't. And then, my coochie began to throb, forming a heartbeat. I thought about pleasing myself but I knew that wasn't what my kitty wanted. She wanted to know what Jayson's manhood felt like.

Rolling over quietly, I removed the pillows, throwing them on the floor, and slid under Jayson's sheet. I looked up at him to see if he moved. He didn't. So, I kept on going. Taking off the oversized shirt he gave me, I positioned my nude body over his, making the sheet fall off both of us.

Yearning for penetration, I slid down on his pole, rotating my hips slowly.

Jayson opened his sleepy eyes as I rode him. Even though he wasn't fully awake, his dick sure was. I took full advantage of it too.

"Good morning, beautiful,"

"Good. Ah! Ah! Ah! Morning." I was jumping up and down now. Ready to cum. "Oh, Jayson, your dick feels so fuckin good." My rocking changed to a nasty rhythm, jerking my pelvis back and forth.

Fully up now, Jayson held my hips pounding into to me. "Yeah, work that pussy."

Hearing him talk dirty got me even hotter. "Yeah, boo, you like this pussy on your dick, don't you?"

"Fuck yeah," he said sitting up. "Get it, baby."

My eyes rolled into the back of my head. My body trembled. "Ah! Ah! Ah! Ah! Aaaaaaaaah! Yeeessssss."

Jayson held me tight, flipping me onto my back still pounding away as I came. "Ooooh. Ssssss. You got some good pussy. Daaaaaamn."

His breath was labored. I knew he was about to cum. "Don't squirt in me."

"Huh? What? Oooooh. It's so goooood, though."

"Pull out!" I damn sure didn't want this nicca's nut in me. I don't care if I was on the pill. Hell no!

"Oh! Oh! Ok. Ok. Ok." He pulled out just in time, oozing semen on my pubic hairs. "Fuuuuuuuck!"

"Shit, you cum a lot."

He smiled as if it was a compliment.

"Hold still," he said, climbing out of the bed to get a face rag. He came back immediately, wiping all his kids off of me.

I rolled over on my side, purposely not facing him. I was glad I didn't make any commitments. I would have really been fucked then. I pretended to be sleep when Jayson got back into the bed. That didn't stop him from curling up close, spooning me.

Mwah! He kissed my face. "I wish you were mine. I'd spoil you rotten. Buy you whatever you wanted. Give you the world if you wanted it."

He stroked my hair. I cringed. He was doing too much. Clingy and shit. I was ready to dip out.

"You're special to me already."

Ugh! What a lame. "Um, I thought we talked about this already."

"I know, but I needed you to know. I fell for you the moment I saw you."

Jayson was cool and all. He was a really nice guy, but I still had no real interest in him other than sex or money. I wish I could detach his dick and take it with me, leaving his stale ass right here.

Although, he was good in bed, I found him dull, which put a damper on my attraction for him. A complete turn off. For real. No swag whatsoever. His conversation was wack. I didn't like how he dressed. Just not my type. Period. Point blank.

I heard my phone buzz. There was a missed call and three texts. It was from Vanity. She said that I had an hour to get back to the hotel, check out, and make it to the airport to board the flight. If I didn't make it to the airport on time, the next fight to Chicago wasn't for another three days.

"Who was that? Your man?"

He's tripping. "No. That was my sister," I said rushing to his shower washing off our morning sex.

"Let me join you," he said, pulling the curtain back.

"No!" Damn, he was getting on my nerves, shit. Fuckin bug-a-boo ass. "Look, I need to hurry up and get back to the hotel and pack. My family is waiting for me to check out."

"I'll drive you then."

"Jayson, straight up, I'm good. Call me a cab. Do that."

Geesh! I was about ready to knock his no swag having ass in the head again. Sit your ass down somewhere.

"Ok, they'll be here in five minutes."

"Thanks."

I was already out of the shower, putting on my clothes from the night before, when he popped up in the doorway. "Here. You don't have to wear what you had on from last night."

I looked at the shorts and the top that he gave me, and said fuck it, putting them shits on. Normally, I didn't wear other chick's clothes unless they were family. The shorts and shirt weren't my style, but hey, I couldn't be picky at this point. It was either wear dirty shit or someone else's shit.

I was in the process of looking around to see if I left something when Jayson started sweating me again.

"I wish you could stay longer. I'll pay for you to leave on a later fight or even tomorrow." He got excited as if I said yes to him rescheduling my flight. "That way we could spend the whole day together."

I grabbed a plastic bag putting my dirty clothes in it. "Ain't gonna happen, Boo-Boo." I heard the horn blow. I looked out the window seeing my cab. "That's me. I'm out."

"Don't be in such a rush. Give me a hug," he said, grabbing me and holding me tight for what seemed like an eternity. "Be safe traveling back. And here's a little something for you to remember me by."

I snatched the paper out of his hand, kissed him on the check as a nice gesture and rolled out. He stood in the doorway, waving bye as I sat in the cab. I opened my hand to waved bye. The paper he gave me fell out on the floor. I bent down to get it as the cab pulled off. My eyes bucked when I realized it was money inside. A thousand dollars. Was he calling me a prostitute? As if he heard my thoughts, I got a text from him that said I hope I didn't offend you, but you deserve the best.

That gesture didn't change my mind. Jayson wasn't boyfriend material in my book. I texted him back, Thank you. I appreciate it. And that was the end of that.

When I got back to the hotel room, I didn't see Vanity or anyone else in sight. Her side of the hotel room was empty. While my stuff was still thrown around the room. Gathering my things as quickly as possible, I tossed everything into my suitcases. I didn't care what went with what as long as it was in there. Sweeping through the room, I made sure I didn't leave anything. I wheeled my luggage out the room towards checkout, praying that it didn't take forever.

I was the only one at the counter. Excited couldn't even describe how I felt at that moment. It quickly changed when I took a good look at the ancient woman staring at the computer like it was a foreign object. She had to be at least one-hundred years old. Dammit! Just my luck.

"May I help you?" Everything on her was shaking from her hands to her neck to her voice. You got to be kidding me.

"Yes, I need to check out." I handed her my key card. Her hands were trembling so bad that I couldn't even give it to her. This some bullshit.

After many attempts, she finally took the key card out of my hand. I sighed loudly. Now, she was trying to type on the keyboard as if she hadn't heard my frustration. She probably didn't. I bet her hearing was bad too. Jesus take the wheel, please!

After ten minutes of this nonsense, I was through with her and the damn checkout process. I was just about to ask her if there was someone else who could help me when a young man walked up.

"Thanks, Greta." He stepped in front of the computer and the old woman shuffled on to the back. "Sorry about that. I had to go to the bathroom and I'm the only one here."

I looked at him like he had and eye in the middle of his forehead.

"How may I help you?" he asked politely.

"I need to be at the airport in less than fifteen minutes," I said, eyeing the clock once more. "Can you hurry up and check me out so I can get there on time?" I wanted to curse so bad but I kept my cool.

"Sure, no problem. Is this your key card, right here?"

"Yeeeessss," I said with an attitude.

By the time he finished, I had ten minutes to get there on time. It wasn't that far away. Still, time was not on my side. Racing outside of the hotel, I jumped in the first taxi I saw and told him to get me to the airport as fast as possible. He got my luggage, tossed it in the back, and took off at high speed.

Why did I tell this man to get me there as fast as possible? He had me flying all over the taxi as he turned corners on two wheels. I would have clicked in if possible, but there wasn't no damn seatbelts in this muthafucka. I just held on to the seat in front of me and prayed that I made it there in one piece.

"Miss Lady, we here," the Bahamian driver said, stopping abruptly. I'm glad I didn't eat. That shit would be everywhere.

Jumping out, I snatched my luggage from him and ran towards customs. Pouring down with sweat, the window closed seconds before I got there. Dang, I was too late. I banged on the window. The woman pulled the shade up. She pointed to the clock. I guess insinuating that I had run out of time.

My mind raced a million miles a minute. I'd already checked out. No longer did I have a place to stay. Well, I had money thanks to Jayson. I'd stay with his lame ass if I had to. He could pay for my flight back too. But then I'd have to spend the next three days with him. Ugh! I growled.

Standing there contemplating what my next move was going to be, I felt someone wrap their arms around me, kissing my neck. I was about to get busy on his face when I saw who it was.

"Gabriel!" I screamed, hugging him tight.

He squeezed me too. "Mmmm-Mmmm. That's how I like to be greeted." We kissed. "Why are you standing right here?"

"She won't let me in."

"Yes, she will. I got you."

Gabriel banged on the window. The woman lifted the shade with an attitude but change her frown into a smile when she saw him. "Let us through, Nikki."

She looked at me and rolled her eyes. "Who is this girl?"

I wanted to say, who the fuck are you, bitch? But I stayed in my place. I was trying to get back home.

Gabriel chuckled. "Stop being jealous Nikki. You know you're my number one."

Her whole demeanor changed. She smiled bright, giving us the stamp of approval to move on through. Without validation from her, we weren't going nowhere.

"Thanks," I told Gabriel when we passed through customs. "I just knew I was stuck here a few more days. Who was that girl, anyway?"

"My mean ass cousin. I'm her favorite so she's nice to me. Everyone else catches hell." He chuckled.

"You don't even have to tell me. If she had her way, I'd still be standing on the other side of that window.

Gabriel had his arm around me when we walked into the terminal where my family was seated. Cash and Marcel's eyes were on Gabriel like flies to shit. I knew they were going to give me a hard time.

Vanity and Stoney were sitting apart. It looked like they weren't speaking to each other. He was on one side of the room with his headphones on. His head leaned back and his eyes closed. She was on the other side, sitting between Lyric and Piper with sad puppy dog eyes, flipping through a magazine.

My crew looked beat. All of them were wearing head wraps and frumpy clothes. They were stretched out in two chairs, turning them into makeshift beds. I guess they had way too much fun time last night.

"I'm going to get me a coffee and a sandwich. Can I get you anything?" Gabriel offered.

"Yeah. I want a white mocha latte. And a breakfast sandwich if they are still serving it. If not, turkey will do."

"I'll be right back."

I took a seat next to Gabriel's carry-on bag. Seconds later, Marcel and Cash flopped down on both sides of me.

"Where did he come from?" Marcel asked giving me the Eagle eye.

"Yeah, were did you get the bootlegged Stoney from?" Cash asked, trying to be funny.

I ignored Cash, addressing Marcel. "He's cool. I met him a few days ago. We've talked and hung out since then. He was the one that got us into that outdoor party after we left the Welcome Boat."

"I don't care who money is. I don't like it," Marcel said, suspiciously.

"Calm down. He's cool. Trust me."

Marcel gave me a hardcore stare. "How cool? Like I'm looking for another baby mama cool? I just want to bump and grind cool? Or I'm genuinely interested in you cool?"

"Gabriel's not like that."

"Awwww," Cash and Marcel said together as if Gabriel was a national threat or something. "First name basis."

Marcel exhaled. "Dammit."

Cash shook his head. "Dammit, man."

I laughed. They were stupid. "What am I supposed to call him? By his last name." I laughed again. "Y'all goofy."

Marcel made himself comfortable next to me. "I need to meet this joker."

"Me too," Cash said, unzipping Gabriel's bag.

I yanked his bag into my lap. "Would you stop it? That's his personal belongings."

"I'm sure serial killers have personal belongings too." Cash nodded at Marcel. They exchanged looks as if they were on to something.

"Monkey See and Monkey Do, stop it."

Gabriel walked back over, looking at Cash and Marcel strange. They nearly bum-rushed him when he approached me.

"I'm Marcel."

"I'm Cash."

They were all in his grill. "And who are you?"

Gabriel sat the food down. "I'm Gabriel. Nice to meet you."

He stuck out his hand for them to shake. Cash shook it. Marcel smacked it away cutting his eyes at me. "Get that up out-ta here, man. Nice to meet you," Marcel said, mimicking Gabriel. Him and Cash laughed again. "That's not flying over here."

Cash folded his arms, looking more like a B-boy than an angry big brother. "That pretty boy charm don't work up in here, homie."

I sucked my teeth. "Why are you two trying to ruin my life?"

Marcel looked back at me. “Zip it.” He gave Gabriel the once over. Looking him up and down from head to toe, playing him real close. “Do you live alone? Are you married? How many kids do you have? Where do you work? Do you have a car? What are your intentions?”

Gabriel surprised me, keeping his cool. “Yes. No. None. Professor at the University of Chicago. Yes. I’m crazy about her.”

Cash looked satisfied.

Marcel still had the screw face. “What does that mean? Crazy about her? I’m crazy about my dog, nah mean?”

“Nah mean, son,” Cash emphasized.

OMG! Somebody shoot me now.

Gabriel pulled Marcel to the side, whispering something in his ear. I wished I could read his lips, but his back was facing me. They spoke briefly. Strangely, Marcel backed off. He waved Cash over and they coolly walked away.

I kept my eye on them as they strolled in the opposite direction. “What did you say to him?” I needed to know.

Gabriel smiled, handing me the sandwich and latte. “I’ll tell you when it happens.”

All I could do was grin at his exotic fine ass. Pulling that boss move gave me the hots for him even more.

Chapter 23

Vanity

The trip back wasn't as rowdy as the trip going. Nobody was hyped like before. People looked wore out. Maybe even sad because the trip was over. I know Shay didn't want to leave Moneaco. Others probably didn't want to resume their current lives either. Being on vacation was an easy escape from the norm.

Well, not everyone. Pebbles seemed content with her new beau. He was handsome too. They were all in each other's faces chatting and smiling.

Stoney and I still hadn't made up. I guess he was still mad at me. I don't know. We didn't even sit together on the plane ride back. Joss was in his seat, talking my head off. I have no clue what she said. My mind was still on vacation in the Bahamas, thinking about Stoney. By the time I got off the plane I was a nervous wreck. Severe nausea.

As we waited in baggage claim, Stoney wasn't nowhere in sight. I wondered if things between us were really over. Just thinking about losing him made me so sad. Heartbroken. Now that we've reconnected, I couldn't see myself without him. I needed him in my life.

Tears filled my eyes. I didn't realize how much of an affect Stoney truly had on me until now. How ironic. The whole trip, I had been miserable dealing with Ivan. Fighting. Arguing. Not enjoying myself. Messing up my trip. I could have been taking more pleasure with Stoney. Had I been a better companion, maybe he wouldn't have looked to Pebbles to fulfill his needs. It was me that he wanted. I thought about that for a long time last night, since I had the hotel room to myself. Constantly pushing him away, he ran into her arms, trying to replace me.

I followed Karen, Natalia, Cash and Marcel as they waited on the curb for their ride. I put on my jacket because the wind was picking up. They didn't call this the Windy City for nothing.

"Aight, fam, I'm out," I heard Stoney say, appearing out of nowhere. I watched as he hugged Karen and Natalia. Then, knocked knuckles with Marcel and Cash.

"Don't forget about tomorrow morning," Marcel said, shivering. "Make sure Dash knows too."

"He knows. He already texted me about it. We never forget. You need to be reminding Cash's late ass. Not us. Did you hear that Cash?"

Cash opened up a bag of nacho cheese flavor sunflower seeds, pouring a handful into his mouth. "I'm standing right here."

"Aight. I'm just saying," Stoney fired back.

"Shit! It's colder than a bitch out here." We laughed as Marcel danced around to keep warm, zipping up his little jacket. He gave his coat to Natalia who forgot to pack hers. "I miss the Bahama weather all ready."

I'm sure everyone did.

"Me too," Cash said, cracking sunflower seeds. "That was the shortest vacation ever."

I stood off to the side keeping my distance as Stoney purposely ignored me, saying goodbye to them. When he finally looked at me and didn't acknowledge me, a lump formed in my throat. I looked the other way to keep from crying.

Suddenly, he grabbed me in a bear hug, singing. "You be saying no, no, no, no, no. When it's really yes, yes, yes, yes, yes." His body swallowed mine as he grinded against me, dancing. "You want to keep it on the down looooow. So nobody has to knoooooow."

A big smile came across my face. I can't even lie, being in his arms felt so right. Instantly, I felt much better knowing that he wasn't mad at me anymore.

"Stop looking so depressed. You know I wasn't going to forget about you." He rubbed his nose with mine in a loving way.

"Look at her now," Natalia said. "She was moping just a few seconds ago. Now, she's all teeth. Stoney!" Natalia yelled, hugging Karen, pretending to be us.

"Cuz he's her bae-bae." Cash walked over to us. "So when's the wedding?"

Stoney smiled.

I smiled even harder.

Cash threw his sunflower seed shells on the ground. "Y'all need to quit playing. This is more than just a hook-up. Everyone seems to know that but you two. Stop fighting what's meant to be. But I'm going to take my so called nosey ass back over here."

It was very apparent that Cash was right. We did fit together. Probably better than the people we were currently with.

I heard Marcel, Cash, Karen and Natalia whistling and cheering when Stoney gave me a long, passionate, and very memorable kiss. "I'm going to miss you so much. You just don't know."

My tears fell. "I miss you already."

"Promise me?"

"What?"

He reached inside of my jacket, rubbing my tummy. "That if given the chance to be with me, you'd take it."

"I promise."

"That's all I ask."

Behind Stoney, I saw an expensive red sports car pull up. Out stepped a very pretty woman who was flawless from head to toe. "Stone-ney!" she called out in a cute but irritating voice. Then she struck a pose as if the world should take notice.

"This bitch here," Karen mumbled, rolling her eyes.

Stoney looked over his shoulder at the woman, signaling for her to wait a minute. He directed his attention back to me. "Call me later, ok? Better yet, text me."

"Ok." I truly didn't want to see him go.

He hugged me one last time, pecking my lips. "Later, my love."

I kept my eyes on him as he wheeled his luggage away from me. Meanwhile, the chick mugged all of us but her eyes lingered on me. I guess she felt some kinda way because he told her to hold on while he said his goodbyes to me.

"Is that his fiancée?" I asked to no one in particular.

"Yeah," Cash said, sounding like he hated her guts. "Fuckin snake ass bitch. Don't look at her too long. You might turn to stone."

I was appalled. "Dang, Cash. That's kinda harsh, don't you think?"

"Don't mind him," Karen said. "That's his ex."

I gasped, putting my hand over my mouth. "His ex-fiancée? No fuckin way. You got to be kidding."

"I wish I was," Karen said. "And another sore spot for them."

Now, I see why their relationship was so strained.

"This is all your fault, Marcel." Cash threw sunflower seeds at him.

Marcel had his jacket over his face. "How you figure that? I didn't tell you to fall in love with her. And for her to fall for Stoney. I just wanted a hot chick for my video."

Cash put more sunflower seeds in his mouth. "Yeah, well, fuck her. Tired ass."

Marcel shrugged his shoulders. "Fuck her, then. She don't mean nothing to me."

Stoney made an illegal U-turn, staring at me as he pulled off.

My heart felt heavy.

Did I make a mistake? Is he really the man I should have married? Why did I let him leave without telling him how I feel?

Tears came to my eyes again.

Determined to forget about whatever I shared with Keystone "Stoney" Diaz-Santana, I shifted my thoughts back to Ivan, wondering if he was still coming to pick me up.

I looked at my phone once more. Still no response from Ivan.

CPSIA information can be obtained
at www.ICGtesting.com
Printed in the USA
LVOW10s1955190917
549279LV00011B/1217/P